CW01494936

Summer Pudding

Can a comfort zone ever be just a little *too* comfortable? After a chance meeting with a village newcomer, Tessa may be about to find out…

Maggie Ingall was born in Kent, and has lived in Bath, London, Suffolk, and Leicestershire, and is now happily at home in West Somerset. She has written for most of her life, has won several prizes for her work and, when living in Leicestershire, was awarded a bursary from East Midlands Arts.

Summer Pudding

Maggie Ingall

MoK Publications

This book is dedicated to my husband and my family, and to all those who didn't laugh when I said I was writing a novel.

Chapter 1

'I wonder,' said the girl standing beside me, 'just how many it would take to break the record.'

'Sorry?' The sound of rain drumming on the roof of the marquee coupled with noise of the crowds inside was a deafening combination, and made me wonder if I had misheard her words.

She grinned. 'I was just wondering,' she repeated, 'how many people it would take to break the world record. You know - the category for the most people squeezed into one medium-sized beer tent in order to avoid a rainstorm? I should think we've got a pretty good chance, don't you?'

She laughed so infectiously that it was impossible not to smile back, depressed as I was. The smell of bruised grass and warm beer was beginning to be headache-inducing, but worse still was the noise and crush of all the people inside, who ought to have been outside, spending their cash and enjoying themselves.

'Never mind,' continued the girl, 'we may be packed like matches in a box, but at least we're dry, aren't we, poppet.' She gave an affectionate glance down to the baby in the pushchair beside her. 'You're being a good boy, darling, aren't you.'

1

Yes he was, I thought, considering how unnerving it must be to be hemmed in by so many legs. It was bad enough for those of us standing up; it must be even worse to be strapped into a pushchair, and dripped upon by macs and umbrellas. I tried to alter my position so that at least he didn't have the damp hem of my skirt brushing his nose.

'I didn't imagine it was going to chuck it down like this,' the girl went on chattily. 'I didn't even think to bring a jacket with me, or anything for Toby. The weather seemed quite promising when we left the house, and now look at it. Good job the fete was half over.'

'Not really,' I said. 'There's still half a dozen events to be held, not to mention awarding the raffle prizes, and all the best fruit and veg certificates to be presented.'

She looked surprised by the gloom in my voice. 'Is it a problem?'

'It is if you're one of the organisers,' I said. 'You try telling a doting mother that the children's fancy dress parade isn't going to take place after all. Especially when they've spent the last three months sewing on a thousand petals so that little Kelly-Marie can go as a rose garden. *And* there's the donkey derby,' I remembered. 'And after all the trouble we had actually getting them here...'

'You could always hold it inside the marquee, I guess.' She giggled, then saw my face. 'Sorry,' she said. 'Shouldn't joke. There must be so much work goes into this sort of thing.'

'There is,' I confirmed bitterly.

2

'And it's been great up till now, it really has. This sort of event is one of the things I like most about living here.'

I realised that her accent had been puzzling me. It certainly wasn't a village accent, or even Bristol. 'Are you from Norfolk?' I asked.

'A bit further than that,' she smiled. 'Australia, actually. Sydney, to be specific.' She saw my chagrin and laughed. 'Oh, don't worry – I've been living in England for ten years now. It's not surprising if the Aussie twang isn't obvious.'

Feeling stupid, I forced a smile, but she was already elaborating. 'My parents moved over here when I was seventeen. But when they went back to Sydney, I stayed on.' She grinned. 'I just fell in love with England. The people, the life, the traditions.' She waved an expansive hand around her, narrowly avoiding hitting the man behind us. 'Things like this fete, for instance. I'll bet the Little Bagford Midsummer Fayre has been held here in the village, on the same Saturday in June, for years and years, and it's still going strong. I just love events like this. Even the rain doesn't really spoil it, because that's traditional too.'

As if on cue, the tattoo of rain on canvas increased in volume, prompting the baby to whimper, wriggling and turning his head to look up at his mother.

She bent to smooth his head. 'How old is he?' I asked.

'Ten months,' she told me, 'but he's already big for his age, don't you think? Shhh now, sweetheart.

Are you wanting to be fed? Is that what you're waiting for?'

'What a gorgeous little boy.' My compliment was no platitude for he really was a most attractive child. Huge blue eyes were framed by lashes as soft and sooty as his wispy curls, while his cheeks were as flushed and downy as a ripe peach.

'A real little heart-stopper, isn't he,' beamed the girl. 'Sometimes I can hardly believe he's mine. But you take after your Daddy, don't you, darling?' She wiped away a small dribble from his rosebud mouth, then thrust out a sudden hand of introduction towards me. 'My name's Erica, by the way. And this little guy is Toby.'

I held out my own hand. 'Tessa,' I said. 'Tessa Lamport. Do you live in the village?'

'Yes, that's right. But we've only been moved in for three weeks. My husband has a job which takes him all round this area, so we figured that as long as we weren't too many miles from the motorway, we might as well live somewhere attractive. We've got one of the houses on the new estate. You know it - Windmill Meadows?'

I did know it. There had been a great deal of controversy about the building of a housing estate in Little Bagford. Ours was a small, pretty village, and most of the inhabitants wanted it to stay that way. The campaign against a huge new estate had been vigorous, and the eventual compromise had resulted in a considerable drop in proposed numbers, and a handful of starter homes to sit uneasily against a larger number of 'executive dwellings'.

'We're on Barleycorn Crescent,' said Erica.

The highest and nicest part of the estate. 'You must have good views,' I said.

'Oh, it's wonderful,' she confirmed. 'We can see all across the Quantock Hills.'

'And are all the other houses sold now?'

'Pretty well. Although,' she added, making a slight face, 'it's not very easy to get to know people round here, is it. Still, my husband did warn me that villages in England can be a bit clannish about new people moving in.'

'He's Australian too?' I asked.

Erica laughed. 'I should say not. No, he was born and bred in England, though he does claim an Irish grandfather.' She paused and peered around the crowded tent. 'In fact, he should have been here with me now, except he had to go and see a client. He runs a computer systems firm, so he has to fit in round the customer sometimes. But he did say he'd meet me here if he finished in time.' She glanced at her watch. 'Still, it is getting a bit late. I don't want to wait too much longer, not if Toby's going to start demanding food.' She stroked his head, and again he began to make small noises of discontent, wriggling fretfully. With some difficulty, Erica managed to squeeze down to squat in front of him. 'Are you hungry then, sweetie-pie? Not long now.'

I let my attention wander back to the weather, listening to the rain on the canvas roof. It must, I realised, have begun to ease off at last, for no longer was it necessary to shout to make oneself heard. Now it was even possible to distinguish the faint sounds of

5

the world outside, distant calls, the low rumble of a traction engine in motion, the faint tinny strains of 'Tie a Yellow Ribbon' played on some valiant steam organ.

A stir of hope rose. I'd need to confer with Aileen and Brian, but at this rate, we might just be able to get the rest of the events back on schedule.

Erica lifted the baby out of his buggy and stood cuddling him. 'Shall I take you home then, Toby, shall I? Perhaps we'll find Daddy already waiting for us there.'

'Don't leave yet,' I said. 'I'm sure things will be starting up again any minute, and it'll be disappointing if there's no-one around to watch. Wouldn't Toby like to see the donkeys?'

Erica smiled. 'It sounds fun,' she said. 'But this young man really does need his feed.'

'Give him something here,' I suggested. 'If you've got his food with you, I'm sure we can find you a chair. There are several over by the bar.'

She grinned. 'No problem about having his food with me,' she said. 'But are you sure? I don't mind for myself, but I know that even these days people can be a bit funny about feeding a baby in a public place. Especially when it would be so *very* public.'

I felt my face grow hot. It hadn't occurred to me for one moment that Erica was intending to breast-feed the child, but now I realised that this was plainly what she had in mind.

'Still, if you're sure no-one will object...' she continued.

'No! I mean yes,' I said. 'I mean, yes, they will

object. Little Bagford really isn't that kind of village.'

The idea of the girl sitting in the middle of the tent, hoisting up her skimpy tee-shirt to bare her voluptuous all was disconcerting in the extreme – especially if it got back to Aileen that it was I who had encouraged the incident. 'I'm afraid,' I continued quickly, 'that you'll find most of the community round here are very conservative. Some of our older residents would be very upset. I suppose they wouldn't mind if you had a shawl or something to put round you…' My voice tailed away, for she so plainly *didn't* have a shawl or anything else that might serve to make the activity less noticeable.

'All right,' said Erica equably. 'I just thought that perhaps because it *is* a village, with animals and nature and stuff going on all around, people would be used to babies suckling.'

'No,' I said. 'I'm afraid not. Not in this village. And anyway,' I observed as the thought struck me, 'surely he's rather old to be still feeding from – well – like that?'

Erica laughed. 'Oh, but he's only little. And he does love his mummy's boobies so, don't you, sweetheart?' She kissed him again. 'In fact, that's another way in which he's exactly like his daddy. He can never keep his hands off them either.'

I tried not to cringe too visibly. Too much information! Far too much, considering we hardly knew each other. And what if I ever got introduced to her husband? It was hardly the sort of mental picture I'd want to have in front of me.

7

'Well, anyway,' I said, 'I must be going – donkey owners to talk to – all that sort of thing – nice to have met you… '

I was attempting to move away when the worst happened.

Erica suddenly thrust up an arm and waved as vigorously as she could while still holding the baby. 'Dan - !' she yelled. 'Danny – over here!'

At the far side of the tent, a man turned his head to look at her. A tall man, dark haired and every bit as good looking as she had boasted. A man who was self-evidently her husband, and who was now squeezing his way through the crowd towards us.

'This is Danny,' said Erica. 'And Danny, this is my new friend – Tessa, did you say your name was?'

But now that the moment was upon us, I found no introduction was necessary. I was staring into a face I knew far better than Erica could have possibly imagined. It was Daniel Dunstan, the man whom I had once looked upon as being the love of my life, and who I'd last seen thirteen years ago, when shouting that I never wanted to set eyes upon him again.

It wasn't until I was on my way home that I was properly able to think about the events of the afternoon. Perhaps fortunately, my attention had first been required in other more urgent directions. With the rest of the fete to put back on track, my immediate task was to round up the Fancy Dress contestants and get them processing round The Green in an orderly line. Then, after the vicar's judging and the subsequent soothing of ruffled feelings, I was still needed to help with the running of the donkey derby and the handing out of various prizes. Even as the last stragglers finally left the site, there was a great deal of clearing up to do, unsold bric-a-brac and rubbish to be dealt with, and then the grand count-up of how much money the Midsummer Fayre had taken. As always, the latter was to take place in the sitting room of Brian and Aileen's house, overseen by the entire committee while being restored by tea and biscuits.

My head buzzed at the thought of it.

'You won't mind if I don't stay, do you?' I asked Jodie, my best friend and fellow committee member. 'Could you pass on my apologies to Aileen? Tell her I was worried about leaving my mother for too long while she's still getting over her virus.'

Jodie looked at me curiously. 'I thought your mother had almost recovered now. Or is there something else? You look a bit bothered.'

I hesitated. Much as I was tempted to confide in her, this was not the time or place. In any case, I needed to get my own head round events before I could think about discussing it with anyone else.

I shrugged. 'Tell you later, I promise.'

'Okay, if you're sure you're all right. Talk to you soon. I'll let you know if the Fayre's made a massive profit this year. But you'd know anyway, by the herd of pigs flying over the village.'

She allowed herself to be absorbed into Aileen's little entourage, while I slipped off in the other direction. I would head home as I had promised, but not by the quickest route.

After the full-on afternoon I'd had, the footpath that followed the stream was blessedly quiet. There had been woods here once, and a few trees still remained, old and twisted. In springtime the ground shimmered with bluebells but now, in late June, they had passed their peak, leaving the cow-parsley and wild angelica to take over. Only dog-walkers used this route regularly and, on dry days, an occasional jogger. Today the path was too full of puddles to tempt anyone, and I found myself quite alone as I wandered slowly home.

I breathed in the cool air, glad of its damp freshness. Even now, I could hardly believe the events of the afternoon. Daniel, of all people! Living in the village. And married to that girl. And with a baby. *A baby.* Daniel, who had always been so reluctant to commit himself to anything approaching domestic ties. He might have spoken vaguely of eventually getting married, but any talk of fixing a date had sent him running in a different direction. He much preferred just living together. A free spirit, that's how he had described himself. Certainly he'd regarded himself as free enough to bed a so-called friend of mine when he thought I was safely out the way.

I broke off a dead twig and swished it angrily against the tall grass. How weird it all was. If just yesterday someone had asked me how the split had occurred, I'd have probably claimed that it was so long ago I'd forgotten the details. And yet now -

seeing Daniel face to face like that - all of a sudden I could almost taste the shock, the sick feeling of betrayal I'd felt when I'd got back to our flat earlier than expected and found them in bed together. Our new bed, which we had bought together only a week beforehand; a fact that had somehow made his treachery even worse. I could almost see the scene again, him and Maxine, lying there staring up at me, their mouths agape and ridiculous. Like some television drama, the sort of scene which is so very clichéd it would be risible, if only you didn't happen to be actually living it.

I swished at the grass again. Bloody Daniel! Who the hell did he think he was, waltzing back into my life, as if he had some right to? As if...

But hang on. He hadn't waltzed into my life. Not deliberately, anyway. One only had to look at his face to see that I was the last person he'd expected to bump into.

For the first time, I felt a small bubble of amusement. His face! That look of blank disbelief said it all. No, he hadn't anticipated the encounter any more than I had. My mouth twitched reluctantly. It might have been a belated and minor revenge, but I was childishly glad to see that he'd been caught so completely off-balance by the meeting. Moreover, he had a wife to witness his discomfiture, who would no doubt want to know just what had caused it.

I, at least, had kept my dignity. I might not have been able to hide my surprise, but I was pretty sure I hadn't looked quite such a fool. Plus I'd also had a legitimate excuse for walking away. I had a job to

11

do, whereas Daniel had been left standing there, left to explain to Erica just why his eyes had popped, and his mouth fallen open like a codfish. Like the sorry piece of low-life that he was.

I flung my stick into a tangle of wet undergrowth and left it there. Poor Erica, married to such a pathetic creature. I pitied her. Yes, I genuinely did, for up until then she'd struck me as a likeable creature; someone who might even have become a friend. Although perhaps not, because she must be ten years younger than me –

I paused mid-stride. Yes, indeed. Working it out, she must be about twenty-seven, while I was the same age as Daniel. Our birthdays were only a couple of months apart, and we would both be thirty-eight next spring. So Erica was considerably younger.

I frowned. Erica was not just ten years younger than me, she *looked* it. Indeed, I might almost have taken her for a teenager. The attractively cropped blond hair, the fresh complexion, the skimpy tee shirt and tight white trousers – her whole being spoke of youth and charm.

Whereas I... For the first time that day, I gave my full attention to what I was wearing. I had thrown on my clothes this morning, already aware that I was running late. My choice of checked shirt, ancient denim skirt and canvas pumps had seemed perfectly adequate for marking out pitches and helping set up stalls on the village green. Even my hair had received no more attention than a quick tug through with a comb. I'd fully intended to change into something smarter before the fete started – except of course, I hadn't found the time.   Now I wished very much that I had done.

Chapter 2

My mother was sitting by the fire when I arrived home.

'I know we shouldn't need heating at this time of year,' she apologised, 'but when it started raining I suddenly felt quite cold and shivery.'

I looked at her in concern. 'Not that horrible virus starting up again, is it?'

'You worry too much,' she smiled. 'No, I'm fine, I just got a bit chilly.'

'Fancy a cup of tea?' I asked. 'That should warm you up.'

'Come and tell me about the fete first. How did it go? What about the rain? Did it spoil things too much? I kept looking out the window and wondering how you were getting on.'

'Not too badly,' I told her. 'Luckily the downpour didn't last long enough to send everyone home. Just enough to make the grass very wet. Still, it all seemed to go okay in the end.'

'I wish I'd been there. I really missed being a part of it this year. How did the tombola stall go?'

'Not as well as if you'd been running it. Everyone kept asking where you were.'

'Well I hope you told them that I was pretty well fighting fit again. I'd have been running it as normal if only you hadn't been so bossy about it. I know it was a nasty bug, but I'm over it now. I don't need

14

any more molly-coddling.'

'Well, better safe than sorry. Next year I'm sure you'll be doing it again. And I do think we'll have made some profit, despite Aileen's moaning.'

'Lots of people there?'

'All the usual suspects, plus quite a few I didn't recognise.'

'What about people from the new estate? Did many of them come and show their faces?'

I hesitated. Should I mention the encounter in the beer tent, or pretend it had never happened? I didn't want her worrying about my emotional welfare, but on the other hand Little Bagford wasn't that big a village. It was perfectly possible that sooner or later she'd find out about Daniel, and I didn't want her thinking I'd been so traumatised by the meeting that I'd needed to conceal it.

'Let me make that tea,' I said, 'I'll tell you more in a minute.' I went into the kitchen, and started to run water noisily into the kettle. 'Biscuits?' I shouted.

She followed me in. 'There's a new packet of ginger nuts in the tin. You must be hungry.'

'Not particularly.'

She fetched the tin, then started putting milk into the mugs.

I said, more sharply than I'd intended, 'Leave it. Go and sit down and let me do it.'

She glanced at me. 'Something's the matter, isn't it. I can always tell when you're upset.'

'I'm not upset, and nothing's the matter. Well, nothing major. Just a rather unexpected meeting,

15

that's all. Let me finish this and then I'll tell you all about it.'

Sometimes it surprised people to learn that I still lived with my mother. Sometimes it surprised *me*. I had left home at the conventional age of eighteen, gone to study in Bristol. There I had gained some qualifications, a not-particularly-exciting job in an advertising agency and, some eighteen months later, a serious boyfriend - Daniel. I certainly hadn't imagined that at the advanced age of thirty-seven I would be back where I'd started. When, ten years after I'd first left home, I had returned to Little Bagford to move in with my parents, we had all regarded it merely as a temporary arrangement. A state of crossroads in my own life had coincided with my father suffering a minor stroke, so my decision to return had seemed only logical. It would not only buy me some thinking time, but also allow me to give my mother some practical assistance and support. It made sense in every way.

But before any of us had quite come to terms with that first stroke, my father suffered a second one. His death was such a shock that it jolted my mother into a state of breakdown, and left me unwilling to leave her until I felt sure she had fully recovered. And so I had stayed on, and somehow never quite got round to moving out again.

Sharing the cottage suited both of us too well. It was only occasionally that I could have wished for a place to properly shut myself away. This was one of them. Reluctantly I poured the tea and carried it back to the fireside.

'That man,' said my mother, 'has never been anything but bad news.'

'*Was*,' I pointed out. 'He's history, Mum. Has been for ages.'

'He damaged your life. That's when everything started to go wrong for you.'

'Nonsense,' I said. 'You're making me sound like a real tragedy queen. It was a bad episode in my life, but it's over.'

'He caused you a great deal of pain.'

I shrugged. 'I got over Daniel Dunstan a very long time ago. Anyway, no-one in the world lives a life of total unblemished joy. Even if I'd never set eyes on him, I don't suppose my life would have been roses all the way.'

'Well, I can't forgive him so easily,' she said. 'He behaved so badly to you.'

'And yet you liked him at first,' I pointed out. I could still remember the first time she and my father had met Daniel. They had come to Bristol especially for the occasion, despite the fact that neither of them were keen on visiting cities. I was the only child of older parents, born when they had almost given up hope of producing any offspring. As a child this had never bothered me, but now for the first time I felt self-conscious about it.

We had arranged to meet for lunch. It was a pleasant restaurant, small and friendly, and Daniel and I had eaten there many times. Nevertheless, I had arrived as taut as a rubber band, wondering what they would make of him – and just what my gorgeous city-slicker lover would make of my staid, respectable parents up from the sticks.

I needn't have worried. Daniel was on his best behaviour; showing just the right amount of deference to my father, and gently teasing my mother until her eyes sparkled. It was a dream first meeting.

'Ah, well,' observed my mother now. 'When I liked him it was before I knew him. Knew him properly, I mean.'

'He wasn't a monster,' I said. 'There were lots of things really nice about Daniel – he just had this fatal inability to understand the meaning of fidelity.' I had never told my mother the exact circumstances of how I had discovered this weakness, and now I was rather glad of it. The last thing I needed was extra fuel being added to her flames by the image of Daniel found in *flagrante* with my friend.

'Well, I hope he knows how to behave himself now,' she said. 'Now that he's got a wife and child to think about. And him so much older than her, too!'

I paused. Again we were back to this age thing. I wondered if my mother had remembered the fact that Daniel was only two months older than I myself. But she pressed blithely onwards. 'I'm just glad that you had the sense to break it all off when you did. You had to cope with some very hard lessons thanks to that man, but at least you came through in the end. You may have had your setbacks, but you've got a lovely life now, what with Oliver and the antiques, and Jodie, and all your village interests…'

Had I a lovely life? Yes, I supposed that of course I had.

'All the same, Mum,' I said. 'I'd much prefer it if, by any chance you should bump into Daniel, you don't have a go at him. Just ignore him.'

'Ignore him?' she said. 'I certainly will ignore him. I'll ignore him so hard that he'll have no doubts at all that he's being ignored.'

I might not have wanted to tell my mother about Daniel, but once I had done, I was oddly comforted by her reaction. Her anger had put my own in proportion and, as I went into work on Monday, I was beginning to wonder why the episode had seemed such a big deal to me. Why should I get hung up on the problems of the distant past when the present was perfectly satisfactory? Why feel threatened by old ghosts, when I had long since exorcised them? Indeed, lots of people might envy my calm, unruffled existence. It might not be a life of great drama or high achievement, but I still had my own little place in the world. Although - come to think of it, the question of what I had, or hadn't achieved was not entirely cheering. Hadn't I once wanted to travel, to see the world, to discover who I really was? Or had that just been the passing whim of youthful naivety? Of course it was, I told myself firmly. There was nothing wrong with stability, and if I allowed Daniel's sudden arrival to make me think otherwise, then I was a fool.

I lifted my head and drew in a bracing breath of fresh air. Even the weather seemed to confirm that all was well. The rain clouds that had brooded over the Quantock hills earlier had given way at last to a sky of blue – a rather pale blue, admittedly, but nevertheless blue. A brisk breeze was feather-dusting through the village, swaying the branches and chasing the last stray petals of blossom across the pavement. Making my way to the small parade of shops in the High Street, I couldn't help thinking just how nice the village was looking, now that the sun was shining and the puddles drying out. Walls glowed, windows sparkled, and peonies and poppies bloomed cheerfully in the little gardens. Little Bagford might never quite achieve the quaint chocolate-box prettiness of some of the other Somerset villages, but as far as I was concerned there was nowhere else I would rather live.

Pushing open the door of Pilgrim's Antiques, I found the shop empty.

'Morning, Oliver,' I called loudly over the sound of the jingling bell. 'It's all right, it's only me – not a customer.'

He emerged from the back room, a tall solid shape against the darker background of the workroom doorway. Holding a polishing cloth and blinking in the brighter light of the showroom, he pushed back the hair from his high forehead, leaving a dark smudge of dust on his temple.

'Tessa,' he greeted me vaguely. 'You here already?'

'I know I'm a bit early,' I said. 'But I thought

I'd come in promptly today, seeing as I couldn't come in on Saturday.'

'Oh that's right – the Midsummer Fayre,' he said. 'Don't worry, it was all very quiet here anyway. So how did it all go?'

'Pretty well,' I said. 'Once the rain had stopped.'

'Good. Excellent. I knew it would all be fine. I don't know why you get yourself in such a state about it each year; it always goes like clockwork. But well done, anyway. There was no need to come in early, though – what's a few minutes between friends?'

I looked at him affectionately. Oliver was another good reason for me to feel happy with the way things had turned out. I had started work in his antiques shop soon after coming back to live in the village, after seeing a card in his shop window advertising a 'temporary vacancy' for a part-time assistant. It seemed a good way to fill a few hours, while still allowing me to be available for my mother should she need me. I was never quite sure how, all these years later, the shop had become a permanent and pretty well full-time part of my life.

'I was just in the middle of sorting out the stuff I bought at the sale last week,' he continued. 'It was all a bit disappointing on the whole. I did end up with one or two decent pieces of jewellery, and a little walnut bureau that I've already started work on, but nothing more. Nothing spectacular, unfortunately.' He sighed. 'We could do with something showy to put in the window. Something really eye-catching to bring the customers in.'

21

'Oh well,' I comforted, 'perhaps we'll get a rush today. It's nice weather – that usually brings the day-trippers out and about. We might even get a coachload, if we're lucky.'

Little Bagford, although on the southern edge of the Quantocks, was still near enough the main tourist trail for some of the regular excursion coaches to stop for afternoon tea on their way home. A favourite calling-in place was the Patchwork Pumpkin, the cafe across the road. Despite its twee name, it had a robust and well-deserved reputation for fabulous home-baked cakes – many of them made by my friend Jodie, a magician of the mixing bowl. Her fresh scones and spicy gingerbread, her carrot-cakes and treacle tarts, coffee sponges and nutty flapjacks were famously delicious, and the reason why many tourists chose to drop in on Little Bagford around elevenses or tea-time.

It was certainly fortuitous for Pilgrim's Antiques that they did call in. Occasionally, while watching the steady stream of customers heading into the Patchwork Pumpkin, I wondered if it might ever be possible to transform our own shop into a similar mecca. I would certainly have persuaded Oliver to make the necessary changes, if only I knew what they should be. As it was, when it came to customers, our own emporium had to make do with the café's leftovers. It was heartening how many of their replete and mellowed patrons were quite happy to amble across the road to examine our cabinets, clocks and candlesticks - but I had to admit that getting them to actually buy something was rather more challenging. They looked at things, they often admired them, but serious money rarely changed hands. And yet their money *was* needed. As the person now responsible for balancing the books, I knew too well just how wobbly they often were.

'Do you think we're going to be busy today?' asked Oliver rather anxiously, glancing towards the shop window as if he had only just noticed the sunshine outside. 'Only I've arranged to go over to a house near Dunster later on. Some woman rang up, she's got a collection of china that she wants me to have a look at.'

'Don't worry, I'm sure I shall be all right by myself.'

'I don't want to leave you in the lurch, but it did sound tempting when she described what she had in mind to show me.'

'Lucky old you,' I teased.

He looked puzzled for a moment, then broke into the sudden smile that was always so endearing. 'Sorry, Tess. I'm not on the ball today. It's just that I had a phone call last night. From Anita.'

'That's nice,' I said. 'How is she?'

'Oh, she's all right.' He hesitated. 'Well, actually, not terribly all right. She seems to have been having a lot of trouble with Todd.'

'Again?' Most of the phone calls from Oliver's daughter seemed full of her marital problems and, to be honest, I wasn't greatly surprised. I hadn't set eyes on Anita for nearly four years now, but despite the fact she was Oliver's only child, I had never been able to warm to her. I had tried, but Anita had always been far too sure of herself to be very likeable; far too convinced that she knew exactly what was best, not only for herself but everyone else around her.

But I hadn't actually seen her since her wedding. At twenty-two, and not long graduated from university, Oliver's daughter had made a tall, fair, and sturdily-built bride, who strode down the aisle with a purpose. Even then, her groom Todd had not seemed the sort of man to be her perfect soul-mate. Meeting this genial and relaxed American, I felt a gleam of sympathy for him which I hoped would prove unnecessary. A few weeks after the nuptials they had moved back to Todd's home town of Chicago, which meant that I hadn't seen her since.

For Oliver's sake, I assumed a look of sympathy. 'So what's the trouble this time?'

'Oh, more of the usual,' said Oliver. "Todd's got no ambition... Todd ought to be out there working, not messing about with his buddies... Todd isn't taking life seriously...' Sometimes I don't know if Anita's exaggerating, or if she really does have a genuine problem.'

'Difficult for you,' I said.

Oliver sighed. 'And in any case, I don't feel I can advise her. What on earth do *I* know about marriage guidance? Even the so-called experts don't seem to get it right half the time. And even if I did have any suggestions, I doubt if Anita would be interested in them. I really think she just wants someone to listen and sympathise.'

'Yes, it's certainly tricky,' I agreed, trying to keep an edge of impatience from my voice. Surely if

Anita needed to unburden herself, she had other people she could talk to? Oliver already had enough problems about keeping the shop going, without his daughter dumping her own half-baked worries on his shoulders.

Oliver sighed. 'You know, it's at times like this that I really wish Margaret was still alive. She always knew what to say to Anita. They understood each other far better than I ever could.'

'Well, yes,' I said. 'Perhaps so. Woman to woman, mother to daughter…'

'Exactly.'

Watching him stand there rather helplessly holding the polishing cloth, I felt a sense of *deja vu*. He had looked like that so often when Margaret was still alive, and Anita a stroppy teenager living at home. Sometimes it was almost as if the two women in his life ganged up on him, for they were two of a kind by nature, even if not by looks. Anita had favoured Oliver in appearance, rather than her slim, dark and elegant mother, but they had both got the knack of making their presence felt wherever they went.

But I should try not to think ill of the dead, I told myself as I started the business of the day by getting out the coffee jar and mugs. Although I had to admit it hadn't been all that easy to think well of Margaret even when she was alive. When I had first started to work there, she'd told me that she wanted to step back from the day-to-day running of the shop. If so, it hadn't happened. As I struggled to get on top of the job, she had never stopped breathing over my shoulder, constantly countermanding Oliver's instructions and then criticising the inevitable muddles. If I hadn't kept reminding myself that the job was only a stop-gap while my mother and I got our lives back on track, I would never have stayed.

But slowly and gradually Margaret had learned that leisure time could be spent in more rewarding ways, and Anita had finished school and gone away to university. My 'temporary' position slipped almost unnoticed into permanence, and Oliver and I fell into a comfortable rut of friendship and trust.

And then, two years ago, Margaret had been killed when her car ran into a tree. She had set out on a shopping expedition to Bath, and had never come home again. There had, it transpired, been a minor shunt on the opposite side of the carriageway which, the coroner ruled, had almost certainly been the cause of Margaret's distraction and subsequent accident. Or – as Jodie observed with most unusual bitchiness - Margaret's inability to mind her own business had literally been the death of her.

I put my hand on Oliver's arm. 'Don't worry. Anita's problems will sort themselves out one way or another. Now, if you want to get back to working on that bureau, I'll do duty out here.'

As if on cue, the bell jangled and I turned to find a well-dressed elderly woman coming into the shop. 'I'm looking for a silver-wedding present,' she told me. 'Something tasteful, but not too expensive. You don't mind if I just browse?'

'Not at all,' I said. 'Though I'll be happy to help, if you can give me some idea of what you might have in mind?'

But the woman had nothing particular in mind, so there was little to do but allow her to look round at her own pace while Oliver retreated to the back room to continue working. At least that part of the business was no cause for concern, thank goodness. Oliver might not be the world's best salesman, but his talents as a furniture and antiques restorer were always in demand. Half-an-hour later, when the woman had, with much dithering and angst, finally decided upon a silver-plated bon-bon dish, he too was almost ready to depart.

'I'm hoping that it won't take too long,' he reassured me rather guiltily. 'It's still quite early in the season, so I doubt if the roads will be too busy. I might be back by mid-afternoon. Before closing time, anyway. You don't mind managing on your own?'

'Of course not.'

'He paused at the door and looked at me. 'Tessa, I hope you realise just how invaluable you are.'

I smiled. It might not be true, but it was nice that Oliver thought so. Nice boss, nice job, nice home. How could I possibly believe my life was anything less than satisfactory?

Chapter 3

Despite my hopes for an influx of coach-trippers, the afternoon seemed destined to be a quiet one. At one o-clock I ate my lunchtime cheese and tomato sandwich, and later made a leisurely mug of tea, still almost entirely undisturbed by any customers.

The sun shone through the shop window, making me yawn. I needed to find myself a task, or I'd be dozing off if I wasn't careful. Not that finding something to do was a problem, for dusting and polishing was always an ongoing job. Even now, I could remember Margaret's insistence that the stock should never look anything less than its very best. 'We can't expect good prices for stuff that looks as if it's just been pulled out from the back of a garage' was a mantra of hers, and although I hadn't agreed with Margaret about many things, I'd always seen the sense of that particular edict.

I began half-heartedly to flick the duster around, then decided I would rearrange the stock in the front window. I could at least make an attempt to lure in potential customers with an impression of gracious living that could be theirs if only they chose to buy from us. I edged a small table to the forefront of the window, draped it with a Victorian lace tablecloth, and carefully placed a few choice pieces of a Coalport tea-set on top. Pleased with the effect, I toyed with the thought of nipping across to the Patchwork

Pumpkin to buy a Victoria sponge cake just to complete the scene. But perhaps that was a step too far. In any case, the sight of one of Jodie's cakes sitting there all afternoon would probably prove more tempting to me than anyone else, especially if I knew it would go stale if left there too long.

At last, with no more shop work to hand, I reluctantly accepted that I might just as well spend my time doing the chore that Aileen had delegated to me. Writing thank-you letters to all the clubs and organisations that had taken part in the Midsummer Fayre was a tedious job which no-one on the committee relished, despite the fact that we all knew it was necessary. There was nothing as good as a hand-written note of thanks to build up a store of goodwill, and we would need to draw on that when it came to organising next year's event.

Next year's event. Oh dear, was my life really so predictable? Would I find myself, in twelve months' time, sitting in the shop doing exactly the same thing? Would it be so terrible if I did? There was no reason why it should be, yet my spirits still sank at the thought of it. I scowled as I rummaged in my bag for the writing pad. It was Daniel's fault, stirring up all these unwelcome questions. I'd been perfectly all right before I set eyes on him. But I would not allow him to rock my boat. It had taken me a long time to reach these tranquil waters, and I wouldn't allow him to disrupt my life again. I squared my shoulders and took out my pen.

By the time I had written the third one, business had begun to pick up a little. A young couple came to examine furniture and left with a promise to return, and then three women spent ten minutes loudly discussing the merits of some silk-embroidered samplers before finally purchasing a pair of wooden candlesticks.

One hour and five letters later, I had sold a Staffordshire dish, a small glass vase and a shell cameo brooch and, for Oliver's later inspection, taken receipt of an album of Edwardian postcards.

I stared out at the empty High Street which seemed to be as deeply sunk in Monday afternoon torpor as I was. The sun still shone, but the breeze that had whisked me to work that morning had blown itself away, leaving the air warm and dusty. I glanced at my watch and yawned again. Knowing how prone Oliver was to be side-tracked, I wondered when he'd get back. At this rate, if no miraculous visitation of customers turned up, I might as well shut the shop at five. Which meant only another two hours of boredom before I could go home. I was wondering idly about what we might be having for the evening meal, when the door-bell gave a peremptory jangle. A girl came into the shop, clumsily manoeuvring a pushchair in front of her.

'Erica!' With a jolt of surprise, I recognised her at once. But what on earth had brought her here? Or was it purely coincidence that we should meet again so soon? Before I could even begin to speculate, the girl turned a pale and distressed face towards me. In half-muffled tones she said, 'Oh – Tessa – Miss Lamport - The woman at the post office said this is where I'd find you.'

"Tessa' will do,' I said. 'But why were you asking about me in the post office?' I looked at her more closely. 'Are you all right?'

'No,' she said. 'No, I've had a sort of accident.'

I felt a stir of sympathy. Whatever her reason for seeking me, it was evident that it didn't involve any discussion about Daniel.

'Whatever's the matter?' I asked.

'My tooth,' said Erica. 'I was eating some cake – fruit cake, with nuts in – and I think there must have been some nutshell left in it. I think it's got sort of wedged in my tooth – so painful…' Her voice tailed away, and I was dismayed to see her eyes bright with tears. Looking more closely, it was obvious that Erica's cheek was pink and swollen.

'Well, I suppose I could recommend a dentist,' I said doubtfully, 'but - '

'No - not that.' Erica fumbled to explain. 'I've got a dentist, but he's back in Long Ashton. I've rung – he'll fit me in as soon as I arrive. But it's Toby – it's a long way to take him, and when I get there, there'd be no-one to look after him….' Her voice became even more muffled.

'So what do you want me to do?' I asked, my heart sinking.

'Will *you* look after Toby?' she said simply.

'But I don't know anything about babies!' I tried not to sound as horrified as I felt. He might be sleeping peacefully at the moment, but who knew when he might wake, and then what would happen? If he started crying, I'd have no idea what to do.

'Isn't there someone else you could leave him

31

with?' I begged. 'Couldn't you ring Daniel to come and take charge? Or a neighbour, or a friend? Try them. You don't want to leave him with someone he doesn't know.'

'But I have tried other people,' said Erica. 'I can't get hold of Danny, not at his office or even on his mobile. My only friend in the village is away for the day, and both my neighbours are out. Then I remembered you, and that you said you were on the Fete Committee, so I thought someone must know you. So I asked at the post office. You see, I don't know anyone else around here yet. Not anyone I could trust.'

'But you don't know that *I'm* trustworthy,' I said desperately.

'You must be,' she said, 'if you're a friend of Danny's.'

I looked at her helplessly. She was obviously in pain. She said, 'I know it's a lot to ask. Especially when you're at work. But please, if you could – if you're not too busy…'

She paused. It was obvious to both of us just how un-busy I was.

I said, 'But how long will you be? What if he gets hungry? What if he needs feeding? *I* can't do it.'

'I've made a bottle,' said Erica. 'And there's baby food, and nappies. I wouldn't ask,' she faltered, 'if I wasn't desperate.'

I felt suddenly ashamed. 'All right,' I said. 'Off you go. But please – you won't be any longer than you have to, will you?'

32

Erica's mouth wobbled in a smile of relief. 'Oh Tessa, thank you! I'll be quick as I can, I promise. I'll just fetch his things from the car.'

She left the pushchair in the middle of the shop and was back within seconds, carrying a dauntingly large bag. I took it nervously. What had I left myself in for? But there was no time for second thoughts. Erica was already on her way out, the door jangling behind her.

I stood at the window and watched her small red runabout disappear into the distance. I just wished I could follow her.

Turning round, I gazed at the sleeping Toby. He was dressed in green today; green dungarees decorated with a tractor, a white tee shirt and green corduroy slippers. Despite the pleasing picture he presented, I regarded him unhappily. How much longer could I rely on him to stay so peaceful? But at least he had managed to stay asleep through the jangle of the shop doorbell as Erica went in and out. Perhaps that meant he was really tired. I felt slightly reassured at the thought. If he was exhausted, he might even remain sleeping for the duration of his visit. I did hope so.

All the same, I could not leave him there in the middle of the shop floor, like some prize exhibit. With infinite caution I took hold of the pushchair handles and wheeled him gently to the side of the counter. He stirred slightly but did not wake, and I breathed a sigh of relief.

Still keeping a wary eye upon him, I returned to my writing pad to embark on my next thank-you note.

33

He really was a sweet little thing. Babysitting wasn't so difficult really.

The bell rang again, and I jumped as a plump well-dressed woman came into the shop. 'I'm after a gift for my niece,' she announced in strident tones. 'Do you have anything suitable? It's her eighteenth birthday, so I want something special, something that she can - ' She broke off abruptly as her roving gaze lit upon the sleeping Toby. 'Oh, what a little lamb!' she exclaimed loudly. 'Is he your – er - ?'

My what? I wondered. My grandson? I might be only thirty-seven, but she had obviously hesitated to assume he was my own child.

'I'm looking after him for a friend,' I said rather coldly. 'Now, what sort of thing do you think your niece would like?'

But my question went unanswered, for her attention was now wholly concentrated on the baby. She bent over him. 'Hello sweetie-boots. Aren't you a beautiful baby, then? Aren't you a little heart-breaker?'

'He's asleep,' I pointed out tightly. 'Please don't disturb him.'

'Of course I won't disturb him,' she said. 'I wouldn't disturb you, would I, my little darling?' She tickled his cheek, and Toby's blue eyes flicked open. For a long moment he frowned at her in bewilderment.

'Hello lambkins,' she cooed.

Toby's mouth wobbled.

'Oh, aren't you just gorgeous then,' said the woman. She straightened and turned back to me.

'How old is he?'

In the silence before I could answer, I was aware of the long intake of breath by the occupant of the pushchair. For a second the stillness hung suspended almost tangibly in the air, then cracked and splintered into a million jagged pieces. His face contorted, Toby roared his confusion and displeasure.

The woman backed away. 'Oh dear, he doesn't seem very happy, does he? Perhaps you'd better see to him. I'll come back another time. When it's more convenient.'

I watched the door swing shut behind her hurriedly departing figure. '*See to him*'! So just how was I to do that? My muttered oaths were swamped and sunk beneath the waves of Toby's bellows as I bent towards him. The obvious thing, I knew, must be to pick him up and try to reassure him, but with such siren screams in my ears, even the task of undoing the pushchair straps seemed beyond me at first. I tugged, pulled and pushed until at last there was a click and a buckle gave way beneath my fingers.

Pulling aside the straps, I looked down at him. My only experience of small babies was the fact that I myself had once been one. A great many years ago. Since then, my days had been free of any kind of dealings with infants, least of all distressed and howling ones.

Tentatively I put my hands around the taut body and lifted him. He was surprisingly heavy. The weight of him almost unbalanced me, yet even as I held him the noise dwindled and ceased. There was a sudden blessed hush as his expression of fury gave way to one of surprise. In the stillness we surveyed one another.

'Hello,' I said experimentally. 'Hello there, Toby. Hello.'

I was aware of myself sounding quite ridiculous, but at least it was keeping him quiet. 'Hello,' I chirruped again.

He stared at me suspiciously.

'I'm Tessa,' I said.

He blinked, frowning, and for a moment I braced myself for the screams that were surely about to begin again. Then I realised his attention had been caught by something behind me. He shifted in my arms and reached out a chubby hand.

'What is it, then, Toby? What can you see?' Following his gaze towards the window I observed, sparkling in a gleam of sunshine, a small millefiori glass paperweight. With renewed energy he leaned towards it.

'No,' I said. 'No, you can't have that.'

He continued to strain towards it, making me stagger slightly.

'No,' I said firmly. 'Not for little boys.'

Toby scowled. His lower lip wobbled ominously.

I took a step nearer the shining glass. Should I let him hold it for a moment? It probably wasn't that fragile. But even as I was tempted, common-sense prevailed. Of course it could not be given to a baby to hold. Whatever was I thinking of? I turned round so that it was no longer within his field of vision.

'Ooh!' I exclaimed in the over-bright tones of the desperate, 'Ooh, what's *that*, Toby! 'What can we see over there?'

I moved towards an ancient teddy bear that sat on a rush-seated stool in a corner of the shop. It was more expensive than the paperweight, but certainly less fragile. 'What a lovely teddy,' I coaxed. 'I bet you'd like to have a look at the lovely teddy, wouldn't you?' I bent down, so that he could reach to touch the fur, but a contemptuous swipe of his hand knocked it to the floor.

His scowl deepened. He took a deep breath.

'Look, Toby, look!' My voice took on a jollity bordering on frenzy. 'What have we got here?' I bent, and with my free hand opened the bag that Erica had left, hoping urgently that there would be something inside to divert him. I tipped the contents haphazardly onto the shop counter; a tub of baby-powder, a small folded changing-mat, two disposable nappies, a box of wipes, a full feeding bottle of milk, a jar of rice-and-banana tea-time-treat, and a small assortment of brightly coloured toys.

'Ooh, look,' I cried. 'All these things that Mummy has left you! Who's a lucky boy then?'

I hoisted him higher onto my hip, allowing him to lean over them. Something among the collection *had* to please him. With utmost relief I watched his plump hand light upon a plastic teething-ring, a circlet of red and yellow horses. He bunched them into his fist, then began stuffing them into his mouth while continuing to regard me balefully.

Cautiously I lowered myself onto the chair

37

behind the counter, wondering what to do next. I was glad that the crying had stopped, but I couldn't sit there holding him forever. How would I manage if a customer came in? No-one would take seriously a sales assistant who couldn't assist; a wild-eyed woman clutching a baby that she couldn't put down.

I looked at him. Toby's attention was now focused entirely upon the toy. With greatest care, I stood up, walked to the pushchair, and placed him gingerly back into it, steeling myself for more protests. He looked up briefly, then returned his attention to the teething-ring.

'Good boy,' I said. 'What a good boy you are.' Cautiously I turned my head away. Perhaps if I didn't actually maintain eye contact, he would forget that I was here and Erica wasn't.

The baby accessories spread across the counter looked distinctly odd among the other items in the shop. The china plates, the brown wooden furniture, the silver ornaments and glassware suddenly appeared drab and boring compared with the simple shapes and bright primary colours of Toby's toys. I gathered them up and bundled everything back into the bag. One couldn't allow customers to think they had stumbled into a crèche. I risked another glance in his direction. Still sitting quietly, he continued to chew on the plastic horses, his gaze roaming the unfamiliar surroundings.

Taking care not to make any sudden movements, I retrieved my writing pad and pen. For a moment or two I attempted to continue my letter to Janice Carter, thanking her for her sterling efforts on Saturday, running the… Just what stall had she run, she and the other bell-ringers? It was no good. However hard I tried, I couldn't concentrate on the task in hand. The presence of the baby was just too distracting.

The door swung open and I looked up to find Oliver coming through the door.

'Well, that was a waste of time,' he announced. 'Nothing like as interesting as she had led me to believe. It took me ages to find the house, and when I finally did, it wasn't worth it. She did have one or two nice plates, but most of the other china looked as if she'd rescued it from the bottom of a skip, and even then - '

He broke off abruptly as he noticed Toby in his pushchair. For a moment he glanced round the shop confusedly, as if he expected the child's owner to suddenly emerge from the shadows. 'Hello - where's this come from?'

I resisted the impulse to claim that I'd just bought him as an interesting item of bric-a-brac. 'He belongs to a friend,' I said. 'Well, a sort of friend. You remember the Midsummer Fayre last Saturday – well, while I was there I got talking to this girl who's just come to live in the village, and then her husband appeared and turned out to be someone I used to know, and then this afternoon she showed up here in the shop, in urgent need of dental treatment, but no-one to leave the baby with…' I paused for breath.

'So you volunteered,' said Oliver.

'Not exactly. But Erica really didn't have anyone else. I am sorry – I know it isn't ideal to have him here.'

He looked at Toby uncertainly. 'Oh well, as long as it hasn't interfered with shop business.'

'No. In fact I wish I could say it had, but we simply haven't had that many people in here.'

Oliver sighed. 'Oh dear, no coach-trips then? And I don't suppose there will be now, not this late in the day. Anyway,' he said stooping over Toby and patting him absent-mindedly on the head, 'in the meantime, yes of course, this little chap can stay here.'

However, Oliver's pessimism as to the likelihood of more customers proved unfounded. Only a few minutes later we saw the familiar green and cream livery of the local tour company slide past the shop window en route to the car park by the church. Soon a straggle of visitors were ambling their way down the High Street, pausing to gaze in the various shop windows or to admire the quaint buildings and flower displays. Within a few minutes, many of the trippers who had not been quick enough to secure a table in the Patchwork Pumpkin were browsing in Pilgrim's Antiques.

I wheeled the pushchair into the back room. Neither it, nor its occupant could be left sitting in the middle of the shop floor. Toby, however, had different ideas. As soon as he found himself being moved away from the interesting new influx of admirers, he started to protest. Soon whimpers of dissatisfaction from the back room grew into roars of anger which reached noisily and distractingly into the shop.

Oliver raised a harassed face from a set of

teaspoons which he was attempting to sell to a woman with grey hair and a doubtful expression. 'Tessa - ?' he implored. 'Could you - ?'

Longing fruitlessly for Erica's immediate return, I grabbed the bag and went to pacify Toby. I picked him up and jiggled him, but it was no good. He was not for pacifying. Proffered toys were knocked to the floor as he continued to bawl his unhappiness. Desperately I delved into the bag once more, and found the bottle of milk. Erica had left no guidelines as to Toby's feeding time, but now certainly seemed as good as any.

I wondered what I should do about warming it. We only had a kettle in the shop, and though Oliver's flat was just upstairs, I was reluctant to ask any more favours. In any case, I didn't even know what temperature it should be. Shouldn't I be testing it with an elbow? Or was that bathwater?

I decided that one cold meal couldn't do too much damage. 'Look at this, Toby!' I cooed. 'Look, lovely milk! Wouldn't you like some of this lovely milk?'

Toby paused in mid-bellow. He eyed the bottle and me with renewed suspicion.

'Yummy, yummy,' I coaxed again.

Picking him up, I perched on the chair which Oliver used when working. Settling the baby as comfortably as I could on my lap, I put the bottle to his mouth and heaved a sigh of relief as he latched onto the teat.

I watched him as he sucked greedily. What a strange afternoon it had turned out to be. Of all the

41

various jobs I had done in the shop over the years, I had never before sat feeding a baby. Which was just as well, because it was hardly a suitable place. The dusty gloom of the room, the distinct aromas of wood-treatments and varnish, the tins of polish and the dirty rags – it wasn't at all the right kind of surroundings in which to tend such a round, pink and healthy infant.

Not that Toby himself seemed worried. Even the fact that he was having to drink from a bottle had not appeared to faze him, as he fed noisily and contentedly. I settled myself more comfortably. He was so heavy, so warm and solid in my arms. I looked down at him, his head moving slightly in rhythm to his sucking, his eyes closed in rapt concentration. The fine tufted baby hair was almost as dark as Daniel's. Even his nose and chin were the same. Now that I knew of the relationship, I wondered how I could ever have missed it.

Once again the feeling of strangeness swept over me. If only things had worked out differently between Daniel and me... If only that awful afternoon at the flat had never happened. If we had gone ahead and got married, as he had said he wanted to, one day, one day... Would *I* have had Daniel's baby? And if so, would he have looked like Toby? Would I have been sitting here in the shop holding a baby that looked just like this one, but which was my very own?

I closed my eyes and pushed away the vision. It would be totally stupid to allow myself to follow that line of thought. In any case, if Daniel and I had stayed together, I wouldn't even have been working in Oliver's shop here in Little Bagford. We would have stayed in Bristol, perhaps even bought a nice little house with a garden. Especially if we'd had a child. But then, that child would have grown beyond babyhood long ago. He would have been a schoolboy by now. Despite my sensible intentions, my mind at once conjured up an older version of Toby, a junior-school boy, with muddy knees and a smile full of mischief. Myself seeing him off each morning, making sure he had a packed lunch and his games kit. Welcoming him home again at tea-time, hearing about his lessons and his homework as I happily prepared an evening meal for Daniel.

Toby gave a resounding burp and pushed the empty bottle away. I looked up abruptly to find Oliver standing in the doorway.

'Well, that's the last of the customers,' he said. 'Some of them even bought things.' He gazed at me curiously. 'Are you all right? Sorry I had to banish you and the baby out here.'

I put down the bottle. 'No, no, that's all right. It should be me apologising. If I'd realised just how much disruption he'd cause, I'd never have agreed to look after him.'

'Well, I don't suppose you could have done anything else,' he said. 'It wasn't really a problem. But I'm afraid *you* might have a problem though.' He nodded towards Toby and I looked down to see the baby's face had gone scarlet, his features frowning in concentration. Oliver grinned. 'There are some things about being a parent that you never forget.'

I recoiled as the smell hit me.

'I'm afraid,' observed Oliver, not without a tinge of smugness, 'that you could be in for a little spot of nappy changing.'

'Nappy changing!' I said. 'But I've never changed a nappy in my life. I wouldn't even know how to do it.'

'You'll manage. Has his mother left you everything you'll need?'

'I suppose so,' I admitted. 'There's a mat to put him on and baby wipes and stuff. Does that sound right?'

'It sounds fine,' he said. 'Just what you need. Have fun!'

I frowned at his retreating back. It was all very well for him to joke, but this was serious. I really had no idea what to do. For a moment I was tempted to call him back, if only to give directions from a distance, but the sudden sounds of a customer's entrance forestalled me. There could be no help from Oliver, at least for the moment.

In the silence, I regarded Toby helplessly.

He stared back up at me, as if aware of my terrible ignorance.

I sighed and, still holding him, went to unpack the bag. With my free hand I lifted out a disposable nappy and began to clumsily unfold it. So which was the front and which was the back? And did it matter? Just how important was it that I got it the right way round? And why on earth did looking after a baby have to be so very complicated?

Chapter 4

I had just about finished the job when I was aware of a car door slamming outside the shop, followed by the jangle of the bell.

There was a moment of silence, then I heard Daniel's voice. 'Hi – er - have you got someone called Tessa here? And a baby?'

'Ah – Toby's father, I presume?' Oliver had obviously worked out at once who the visitor was. By the time I had gathered up bag and baby and made my entrance, the two men had already introduced themselves.

Daniel turned towards me. 'Thank you,' he said, without noticeable warmth. 'Erica rang me to explain what had happened.' He took Toby from me. 'I'm sorry you had to be imposed upon like this. I'm sure it must have been extremely inconvenient.'

'Not at all,' I said, feeling both chilled and irritated by his tone. 'He was no bother at all.'

'Well, anyway,' said Daniel. 'I'm just telling you I appreciate it. I can't imagine why Erica chose to leave him with you, when you're so plainly at work.'

'She didn't exactly have a choice, did she?' I said. 'Poor girl hardly knows anyone in Little Bagford. Apparently she did do her best to get in touch with you, but you had your mobile switched off.'

'Of course I had it switched off. When I'm talking to a client, I can't keep being disturbed by domestic calls. How unprofessional would that look!'

'Oh well, it wasn't a problem anyway,' said Oliver. 'And if Erica needs emergency babysitting in future, I'm sure she'll have more contacts in the village by then.'

'It doesn't exactly look 'professional' for us to have a baby in a shop,' I said to Daniel. 'Don't you think your responsibility as a father ought to come above your responsibility to your clients?'

For a moment we stared at each other angrily.

'How *is* your wife's tooth anyway?' asked Oliver.

I realised with a pang I had given no thought to poor Erica at all. 'Yes, how is she?' I said belatedly.

'Fine,' said Daniel. He turned back to Oliver. 'Yes, she's absolutely okay now, thank you. The dentist managed to sort it out straight away. She's been told she'll have to go back later, but at least he managed to deal with the pain and do a decent temporary repair.'

'Good,' I said.

There was a pause.

'Well,' said Daniel, 'I shall take Toby home then.' He turned towards the door.

'Hang on a moment,' I called. 'There's still all his stuff here - his pushchair, and his bag of toys and things. I'll bring them out for you.' I gathered up all Toby's paraphernalia and followed Daniel out to the car, where he was already deftly fastening Toby into his car seat.

'I can see,' I said with an effort to sound more pleasant, 'that you've done that before. It took me ages to undo his pushchair straps earlier on.'

'You get used to it.' He straightened. 'Well, then. Thank you very much again. As I said – I'm just sorry you had to be inconvenienced.'

'I wasn't really,' I admitted. 'Well, not *very* much, anyway.'

'I did come straight here the moment Erica told me what she'd done.'

'It's all right. I was managing perfectly well.'

'Yes, you always were little Miss Perfect.'

I stared at him.

'Sorry,' he said shortly. 'I do know I should be grateful, but it's ridiculous that she should have chosen to leave him with you of all people. There must have been someone else she could have asked.'

'Thanks,' I said. 'Thank you very much indeed.'

He made an impatient gesture. 'You know what I mean. It's not that I think you're incapable. Christ, you were never ever that. It's just... Well, it was insensitive – tactless of her.'

I looked at him. 'Daniel,' I asked, 'just how much exactly have you told Erica about us?'

'About us?'

'About how we used to be.'

He busied himself making sure Toby was comfortable. 'I told her that we used to be friends, if that's what you mean.'

'You didn't mention that we were actually in a full-on relationship?'

He shrugged. 'I'm sure she managed to read between the lines. I didn't go on and on about it, obviously.'

'In other words, you didn't actually tell her.'

'Oh, for God's sake, Tess! Erica's not naive. She quite understands that I didn't live like a monk before I met her.'

'Well, that's true enough.'

'Meaning?'

'Do you honestly need reminding? Seriously?'

He slammed the rear door shut with a bang that made Toby squawk. 'I've got to go,' he said. 'I want to be there when Erica gets home.' Climbing into the driver's seat, he paused and with an effort said, 'Anyway, thank you once again for your help.'

'My pleasure,' I said icily.

I watched him drive away. Anger burned within me, but it was directed as much against myself as him. Daniel had obviously not changed a bit, but why on earth had I allowed myself to descend to his level, especially when I'd recently been applauding myself for being so rational about the situation? Why hadn't I kept that mature and sensible detachment? It should have been easy enough to stay cool but polite. And what did he mean by calling me perfect? Why had he made it sound like an insult?

Oliver was beginning to shut up shop when I went back inside.

'So that was your 'someone you used to know',' he said. 'Did I imagine it, or did I get the impression that there was some kind of history between you two?'

48

Occasionally Oliver surprised me with his perception.

There seemed no sense in fudging the issue. 'No, you did get that impression,' I admitted. 'Not to put too fine a point on it, Daniel and I were once very much an item. All set to live happily ever after, or so I thought at the time.'

He looked at me.

'You're quite right,' I said. 'It would never have lasted.'

'I didn't say that,' he said. 'But all the same, I'm very glad that you didn't end up with him.' He picked up a roll of brown paper and disappeared into the back room.

Absent-mindedly I turned the shop sign to 'Closed', then wandered after him. 'Oliver,' I asked. 'Do you think I'm perfect?'

He turned and raised an eyebrow, smiling. 'But of course you are, Tess. Don't you know that by now?'

I tried to smile back, but somehow his answer did not reassure me as I felt it should.

It was Thursday evening before I finally managed to meet up with Jodie for a proper chat.

'You know, you don't have to invite me to supper every time James is away on business,' she smiled. 'It's always lovely, but don't ever feel that you've got to.'

'It's a good excuse,' I said. 'I think your husband should go to conferences more often. We can't have a good girly gossip with husbands hanging about – or mothers, come to that.'

'Your mum's at the Fossils Club?'

'She is,' I confirmed. The club had been founded years ago by a vicar who had given it the well-intentioned but long-winded title of the Little Bagford Senior Citizens Society of Friendly Apostles. This, however, had so quickly morphed into 'The Fossils' Club' that few people would have known it by anything else. 'Yes,' I said, 'she never misses it, not if she can possibly help it. Which means we can speak freely.'

'Ooh,' said Jodie. 'A proper gossip? Does that mean there been *developments*?'

I had already told Jodie over the phone about what had happened at the fete. I had given her the full details about my unexpected encounter with Daniel but hadn't yet had the chance to let her know about my unscheduled stint as a babysitter. 'Come and help me prepare the salad,' I said, 'and I'll tell you all about it.'

By the time the lettuce and tomatoes were washed and the quiche and new potatoes cooked and ready to serve, Jodie had been brought up to date with the events of Monday afternoon. As always, she was a good listener, knowing exactly when to stay silent, when to ask the right question, and when to express just the right degree of sympathy or outrage on my behalf.

'So there you have, it,' I said, picking up the plates. 'That's the full story. Shall we eat outside?'

The air was warm and still; it was a perfect

evening on which to dine alfresco. Shafts of late evening sunlight made the flowers gleam, turning the oriental poppies, the helenium and day lilies into fiery beacons of colour that burned vividly against the tall stems of white phlox.

Even in the green and shadier corner in which the table was set, Albertine roses rambled high above us into the apple tree, their fragrance hanging warm and sweet. Jodie brushed a scattering of pink petals from the chairs, and we sat down. 'Poor old Tess,' she said. 'You've not had much luck when it comes to men, have you.'

'Not really. Not that there's been a long procession of them,' I added wryly.

'Well,' she said, 'I know there was Alan. And you've told me about Matt, and now there's this Daniel crawling out from the woodwork....'

'Alan was hardly around long enough to be counted,' I observed, pouring the wine. 'You know very well that we only went out together for a little while, and even then it wasn't as if he behaved badly. In fact he hardly behaved at all, really.' We both smiled as we remembered Alan, a local estate agent whose deeper passions had only really been ignited by the ups and downs of the property market. I had already begun to realise that although our relationship was easy-maintenance, it had little scope for development, so I was not too upset when a career step had taken him north to work in a Lancashire branch of the firm. Once he had relocated, things had fizzled out naturally, and the last I had heard from him was a brief greeting on the back of a postcard depicting a golf course near Morecambe. I hadn't replied.

'But Matt - ' said Jodie. 'I know that he happened before you came back to Little Bagford, but from the way you talked to me about him...'

I stared down at my slice of quiche. Yes, Matt had lasted longer. But like most of the men I'd dated in Bristol, he'd been a rebound choice when I had still not fully got over the bust-up with Daniel. If it hadn't been for that, perhaps we'd have made a go of it. But then again, perhaps not. I'd already been wondering about the possibility of looking for a different job, even if it was one that took me away from Bristol. And then, before I'd had the chance to come to any decision, fate had intervened in the form of a phone call telling me that my father had been taken ill.

When I told Matt that I was needed back in Little Bagford, I think both of us realised that it might signal the end of the relationship. He helped me to pack, said all the right things, and promised to phone me often – which he did, for a while. But I'd been too preoccupied with looking after my father to make much of a response, or even notice when the calls finally ceased. Now, I realised rather sadly, it was almost an effort to remember Matt's face.

I pushed a potato round my plate and sighed. 'No, even he and I weren't really right for each other. I sometimes envy you and James, you seem so – so contented.'

'Contented - or boring, do you mean?' She grinned. 'But yes, we do get along okay most of the time. Certainly he's never put me through the sort of trauma that Daniel inflicted on you. And now, all these years later, he's turned up to haunt you again. It's not even as if you can just ignore him, not with his wife flinging their baby in your face.'

'Not exactly 'flinging',' I laughed. 'But I know what you mean.'

She reached for the salad dressing. 'I suppose Erica can't be blamed, not if Daniel really hadn't explained to her exactly how things were between you and him, but even so… It must have been awful for you, being landed with a totally strange baby to look after.'

'Ah, he wasn't strange - rather cute actually.'

'Stop being flippant,' she said. 'You know what I mean. After all, it's not as if either of us know much about babies.'

There was a small pause, her words hanging in the quiet evening air. I had first met Jodie when she and James moved into the village as newly-weds, not long after I myself had returned to live with my mother. We had become good friends almost at once, and she had cheerfully confided her hopes about starting a family. But somehow those longed-for babies had never come along. During the first year or two she had spoken of her disappointment, and later had told me of visits to Bristol for various hospital tests. But gradually, as time crept by, a sad silence had settled over the matter. More than once I had been tempted to probe, and now that she had sort-of raised the subject I began impulsively, 'Talking of which - '

But at the same moment Jodie herself started

speaking. 'You know, your garden is looking absolutely beautiful. That big pot of lavender smells fabulous, and the roses are just magic. I don't know how you find time to put so much work into it all.'

Her change of subject was abrupt and clumsy, but if she didn't want to talk about babies, then I wasn't going to push her into it. I shoved back my chair and stood up. 'Cheese and biscuits?' I offered.

I fetched them out, and we sat companionably finishing our meal, nibbling olives and Applewood Cheddar, chatting amiably about the merits of growing one's own vegetables, and whether or not organic food really was better for you. Slowly the last of the light drained from the sky, and a little chill breeze got up.

I shivered. 'Coffee indoors?'

'Yes, that would be lovely. Just a small decaff, if you've got any.'

'No problem.' I decided not to comment upon her restraint. Judging by the generous amount of salad that she'd put away, coupled with the miniscule amount of wine, I guessed that she must be back on one of her Healthy-Eating-to-Aid-Conception diets. I just hoped that sooner or later one of them might work.

Standing up, I began to stack the dishes ready to take inside.

She started rewrapping the remaining cheese. 'It was all very delicious,' she smiled. 'And eaten in the perfect surroundings'

From inside the house, a door banged. 'Sounds like Mum's home,' I said. 'I hadn't realised it was

54

quite so late. Oh well, thanks Jodie, for sitting there listening to me moaning on. I'll do the same for you some time. Come on, let's go inside and warm up a bit.'

We gathered up the dirty plates, and headed indoors, glad to get out of the evening chill. In the kitchen my mother was already filling the kettle, and was plainly in good spirits. 'We've been making final arrangements for our trip,' she told me. 'Oh hello, Jodie dear, have you had a nice evening? It's good of you to come round and keep Tess company.'

I sighed, but said nothing at my mother's invariable assumption that I was incapable of enjoying an evening on my own. 'Arrangements for the trip?' I prompted instead. 'You mean Bournemouth?'

'Yes, of course. It hadn't slipped your mind, had it? Not long to go now – only just over a week, in fact.'

I smiled at her obvious excitement. No, I certainly hadn't forgotten that my mother, along with two dozen or more of Little Bagford's senior citizens, would soon be off in pursuit of geriatric jollity on the south coast.

'Oh, it should be wonderful at the seaside,' said Jodie, 'especially if this weather holds. And you're going for a whole fortnight this year, aren't you? That should really give you time to relax.'

'Yes, we only went for one week last year,' said my mother. 'But we all enjoyed it so much we decided to make it longer this time, especially as it turned out it wouldn't cost that much more. It's a lovely hotel, and really close to the sea-front. And the food – delicious! I'm going to see if I can get hold of their bread-and-butter pudding recipe this year. I don't know what they put in it, but it had a real sort of fruity tang about it...'

We drank coffee and listened as my mother extolled the menu, and all the other delights of the holiday that she had enjoyed last year. She was looking forward to going away again, and I had to admit that so was I. Dearly as I loved my mother, I felt it did us both good to have a break from each other, even if it was only for a fortnight.

'I think *you* could do with a holiday, Jodie dear,' observed my mother. 'When was the last time you had a bit of fresh sea air? You and James always seem to work so hard, what with him so often away on business, and you busy cooking for the café all the time.'

Jodie laughed. 'Well, I don't think I work any harder than most other people, but I must admit that I'm beginning to feel a bit sleepy right now. Time to go home, I think.'

On the doorstep she thanked me once again for the meal. 'And for the gossip,' she added. 'Though I do think you've forgotten one person who ought to be on that list of men in your life.'

'Who?'

She smiled. 'Can't you guess? Oliver.'

'Oliver?' I stared at her. 'But Oliver and I have never gone out together. Well, not in a romantic way.'

'All the same – Yes, I know he's a bit older than you, but it's not an impossibly wide age gap.

Anyway, I sometimes get the feeling that he likes you more than just as a friend, you know.'

'Of course he doesn't.'

She raised an eyebrow, but without further comment turned to begin making her way down the road; a slim, brisk figure disappearing into the dusk. She would be home in five minutes, home to the little house she shared with James.

I paused a moment before shutting the door and making it secure for the night. I was glad she'd enjoyed the meal, but it was me who had been left with food for thought.

But by the morning light, it was easier to dismiss Jodie's theory for the soufflé of nonsense that it was. She had whipped it up from some misplaced zeal to create a love affair for me, and seasoned it with a large dash of wishful thinking. But I wasn't having any. Jodie might have meant to spark a romance, but I valued my friendship with Oliver far too much to start reading in any more than actually existed. He was a kind and considerate boss and a good companion, but nothing more, and I had no intention of allowing any such silliness to affect our comfortable relationship.

In any case, there were other distractions. Arriving at work I found that Oliver had received another phone call from his daughter. This time Anita's complaints about her husband Todd seemed to have staggered from bad to worse, and she had downloaded every detail onto her unfortunate father.

'You know, 'he observed rather gloomily, 'it wouldn't surprise me if she ended up coming back home.'

'Well – I suppose a holiday might give her a bit of a breathing space,' I said. 'By the time she goes back to Chicago, she may well have decided she's madly in love with him again.'

'*If* she goes back.'

I looked at him.

'When I say Anita is seriously fed up with life in the States,' he said, 'I do mean it.'

'Oh dear,' I said, beginning to understand for the first time just how critical things were. If Anita *was* thinking of a permanent return, then I strongly suspected that I would get seriously fed up with life in Little Bagford. I had become so accustomed to living without the daily irritation of Anita's autocratic attitudes, that the thought of having to start coping with them again was disturbing. 'But surely Little Bagford would be too small for her, especially after Chicago?' I asked.

His expression lightened a little. 'You're right,' he said. 'Anita won't want to be stuck in the countryside again. Not for long, anyway.'

'No,' I agreed.

We looked at each other.

'And yet – oh, I don't know,' he said. 'When does a father ever grow out of feeling somehow responsible for the well-being of his child?'

'When she's grown up?' I hazarded.

'Yes, I know that's how it *ought* to work. After all,' he continued, almost to himself, 'She's my daughter, and I shall always love her, but even I would have to admit that she's never been the easiest person to live with. Especially when she's bored. I just wish I could come up with some kind of a project to keep her occupied.'

'But surely that's her own responsibility. In any case, Chicago is such a huge place that there must be far more things over there that she could get involved in if she wanted to. Or perhaps even Todd could help her find something?'

'It's Todd who has been her project,' Oliver said gloomily. 'And now she's discovering that Todd will always be Todd, and totally impervious to any kind of moulding, then I think she's about ready to give up on him.'

I stared at the dust motes floating in a ray of sunshine, unable to think of anything sensible I could say. To me, it seemed a very odd approach to marriage, but there was no comment I could make that wasn't directly rude about his daughter.

He shrugged. 'Anyway,' he sighed, 'there's very little point standing around worrying about things. It'll sort itself out one way or another – it always does. Meanwhile, I have a bureau with woodworm awaiting my attention, so I'll be in the back room if you need me.'

He disappeared into the comforting refuge of the workroom, leaving me to carry on with my regular chore of bringing the books up to date. It was never a task designed to raise my spirits, so I was glad of the distraction of the shop bell, until I looked up from my paperwork to see Erica manoeuvring the pushchair in through the door.

'It's all right,' she grinned, seeing my expression, 'I'm not after any more favours, not this time. I've just come to say thank you.'

'Thank you?'

'For babysitting,' she explained. 'You were a lifesaver that day. And I feel just awful that I haven't been in to thank you before now.'

'But there was no need,' I said. 'I wasn't expecting you to. Daniel thanked me when he came to pick up Toby. I hope,' I added, 'that your tooth is okay now?'

'Oh, fine – fine -   But it wouldn't have been without your help, so I wanted to say a proper thank-you. This is from me and Toby – and Daniel, of course.'   She dived into the tray underneath the pushchair, emerging with a brightly coloured gift bag. 'Just a very small token of appreciation.'

Conscious of her expectant gaze, I opened the bag and pulled out what I recognised as being an extremely expensive brand of chocolates. 'Goodness – how kind – but - '

'Are they all right? I wondered if you might prefer something else, but Daniel said he remembered that you always liked these particular chocolates.'

'Yes – yes, thank you very much - '

'Oh good, I'm glad he got it right.'

' - but there was really no need. Looking after Toby was no trouble. No trouble at all.'

'Well, I know he's usually a good little guy.' She looked down at him fondly, 'but even so, it *must* have been inconvenient for you. You were working, for goodness sake. The last thing you needed was a baby to look after. Anyway,' she continued, 'that isn't all. I'm also here to ask you to dinner.'

'Ask me to dinner?' I repeated stupidly.

'You and a guest. A friend. A partner – anyone you like, in fact. I thought it would be the best way of returning your kindness.'

'But there really is no need. The chocolates are more than enough,'

'But we *want* you to come. We want to have a dinner party. I'm going to ask our next-door neighbours, and Danny's colleague and his partner are going to be invited, and of course we definitely want *you* to come.'

'But - ' I stared at her helplessly. Had Daniel still really given her so little idea of our past relationship? And if not – should I be the one to tell her? And if so, how on earth to do it tactfully? Or did she know, and simply not care? Or had she long since dismissed me as being far too old and frumpy to pose the slightest threat to anyone? Reluctantly I had to admit that this was probably the most likely scenario.

But Erica wasn't giving me time to hesitate. 'Now don't say you can't come. *Please.*'

It was like trying to kick away a friendly puppy. Helplessly I said, 'I do think I'm rather booked up over the next few evenings. I may not be free, I'm afraid. When are you thinking of having this dinner party?'

'You can choose your own day,' she said.

'You'll be the guest of honour, so I want to make quite sure you can come.'

'But honestly, you don't have to ask me to dinner. The chocolates are more than generous - '

'But we really want you to come. And a friend. Anyone you like. Please. It's just so nice to feel I'm getting to know a few people at last.'

I hesitated. Again, it was impossible to ask her if she had actually checked with Daniel before issuing this invitation. But had she?

Erica looked at me expectantly. 'So which evening would suit you best?'

'I don't really know.'

'Perhaps you'd like to check with the person you want to bring? I don't mind male or female. Or perhaps there isn't anyone you want to ask? You're welcome to come by yourself, of course. That would be just as nice.'

Oh no. Bad enough that I couldn't think of an excuse to refuse, without appearing such a complete loser that I didn't even have anyone to come with me. 'Thank you,' I said. 'Yes, I think I'd better check first. And then I'll get back to you.'

'That's great,' she said. 'Just give me a ring when you've decided. Oh, I'm so looking forward to it! Have you got my phone number? Then you can call me as soon as you know.'

I watched as she sorted out all her various contact details. If I had wanted something to take my mind off the potential problem of Anita, then I had certainly been given it.

Chapter 5

Happily, I did have a legitimate reason for keeping my head down for the next few days. My mother had always been a ditherer when it came to packing, and the holiday in Bournemouth was throwing her into a positive whirlwind of indecision.

'You're worse than ever this year,' I sighed, looking at the two large suitcases which now lay open on top of her bed. They were both almost full. 'You're only going for two weeks – not six months.'

'But the weather…' She hovered by her wardrobe, two different coloured tops in hand. 'You know what it's like when you go anywhere in this country. You have to pack for every possible kind of condition.'

'Well looking at this lot, I'd say you've managed it.' I lightly excavated the top layers of the nearest case. 'Do you really need all these things?'

'Yes, I do,' she said firmly. 'After all, I want to look my best. Suppose it should be only one kind of weather for the whole of the holiday. Whether it stayed hot or cold, then I'd need enough clothes to be able to ring the changes occasionally.'

'At this rate you could ring the changes several times every day.'

'I want to be able to look nice,' she insisted. 'Sheila and Elaine and Bridget – they all seem to save their best clothes for these occasions. I don't want to look dowdy in comparison.'

'But you never look dowdy. I'm only worried,' I explained, 'about what'll happen if there isn't anyone around to help you carry it all.'

'Oh, one of the men from the Fossils will help me. Hector will, I know. He's such a gentleman, he wouldn't mind me asking.'

'But he'll have his own luggage to look after.'

'He'll be travelling more lightly than me. Men always seem to need less.'

'But what if he's decided to take his entire wardrobe this time? Do let me help you cut it down just a little.'

With the bribe that she could borrow my lightweight mac and new blue jumper, we at last managed to get the luggage down to a reasonable amount. In truth, I was pleased that she was looking forward to the holiday so much. The winter and spring had been long and chilly, and the virus she'd caught earlier seemed to have sapped her enthusiasm for most things. It was good now to see the return of her old vitality, and I hoped that a bit of sunshine and fresh sea air would consolidate the transformation.

But she certainly wasn't the only one to be excited about the break. When I walked down to the village green with her for the Friday morning departure there was, despite the grey skies and steady drizzle, a distinct school-outing air about the small group of Fossils also waiting there to board the coach. They greeted each other with noisy excitement.

Hector Curtis waved as he saw my mother. 'So there you are, Pat! I'm glad we're getting on at the first pick-up point. This way we can choose where we sit. Where do you want to be - lording it at the front, or up to mischief in the back?'

My mother giggled girlishly.

I was glad to see he was looking healthy and strong, and with only one medium-sized suitcase of his own. He grinned at me. 'Looking forward to having the house to yourself, young Tess? I expect you've got the wild parties already planned, haven't you?'

I laughed back. It was impossible not to like Hector. Even now, he had gathered a small crowd of appreciative elderly ladies around him.

'I'd say *he's* the one who needs to behave himself.' A man of about my own age, whose face was only vaguely familiar, was also smiling at me. 'It's Fraser,' he prompted, holding out his hand. 'Hector's nephew. Long time, no see, Tess.'

Even as he said his name realisation dawned. 'Fraser?' I said. 'Oh goodness! Sorry I didn't recognise you for a moment. Yes, you're right, it's been such a long time! You were the last person I was expecting to bump into.'

'Well, I do come to visit my uncle occasionally,' he said. 'But I suppose the last time you and I saw each other regularly was back in our schooldays.'

'And then you left,' I said. 'Where was it your family moved to? Newcastle? And do you still live there? Or have you moved since then?'

'Um – yes – no – and yes.'

I laughed. 'So what does that mean?'

'It means that yes, my parents did move to

Newcastle. No, I don't still live there, and yes, I moved back south quite a while ago. Oh, but here comes the coach – let's see them get on board first, and then we can catch up with things afterwards.'

For the next few minutes mayhem ruled as the senior citizens of Little Bagford vacillated between rushing on board to bag a good seat, or pausing long enough to ensure that their luggage had been safely stowed. Farewells were made and hugs exchanged, along with repeated instructions to have a nice time. Then, with bags and baggage at last on board, we watched the coach finally pull away, its passengers still waving as they rounded the corner and disappeared from view.

The rest of us began to drift away.

'Well,' said Fraser, turning back to me, 'I don't envy Bournemouth when that lot get there.' He grinned. 'So, do you need to rush off somewhere? Or have you got time for a chat?'

I glanced at my watch. 'Yes, I'm okay for a while. I actually work at the shop just over the road,' I said, waving a hand towards it. 'Pilgrim's Antiques. But Oliver - my boss - said he didn't mind if I was late going in this morning. So if you fancy a quick cuppa at the Patchwork Pumpkin, I'm sure he won't miss me. It would be a lot better than standing in the rain while we talk. Anyway,' I added, 'the Pumpkin does do much the best cakes in the village, and I feel I deserve one after all this.'

'You're right,' he agreed, as we entered the café and sat down at a table next to the window. 'There's something about seeing other people off on holiday that does make one feel in need of a treat. Perhaps it's a kind of recompense, because *we're* not going away.'

'Or simple greed,' I smiled. 'By the way, most of these cakes have been made by my friend Jodie, so I can recommend them with complete authority. The carrot-cake is particularly good. Or are you more of a shortbread fan?'

'Ginger parkin's my favourite,' he said. 'Although I've certainly been known to be led astray by a treacle tart.'

I laughed, remembering how I had always liked Fraser. In fact I'd even had a bit of a schoolgirl crush on him in the days before he moved away. But that seemed a lifetime ago, long before I'd met Daniel. Now, I relaxed back in my chair, enjoying the coffee-fragranced warmth of the café, and revelling in the unexpected feeling of freedom produced by my mother's departure. Over cappuccino and cake, it was easy to exchange news and swap details of our present lives.

'So you're a professional writer and photographer now?' I said. 'That sounds exciting. And married? Children? Hobbies? Interests? Shoe size, eye colour?' I added rapidly, realising that my request for his marital status had a distinctly predatory ring to it.

He smiled. 'Was married, now divorced,' he said. 'It was a few years ago, and I guess we were simply too young. But unfortunately that's the sort of thing you only realise with hindsight. Anyway, we grew apart fairly quickly. No kids, which was just as well, I suppose. But the break-up did turn me into a bit of a workaholic for a while.' He paused, and gazed for a moment out of the steam-obscured window. 'Oh well. It wasn't the way I'd have chosen to further my career, but all those months of sinking myself into work did pay off in the end. These days I'm much more able to choose my commissions. I tend to travel quite a lot.'

'Work - or pleasure?'

'Both. I enjoy my holidays, but I'm actually here because I'm working on a book about medieval buildings in this area. That's why my uncle suggested I might stay with him. And then it turned out that the date I could manage to get here was going to coincide with the time he'd be away. But we both agreed that I might just as well stay in his cottage anyway, even though he wasn't going to be there. And it did solve the problem of who was going to feed Buster while he was in Bournemouth.'

'Oh yes, of course. I'd forgotten about his cat. Bit of a character, that animal.'

'He and my uncle are two of a kind.' Fraser finished his coffee and pushed aside the empty cup. 'So there we are - I've told you all about me - what about you? What are you doing with your life?'

I shrugged. 'Well, you already know that I'm back living with my mother and working at the antique shop.'

'And - ?'

'And what?'

'Well, no-one's life is quite as two-dimensional as that. What else?'

I felt suddenly inadequate. Surely at my age I ought to have more to say for myself. But even the best spin doctor in the world would have had difficulty infusing excitement into my few romantic relationships and my very nondescript career in antiques. Fortunately a glance at the clock behind the counter came to my rescue.

'Oh wow, is that the time?' I said, pushing back my chair. 'I really must be going now. Poor Oliver will be wondering what on earth has happened to me. But thanks for the coffee, Fraser. If you've got a moment, you must come and have a coffee at my place next time. Or - tell you what,' I said impulsively, 'if you're going to be around for a few days longer, I've been asked to go to a dinner party, and the invitation extends to a guest of my choice – except that I haven't asked anyone yet. Would you like to come with me?'

He looked at me. 'Sure. In theory, anyway. When is it?'

'I've been told to set my own date. When are you available?'

He thought for a moment. 'Well, I'm pretty sure I'll be tied up most of this coming week. And even the following week I've got commitments. But if you could make it the Saturday in between those two weeks, I'll definitely keep it free.'

'That sounds great. You're quite sure you don't mind coming with me?'

'Of course not. Give me your number and I'll ring you next week to sort out the arrangements.'

I left him at the table, waving to him through the

blurry window as I hurried across the road to the shop. It was a relief to have solved the problem of finding someone to come with me – and yet I was already beginning to wonder if I had done the right thing.

I phoned Erica from the shop that afternoon, before doubts could really set in. She was delighted to hear that I would be bringing a friend, delighted with my choice of guest, delighted that the whole dinner party was falling into place so easily.

'Saturdays are always good for socialising,' she informed me happily. 'On weekdays, Danny sometimes works late, but even if he does get a Saturday call-out, he's always back in good time. He'll be home well before you all arrive.'

'Oh good,' I murmured weakly. Should I ask her if she had actually informed him of her guest list yet? But then, why should it be *my* problem? The dinner party hadn't been my idea, and I would certainly have wriggled out of it if only Erica had left me any kind of loophole.

I switched off my phone feeling vaguely dissatisfied.

Walking in, Oliver overheard my sigh. 'What's the matter, Tessa? Fed up already with the thought of being stuck at home while your mother's off gallivanting?'

'No, not really. Just life in general.'

'How about sharing a meal with me tonight? If you don't fancy being all alone at home?'

For a moment I was too taken aback to answer him. I had, very occasionally, been up to Oliver's flat over the shop, but I had never been invited for a meal.

'No?' he said. 'Well, I suppose I can't blame you. My cooking is pretty appalling, and I must admit I haven't got anything special on the menu. Just a spur of the moment thought, you see.'

'Oh Oliver,' I said. 'That really is so kind of you – but yes, perhaps it is a bit *too* spur of the moment. I've already organised my tea for tonight, you see…' I saw his glum expression and said, 'Look, I'd love to have a meal with you, but could we make it tomorrow night instead? That will give you time to sort out the food, and give me time to look forward to eating it.'

His face brightened. 'Oh yes, that's a much better idea. And Saturday night always feels like the sort of night to do something special, don't you think?' he said, unconsciously echoing Erica. He frowned. 'Now, what shall we eat? Do you like sausage and mash? I'm not too bad at that. And then perhaps some strawberries. Even I can't burn strawberries.'

My goodness, I thought. Perhaps my social life was looking up after all. That was two dinner invitations I had received within the past few days. And if things went in threes, well who knows what might turn up…

Oddly enough, that very evening brought the third invitation.

'Hi, Tess.' Jodie's voice on the other end of the phone was always a welcome sound. 'I was just wondering how you're getting on with having the house to yourself?'

'Fine thanks, Jodie. Rather enjoying it, actually. I've just eaten a very lazy ready-meal from the freezer, and now I'm about to slump in front of the television with a glass of wine. Mum's already rung me to say that she's arrived at the hotel safely, so I don't even have to worry about that.'

'All the same, I bet you'll miss not having her around for a fortnight.'

'Not at all – I shall very much enjoy having some proper *me*-time for a change.'

She laughed. 'So I can't persuade you to leave your solitary paradise and come and have Sunday lunch with us?'

'Ah, that's different! Yes, I'm sure I could make that sort of sacrifice. Is James away again?'

'No, he's at home for the next fortnight. So you can come and dine with the two of us for a change.'

'You're sure he won't mind me playing gooseberry?'

Jodie snorted. 'Tess, you do have a very romantic view of married life. James will be just as pleased as I'll be to have your company. Anyway, things are going to be changing soon. For a start, he's got a new job.'

'A new job? I didn't even know that he was looking for one! I thought he was happy as he is. Or did all the travelling get too much?'

She hesitated. 'Well, there were a variety of

72

reasons, but it's going to be better money, and he won't have to be away anything like as much as he has to now. Anyway, I'll tell you all about it on Sunday.'

'I can't wait till then.'

I could hear the smile in her voice. 'You'll have to.'

Despite my probing, I couldn't persuade Jodie to give me any more information. I put down the phone wondering what James' new job could be. I hoped very much that it wouldn't mean that they'd be moving away. That would the very worst kind of news as far as I was concerned, for I would miss Jodie dreadfully. But to a certain extent, James had always been a bit of an unknown quantity to me. I knew him well enough to chat to, of course, but our conversations were always on a fairly superficial level. Even if he had minded about being away so much, he probably wouldn't have told me. Nor had Jodie appeared too bothered by his absences either. But it couldn't be that easy to have James going off all over the place, while she was left at home. And yet, I thought guiltily, there she was, worrying about *me* being alone, merely because my mother was away for a few days. In fact, I was beginning to feel slightly paranoid about the number of people expressing concern that I might find myself adrift without her. Didn't they see that the reason I'd never bothered to move out of Little Bagford was for her sake, rather than mine?

Ridiculously, I felt almost shy when on Saturday evening I stood knocking on the side door beside Pilgrim's Antiques. I hadn't even been sure how to dress for the occasion. Obviously something different from what I would normally wear to work, but then nothing *too* elegant, in case it implied that I had unreasonable expectations of the evening. But nothing too scruffy either, in case Oliver should think that I couldn't be bothered to make an effort. In the end I settled upon black trousers and a primrose-yellow silk shirt, and spent the whole of the walk from my house to Oliver's wondering if I had got it right.

But when Oliver opened the door, I saw that he too was smarter than usual, in jacket and tie. I followed him up the stairs, carrying the bottle of red wine that was my contribution to the evening.

'Thanks, Tess - er – that's very kind of you. I'll just get some glasses…' He disappeared into the kitchen.

I stood and looked around me. The flat's living-room was larger than I'd remembered and despite its rather dated décor, had a pleasantly airy feel. At the far end was a dining table already set for two, while at the other was a comfortable looking sofa and armchair, a bureau and bookshelves.

'Well - ' he said, reappearing before I'd had time to further indulge my curiosity, and handing me a full wine glass. 'Here's to you, and me, and – er – hopefully to neither of us getting food poisoning tonight.'

I laughed, and immediately felt more

comfortable. 'Come on, Oliver, you can't be *that* bad at cooking.'

'I'm getting better. Margaret used to do all the meals, so when she died I was thrown in at the deep end. I'm much better than I was at first, if that's any kind of reassurance. Of course, if I'd had any sense, Margaret and I would have shared these tasks more equally, but then she was always busy doing *her* jobs, and I was always busy doing mine, so I never quite got round to learning.'

'I know what you mean,' I said. 'It's silly how people who live together can fall into their own little routines. But my mother and I are just the same. She tends to do the dusting and washing, I tend to be in charge of the heavy shopping and the bill-paying. I suppose we could chop and change from week to week but then, perhaps, that would just lead to confusion and stuff being left undone…' I paused, becoming aware that my conversation was perhaps not quite as scintillating as it might be.

But the very ordinariness of the subject matter seemed to be reassuring to Oliver. Absent-mindedly he took off his jacket and draped it over the back of a chair. 'Yes, you're quite right, there are always practical reasons for routines, that's why they become routines in the first place. All the same, cooking, of all things, is a skill that everyone really ought to know. It's a real shame that they don't seem to teach it in the schools any more. I know they did when I was a youngster, but even then it was a subject that only the girls were taught. Foolish, really – after all, everyone needs to eat, so why on earth shouldn't everyone learn to cook?'

Our conversation wandered into the comfortable territory of television chefs and cookery programmes, and I began to feel much more at ease. Before long, Oliver's tie had also been abandoned on the back of the chair, and I was donning a striped pinny and helping him to decide on the best way to cook sausages.

'This apron must have been enormous on Margaret,' I observed, wrestling to do up the strings behind my waist.

'It's mine,' he admitted. 'Anita bought it for me. A present, before she left for America. I suppose she thought it would encourage me, only I very rarely bother wearing it. Never remember to put it on, to be honest.'

'No, I wouldn't usually bother either - it's just that I don't want to splash anything on my clothes.'

'That would be a shame,' he agreed. 'Especially when you're looking so nice too.' He pushed his hands through his hair awkwardly, as if he had made an indecent remark.

I busied myself with looking for cutlery. His embarrassment was contagious.

'Well, er - potatoes,' he said confusedly. 'Where did I put them? Ah, here they are, and I do know how to peel a spud properly, if nothing else.'

The meal, thanks to both our efforts, turned out to be surprisingly successful.

'You know, your idea of adding some cider to the gravy was a masterstroke,' observed Oliver. 'I'd never have thought of doing that myself. I'm just not very culinary-minded. All the same, I'm sure I shouldn't have allowed you to help so much.' He frowned as he rose to clear away the dessert dishes. 'It's hardly good manners to let the guest do all the work.'

'That's all right, I enjoyed myself,' I said. 'It's been a really relaxing and pleasant evening. In fact, probably much more so than next Saturday will turn out to be. Did I tell you that I've been invited to dinner by Erica and Daniel? Or Erica, at least. I'm not so sure if Daniel actually knows about it yet.'

Oliver looked at me.

'I'm not going by choice,' I pointed out quickly. 'But you try getting out of an invitation when it's issued by someone like Erica. She doesn't leave loopholes and she doesn't stand for excuses. But I'm really not looking forward to it. Whereas tonight has just been very comfortable and very enjoyable.'

'Well, it's good of you to say so,' he smiled. 'I must say that having your help made all the difference. But at least you can allow me to get the coffee all by myself. And I do have proper coffee, not just the instant stuff that we have downstairs. Make yourself comfortable, it won't take a moment.'

I wandered over to the window and stood gazing out while the tempting smell of freshly-ground coffee drifted across from the kitchen. Outside I could see that it wasn't quite dark yet, although the sky was streaked with the soft blues and peachy-orange of impending sunset. There were still one or two people walking their dogs on the village green, while on the far side of the road the fairy lights of The Dragon's

77

Head beer garden danced and twinkled in the dusk. From this high angle the village looked strangely unfamiliar, and I stared out, enjoying the novelty of it.

'Milk or cream?' called Oliver from the kitchen. 'Unless you want it black?'

'Um – cream, please. There was some left over from the strawberries, wasn't there?'

'Plenty.'

Moving away, I turned my attention to the room. I supposed Oliver must have been living in this flat for a good few years now. Didn't I remember him once telling me that he and Margaret had bought the business soon after they had married? It must have been their first proper home; the place where he, she and Anita had all lived as a family. Or at least had done so until Anita had left home, and Margaret died in a road accident on her way back from a day's jaunt to Bath.

Not that there was much outward trace of those years of domestic life. Other than a rather stiffly posed studio photograph of the three of them, taken when Anita was still a child, there were few personal touches. The other pictures were of conventional landscapes, water-colours depicting purple moorlands and misty mountains, wide skies and shining black lochs. I was just wondering if there was something psychological to be gleaned from all this when he reappeared with a large pot of coffee.

'That smells wonderful.' I smiled rather guiltily, aware that my curiosity had been degenerating into downright nosiness.

'Good.' He paused. 'Well - so this time next week you'll be having dinner with your ex-boyfriend, I suppose?'

'Not so much 'ex-boyfriend' as 'Erica's husband',' I said. 'Although I've a horrible feeling that she *still* may not realise that we were once very much an item. But at least there will be more than just the three of us, thank goodness. Apparently their next-door neighbours, as well as some colleagues of Daniel's will be there, and I've managed to rope in an old school-friend of mine to come with me. I suppose it won't be too bad. Just not as nice and relaxing as tonight has been.'

He smiled. 'It's the first time I've entertained since Margaret died.'

'Then I think you can truthfully claim,' I said, 'that it's been a total success.'

Chapter 6

Despite the sunlight coming through the curtains, I awoke late next morning. Luxuriating in my temporarily solo state, I surfaced slowly, coaxed into consciousness by the sound of birdsong drifting in through my window. From further away came the distant hum of a lawnmower. Someone somewhere was already up and busy, but I stayed where I was, enjoying the prospect of a leisurely day ahead, punctuated only by a pleasantly sociable Sunday lunch cooked by Jodie. It wasn't until quite late that I emerged from the shower just in time to hear the phone start ringing.

I hurried across to my bedroom, and picked it up with damp hands.

'Tess?' To my surprise it was James on the other end. He came straight to the point. 'Listen, Tess, I'm afraid the meal is off today. Sorry about that, but Jodie isn't really up to it.'

'Oh dear! Is she all right?'

'Oh yes, yes – well, more or less. But she isn't feeling good, so the last thing she needs to be doing is cooking. So perhaps you could come round next Sunday instead?'

'Yes, of course. But – what's the problem? Is she okay? Is there anything I can do to help?'

'No, she's fine. She just needs a quiet morning in bed and no cooking. So I'm afraid it would be best if you don't come round today. I'm sure she'll give you a ring herself when she's feeling better.'

I put down the phone and towelled myself properly dry, my bubble of contentment effectively burst. Poor Jodie. I hoped she would be all right soon. But oh dear, it was disappointing. So much for the pleasant day that I'd anticipated. For apart from wanting to find out more about James's new job, I'd looked forward to telling her all about my dinner with Oliver; about how well it had gone, and how - despite her teasing - there had been nothing romantic about it at all. And I had also wanted to tell her about my bumping into Fraser, and how I had invited him to go with me to the dinner party at Daniel and Erica's. And did she think that had been a sensible thing to do? For I had to admit that my rash offer had been preying on my mind ever since I'd made it. Had I been too pushy in asking him to go with me? After all, that was the first time that I'd seen him in ages. What if he'd thought I was desperate? And the worst thing was that I hadn't even allowed him a get-out clause. Despite the fact that I had cursed Erica for not giving me a definite date on which I could claim to be unavailable, I'd ended up doing exactly the same thing to Fraser. It was too late now to change anything, but I still felt I could have done with Jodie's reassurance.

I wandered downstairs and started filling a bowl with cereal. Oh well. My lunch plans might have fallen through, but at least the weather hadn't reneged on me. The sun was still shining and the sky was still blue. I decided to wander down to the shop for a

81

Sunday paper. If there was nothing more exciting in prospect, then I might just as well sit in the garden with a mug of coffee and read through the supplements.

The village was looking particularly nice today. Too often I took the charms of Little Bagford for granted, and indeed, as a teenager I could hardly wait to leave and head off to pastures newer and greener. Bristol University was to be only the first step on my intended journey. With some qualifications and work experience under my belt, I had planned to go abroad, to take jobs in other countries, and travel the world.

So what had gone wrong? If my father hadn't died, if my mother hadn't had her near breakdown, what would my life be like now?

Although Little Bagford's attractions were undeniable, was it really where I wanted to remain for the rest of my life? I began to look around me as I walked down the lane, consciously taking notice of my surroundings. No normal person could fail to appreciate the little stone cottages and shops, the crooked roofs, the small windows with their quirky glass panes, the narrow front gardens crammed, country-style, with pinks and poppies and unruly banks of lavender. Even where there was no room for a garden, hanging baskets and tubs of greenery adorned doorways and railings. And if one could bottle a fragrance called 'High Summer in Little Bagford' it would be a sell-out. Yes, we might only be a tucked-away village in Somerset but nevertheless many people would regard it as a most desirable area in which to live.

I sighed.

'Oh dear,' said a voice in my ear. 'You sound very sad. Finding things lonely with your mother away?'

I jumped, and turned to see Aileen standing just behind me. 'I expect it feels strange for you,' she continued, 'being all alone in the house.'

I fixed a smile. 'Hello Aileen, are you off to buy a newspaper too?'

'We have ours delivered,' she said. 'I'm just on my way home from Sunday Worship. You should come along sometime, Tessa.' She smiled at me encouragingly. 'It's always a lovely service. Anyway, I'm glad I've seen you because I've been trying to arrange a committee meeting about the Midsummer Fayre. We haven't had our de-briefing yet, and we do need to do it soon while it's all still fresh in our minds.'

'Oh yes,' I said, 'I'd forgotten we hadn't had it yet. Yes, I suppose we do need to do it before much longer.' The de-briefing meeting was as permanent a fixture as the Midsummer Fayre itself, although obviously more private, being for the organisers only. Here we had a proper discussion of what had gone well, what had gone badly, and how, with hindsight, the whole thing could have been done very much better. In theory it was an attempt to learn from mistakes and ensure that next year's event went even better. In practice it always turned into a prolonged grumble about all those who had not done half as much as they could and should have done. It was always rather enjoyable.

'So I need to know which evening would suit you best,' continued Aileen. 'Brian says he'd rather it isn't a Wednesday. He's just joined the bridge club, and it's so nice for him to have something that gets him out of the house that I really don't want to discourage him.'

'No, that's all right,' I said vaguely. It doesn't have to be Wednesday.'

'And neither Carol nor Maureen are available this coming week, so that rather rules that out. But everyone else on the committee can make the following Tuesday. So can we count on you coming? My house, of course.'

'Er - yes, okay. I'll put it in my diary.'

'Good. I hoped you'd be free. I wasn't sure if you might be out enjoying yourself with a certain young man.'

I looked at her, bemused.

'Fraser,' she said. 'Fraser Curtis. It *was* him you were having coffee with, in the Patchwork Pumpkin?'

My mouth fell open.

'Oh don't worry, dear,' she said, 'no-one's been spying on you. It's just that Carol happened to see you both, and thought how nice it was that he was back in the village after all this time – if it *was* him, of course, but she was pretty sure that it was because she said he hadn't changed a bit, not even after all those years away.'

'It was a chance encounter,' I said irritably. 'I just happened to bump into him when I was seeing Mum off on her coach trip. He was there seeing off his uncle.'

'Oh, so it was just an accidental meeting,' she said, making little effort to hide her disappointment. 'And there was Carol thinking that the two of you must have kept in touch all this time. You know what she is. She loves a bit of intrigue and romance. I expect she was dying to think that you and Fraser might be getting together. She was probably wondering if the two of you might even beat your mother and Hector down the aisle.'

For the second time my breath was taken away. This was putting two and two together and making five hundred! 'My mother has *no* plans to get married,' I said. 'Doesn't Carol understand that she and Hector are simply friends? I know they've gone on holiday together, but they're also accompanied by at least two dozen other members of the Fossil Club. And as for Fraser and me,' I continued, 'we were simply sharing a pot of coffee while catching up on each other's news. Surely we can do that without Carol planning bulk orders of confetti!'

Aileen looked put out. 'Well I'm sorry, I'm sure,' she said. 'I certainly wasn't intending any offence, I just thought you might find it amusing. You know how Carol likes to run on.'

'Yes, I do,' I said. 'And she may not mean any harm, but it really is very irritating to find minor mole-hills turned into mountains that would put the Himalayas to shame. Perhaps she should try making her own life a little more interesting. Perhaps *she* should join the Fossil Club, I'm sure she must be old enough to be eligible.'

Even as I spoke the words I felt ashamed of my bitchiness. Carol's enjoyment of a good gossip was notorious, but it was never with any deliberate malice. Indeed, I myself had often listened to her ramblings without making any real attempt to stem them. Perhaps if I had done, I might not have been the object of them now.

'Oh well, I'm very sorry - ' said Aileen stiffly.

'No, *I'm* sorry,' I said. 'It was a nasty thing to say, and I shouldn't have said it. I suppose I'm just not in a very good mood this morning. My lunch plans have fallen through. I was invited round to Jodie and James' house, but now it seems that Jodie isn't very well.'

'Oh dear,' said Aileen more kindly. 'That is a pity. Well then, why don't you come and have lunch with Brian and me? We're having a nice traditional roast beef and Yorkshire pud, and I'm sure I could make it stretch to three if you wanted to join us.'

'Oh – thank you. But don't worry, I've already defrosted a lasagne to put in the oven. It would be a shame to waste it.'

'Oh, well – if you're really sure I can't persuade you, I'd better be getting back.' She gave a gracious smile and moved on, leaving me to continue on my way to the shop, wondering just how many other people had been given the benefit of Carol's speculations about my love life. When Becky-behind-the-counter took my money for the paper, was there really a strange significance in the smile she gave me? And did old Mrs Bromley really seem to wink as she bade me 'good morning' on my way home? Or was I simply becoming paranoid? But at least, thank God, no-one other than my mother and Jodie knew about the unexpected return of a long-lost lover into my life. If they only knew about Daniel Dunstan, it would have certainly given Carol – and probably half the village - something to gossip about.

And that was one thing to be grateful for, I reflected as I ate my solitary lunchtime sandwich, wishing that the lasagne had been a reality rather than just a polite evading tactic.

Chapter 7

Erica and Daniel's new home proved to be a nice house on a nice road on the nice new estate of Windmill Meadows. The actual windmill had not existed within living memory, but nevertheless every native of Little Bagford could remember the green and pleasant hillside that had been there before the developers moved in. There was still residual ill-feeling about the loss of such an attractive piece of our countryside, but it had to be admitted that in the end, and despite everyone's worst fears, the builders hadn't made too bad a job of it. Barleycorn Crescent was wide and attractive, with each of the detached houses being a little different from its neighbour. The front gardens were neatly landscaped and, to judge by the kind of cars parked on the driveways, the residents, as my mother would have put it, 'did not go short of a bob or two'.

Daniel and Erica's house was easy to pick out, being made recognisable, as she had told me, by several tubs of flowers dotted outside the porch: bright red pelargoniums, trailing ivy and lobelia. Almost before we had time to notice and admire them, the door was flung open.

Erica's smile was wide and welcoming. 'Oh, here you are at last! It's so great to see you guys! Everyone else is here already, so come on in and I'll introduce you. No, you're not at all late – did you walk here? Well, I suppose it's not far really, though it's quite a chilly evening, isn't it. Can I take your jackets? Here, let me... She barely paused for breath as she ushered us in, taking our outer garments and thrusting them into a cloaks-cupboard. 'Oh, flowers! Aren't they beautiful, that's so kind of you,' she continued, accepting our guest-offering. 'You look nice, Tessa.'

I didn't particularly. I had spent most of last week intending to sort through my wardrobe, to come up with something simple but stunning. But when I finally got round to it, I'd realised that my confidence in its contents had been misplaced. With no time for a shopping expedition, I'd fallen back on wearing the same black trousers that I'd worn the previous Saturday, topped this time by a pink blouse with frills, which I was already regretting as being far too old-lady-ish.

But if Erica had similar thoughts, she gave no hint. 'And you must be Fraser,' she was continuing, turning to my companion, leaning forward to offer an enthusiastic hug. 'It's good to meet you! But come in, come in - '

I managed to interrupt her at last. 'No,' I said, more loudly than I'd intended. 'No, this isn't Fraser. He couldn't come, I'm afraid. He's twisted his ankle, it seems. So I asked Oliver instead. I was sure you wouldn't mind.'

'No, of course I don't mind, not in the least.' She stood back and beamed at Oliver. 'It's a pleasure. I know we've not actually met before, but that doesn't mean I haven't heard all about you. You're the antiques expert, the kind man who doesn't mind when his assistant gets landed with looking after a grumpy little boy while she's trying to do her job.'

Oliver smiled, and I could see he wasn't quite sure as to how to take this barrage of talk. Fortunately, no reply was required, for Erica was already leading us through the hall and into the large dining room where four other people were already standing around chatting, glasses in hand. We slid in as unobtrusively as we could.

'Everybody - ' Erica clapped her hands for attention. 'This is Tessa and Fraser - sorry - no, no, Tessa and Oliver. And, Tessa and Oliver, this is John and Paula, our very good neighbours from next door, and this is Poppy and Rufus. Rufus works with Danny, and Poppy is his partner.'

Oliver and I smiled uncertainly at the assembled company. John and Paula appeared to be in their mid-twenties; John wearing a suit and tie and looking as if he wished he wasn't. Paula, although slender and pretty, also looked uncomfortably overdressed in a sparkly top and tight skirt. So at least I wasn't the only one who hadn't known what to wear. Only Poppy and Rufus, who must have been closer to Oliver's age, were casual and stylish in what even I could recognise as designer chic. They greeted us easily, and we made polite noises and shook hands all round while I wondered where Daniel was.

'If you're wondering about your host,' said Erica, presciently, 'he's just upstairs, checking that Toby's still asleep. Although once he *is* asleep, then he's usually out for the count until about six in the morning. Ah, good - here we are.'

The door was pushed open, and Danny came in, holding a bottle and glasses. 'Tessa, how very nice to see you.' He kissed my cheek coldly. 'And – it's Oliver, isn't it? But, I thought - ?'

It was quickly explained again that Fraser was at present incapacitated, and that Oliver was here in his place. I hoped the explanation sounded more plausible than it felt to my own ears. I had so wanted the evening to pass off uneventfully, and yet here I was, even before it had properly begun, lumbered with giving excuses that sounded more unlikely with every repetition. For even I wasn't sure I believed the excuse. It sounded lame in every possible sense.

The phone call had come yesterday afternoon. 'Tess? It's Fraser. Look, I'm really sorry to let you down, but I can't make the dinner party. I've sprained my ankle, and at the moment I can't actually walk on it.'

Even as I made sympathetic noises, my heart was sinking. Was it actually true, or was it all just a bit too convenient? And if he really hadn't wanted to come with me, then why not be upfront about it instead of inventing silly excuses?

'Should have looked where I was going,' his voice continued. 'But I was just lining up a shot of a medieval barn, and I stepped backwards, and there was this bloody great rut in the ground....'

'Oh dear.' I reminded myself that it was me who had made it difficult for him to refuse my invitation without being rude. If I had just picked a definite date, then he could have got out of it more easily.

'Fortunately the camera didn't get damaged,' said Fraser. 'Just me.'

'Good,' I said. 'No, I mean, bad. Well – you know what I mean.'

We had both laughed, but nevertheless I had put down the phone feeling distinctly snubbed. What to do now? Phone Erica and cancel completely? I could try but, knowing her, she'd see no reason why I couldn't come on my own. Then I realised my more obvious option. I could ask Oliver. He already knew I was going, and he wouldn't take it amiss that he'd happened to be my second choice. He was too reasonable and our friendship too long-standing for him to see insults where none were intended.

Now, I was pleased to see that his initial bemusement with Erica was warming into a gentle enjoyment of her lively personality.

'So, Oliver - ' she was saying, 'what would you like to drink? Are you a beer drinker, or would you prefer wine? Or a gin and tonic? Danny can pour you one of his specials. The food won't be long. I hope you like salmon…?'

I settled down for what I hoped would not be a long evening.

Perhaps because my expectations had been so low, by the time we reached the dessert course, I had to admit that the dinner party was not as bad as I'd been fearing. Conversation between everyone except Daniel and myself flowed easily; certainly freely enough to ensure that the gap was not noticeable.

Poppy and Rufus and Erica were the main contributors; they had all travelled the world, and there was much discussion about the differences between life in England and Australia, and the pros and cons of city-living compared with the countryside. John and Paula, though less experienced, threw in comments where they could, while Oliver was happily able to contribute his own thoughts on his visits to see his daughter in America, and how she was finding the experience of living in Chicago. I spoke less, but sat back and took pleasure from listening, and from the food. Erica was not a sophisticated cook, but her unassuming menu had proved very tasty. A simple walnut and pear salad was followed by a main course of grilled salmon and new potatoes, and the meal finally finished off with a home-made summer pudding, bursting with fruit.

'Ah, my favourite dessert,' smiled Oliver. 'I suppose if we were in Australia, we'd be eating this in the middle of December.'

Erica laughed. 'Naturally - although probably not with Cornish cream. But to get back to travels,' she went on, emptying her dish with a final lick of her spoon, 'I always think you Brits can be really blind when it comes to your own country. I mean, I love travelling around Oz, but if you want to see somewhere completely different from your own home town, you have to go miles. I mean, literally, *miles*. While here – well, if you want to see somewhere different, you only have to go down the road a bit. Completely different town or village, different people, different kind of countryside.'

'Different countryside?' queried Daniel, lifting an eyebrow.

'Well, alright – not *just* down the road. But I could get in the car right now, and within an hour or two I could be in a big city, or in the Peaks or the Lake District, or even the very tippy-toe of Cornwall.'

'Dear girl I know you drive too fast, but that would be pushing it, even for you.'

Amid the laughter, Erica made a face at him.

'But you're right,' agreed Oliver. 'I do think a lot of us tend to assume that a proper holiday has to be spent abroad. We don't think about what's here all around us. And I know I'm as bad as anyone. I keep telling myself I'll make more effort, that I'll spend a week or two visiting Kent, or Cardiff, or wherever. But do I ever actually get round to it? No. And yet there's no reason why not.'

'You're right,' I agreed. 'Take Scotland. I've been promising myself a proper holiday in Scotland for ages and ages, but I never take the trouble to actually organise anything.'

There was a small and unexpectedly awkward silence. Poppy and Rufus, Erica and Daniel glanced at each other.

'Bit of a sore point, is Scotland,' announced Rufus to nobody in particular. 'You see Poppy and I had agreed to go on holiday there with Dan and Erica. Booked this really large house for a fortnight, and everything.'

'And then I spoiled it,' said Poppy. 'I made us drop out of it. I still feel dreadful, but – what else could I do?'

94

'Nothing,' said Erica warmly. 'Don't feel guilty. You can't possibly be away for the birth of your first grandchild. No-one would expect you to. It's just bad timing, that's all.'

'You're about to become grandparents?' I commented politely, vaguely surprised. For no good reason, they had not struck me as natural grandparent material.

'Second week in September,' said Poppy. 'The very time we'd booked to go away. It's our daughter's first baby, and she didn't even realise for ages that she *was* pregnant. I mean, can you believe it? Just typical of Jo-Jo. Then literally, the very day after the booking for Scotland had been made, she rings me up and tells me that she's having a baby. And there's no father on the scene - she'd split with him weeks ago - so I couldn't turn round and say, 'Tough luck darling, you'll have to go through it all on your own. Daddy and I won't be there either because we'd much rather go on holiday."

Rufus looked as if he might have disagreed, but confined his feelings to an eloquent shrug, leaving another small silence.

It was Paula who broke it. 'But there's your answer,' she said, smiling at Erica. 'It's quite obvious. Tessa and Oliver want to go on holiday, Tessa particularly fancies Scotland, and you two need another couple to share this house you've rented. Why don't you go together?'

It was such an innocent suggestion.

Daniel and Erica both spoke at once. 'There's no question of 'needing' another couple,' said Daniel.

'Erica and I will still be going to Scotland anyway. We certainly weren't touting for anyone else to come with us.'

'What a brilliant idea!' said Erica at the same time. 'Of course! What could be better!'

While they were still frowning at each other, Oliver and I launched into our own duet.

'No,' I said firmly. 'It's a lovely thought, but no, I'm afraid it's totally out of the question. For a start, we couldn't possibly both be away from the shop at the same time.'

'Yes,' said Oliver thoughtfully. 'Yes, why *don't* we come with you?

It was an evening of small silences.

'Oliver!' I exclaimed. 'How could we both be away from the shop ? You'd have to close down for a fortnight.' I refrained from adding that I didn't see how the finances could possibly support it, although it was true enough. I turned back to Erica. 'No, it just can't be managed, I'm afraid. It's a really nice idea, but it's just not practical.'

'What a shame,' said Daniel smoothly. 'Now, who'd like another drink? Paula? Tessa?'

'Love one,' I said enthusiastically. 'It's a really nice wine. Did you get it from the little deli in the village? They have an amazing selection for such a small shop.'

'Really? I hadn't realised. I shall have to go in and have a proper look sometimes.'

'Yes, do - '

Daniel and I were babbling to each other with more animation than we had managed to summon up all evening.

'It *is* a shame, though,' said Erica. 'It would have been so nice to have you join us.'

'And cheese, too,' I said. 'Such a range they stock! Just amazing.'

Daniel regarded me with what could almost have been described as warmth. 'Really?' he said. 'Cheese? I love cheese.'

'So what's your favourite?' I asked inanely.

'I think it *could* be managed,' said Oliver. 'With a bit of planning.'

'Could it?' said Erica. 'That would be wonderful.'

'Stilton,' said Daniel. 'Prince of cheeses. Or Wensleydale. That's pretty good too.'

'Brie,' I said. 'That's my choice. Did you know you can get a really nice Somerset Brie?'

'Oh dear,' said Erica, side-tracked at last. 'I didn't think to do a cheeseboard as well as a dessert. That was stupid of me. But I've got a block of mature Cheddar in the fridge if anyone would like some?'

Compunction struck me. 'Oh no, Erica. I'm absolutely full! No, no, I was just talking in general terms.'

The rest of the company declined her offer politely, except for Oliver who, ignoring altogether the question of cheese, was still refusing to abandon the idea of Scotland. 'You know I reckon it could be done, Tess,' he said to me. 'I'd already been thinking about an idea I'd had – just mulling it over in my mind, or I'd have talked to you about it earlier. But I had actually been thinking of giving the shop a revamp. Redecoration – reorganising the space - re-thinking the way we display the goods – there's so much scope for improvement. So you see, we'd have had to shut down for a few days anyway. And going up to Scotland while it was all carried out wouldn't be impossible.'

I stared at him, lost for words.

'A whole business re-vamp?' queried Rufus interestedly. 'You'll be wanting a good firm of consultants, then. Anyone in mind?'

Oliver shook his head.

'If you need any suggestions,' said Poppy, 'I could give you a few names. Rufus, what do you think? What about Monty? He's young, but full of ideas. I could give you his number, if you like.'

'I hadn't quite got that far,' said Oliver, beginning to look as if he wished he had never mentioned the subject.

'Well, do make sure you go for the best you can afford,' advised Poppy. 'It's always money well spent. Then you can just relax while the experts get on with the job.'

'Yes, I suppose so.' He looked at me. 'So you see, we *could* get away.'

I stared down at my crumpled napkin. Any delusions I'd nursed that the evening would not be as bad as anticipated were vanishing rapidly. It was turning into a nightmare.

For once Erica did not rush to press her advantage. 'Coffee?' she asked. 'Who'd like coffee and mints?' She pushed back her chair and stood up. 'Danny, do take everyone into the sitting room, then we can sit back and enjoy it in comfort. Tessa, could you give me a hand?'

A little surprised, I followed her into the kitchen, where she immediately pushed the door shut behind us.

'Tessa,' she told me in a dramatic whisper, 'if you're worrying about what I think you're worrying about, I have to tell you – *I know*.'

'You know?' I repeated stupidly.

'Yes, I know,' she said. 'I know about you and Danny and how you came to be acquainted with each other. He told me about you having had a bit of a crush on him, years ago.'

'Oh,' I said.

'It's okay. I could see Danny had some issues about you, and I kept on and on at him until he told me that the two of you had once been a bit of an item. But I don't mind, really I don't. Why should I? After all, he is quite a bit older than me. It's only natural that he's been out with other women in the past. So if the reason you don't want to come on holiday with us is because – well – because of *that*…' She smiled reassuringly. 'Don't worry on my account. I know it's all ancient history.'

I wasn't too keen on the 'ancient' but, encouraged by the rest of her words, decided to bite the bullet. 'Then I assume Daniel told you that we were actually in a serious relationship?'

She hesitated, and I wondered if he *had* told her. Knowing him, I wouldn't have put money on it. But her voice, when she spoke, was still firm. 'The point is,' she said, 'your relationship, such as it was, happened a very, very long time ago. Years go by, and people change – we all move on. I absolutely know that Danny doesn't hold any kind of torch for you, and I don't believe you have any feelings for Danny either. Other than friendship, of course.'

Friendship…? Obviously he had not told her of the circumstances in which we had broken up. Even Erica could not be such a Pollyanna as to believe that finding your lover in bed with your friend could lead to feelings of lasting affection.

'In any case,' she continued, 'I can see that Oliver's longing for you to go on holiday with him. It's easy to see just how fond he is of you. So there would be no need for awkwardness between any of us. It would just be you and Oliver, and me and Danny – and Toby of course – all having a lovely civilised holiday together.'

I sighed. Erica was such a *nice* girl, so well intentioned. She was almost beginning to convince me that such a holiday would not be an impossibility. Until I suddenly realised what she had said about Oliver. Why on earth did people keep assuming that Oliver nursed some kind of hidden passion for me? Just because we both happened to be single, why did they feel this urge to create a romance? I was about to disabuse her, when it occurred to me that as long as she thought Oliver and I had feelings for each other, then the easier it would be to smooth over any lingering awkwardness about Daniel.

I saw she was studying me, waiting for a response. I forced a smile. 'Thank you, Erica,' I said. 'Thank you for wanting us to come with you.

100

But I still think that there are plenty of purely practical reasons why Oliver and I couldn't be away from the shop together. Even if he does decide that he wants to shut it down while it gets a face-lift, someone would still need to be around to supervise the decorators.'

'Oh. You're quite sure it couldn't be left?'

She looked so disappointed that I felt mean. 'Tell you what,' I said. 'I'll think about it. I'll talk to Oliver and I'll think about it.'

Chapter 8

'So what *do* you think?' asked Jodie. 'Will you go on holiday with them?'

It was the following day, and I was at Jodie's house to take up the Sunday lunch invitation which had been postponed from the week before. I had, of course, rung her during the week just to see if she was feeling better, but although she sounded reassuringly cheerful, she had been in the middle of cake-baking, and too busy to speak for more than a moment. In any case, with so many things to tell her about, I really wanted a proper face-to-face chat. Now, with James still in the kitchen to supervise his famous roast potatoes, I'd been able to give her a full report of most of my doings, and had got as far as the dinner party of the previous night.

'So will you go to Scotland?' she pressed.

'No!' I said. 'No way.'

'Although, you know,' she mused, 'Erica must be an extraordinarily trusting sort of person. After all, how many women would invite their husband's ex-girlfriend to go on holiday with them?'

'Ex-girlfriend, plus Oliver,' I corrected. 'Even so – you're right – it is a weird thing to do. But Erica is such a complete one-off. And also, I think she's lonely. Don't forget, she's got no friends or family in the area, and I suspect she spends most of her time by herself, looking after Toby. So perhaps she sees this as a chance to make new friends, and is grabbing it with both hands.'

'Even though you and Daniel - ?'

I shrugged. 'I'm not sure she's really taken it on board. She told me herself that she sees it as 'ancient history', a far-distant episode that's quite irrelevant to the here and now. And you can bet your boots that Daniel has downplayed the whole thing anyway. She probably thinks it was never anything more than a boy-girl infatuation. Certainly not real enough for her to think of me as any kind of threat. As it happens, she's entirely right, of course, but even so…' I smiled wryly. 'Basically, I suspect that she thinks I'm really old.' I remembered, and regretted again, the frilly pink blouse I had chosen to wear to her party. 'Yes, I'm quite sure she regards me as so past my sell-by date that I couldn't possibly be regarded as a rival. But apart from that, there's not a nasty or suspicious bone in her body. Much as I'd love to dislike her, I simply can't. Nobody could. She's so completely – *sweet* – for want of a better word. Although in this case, she really doesn't have anything at all to worry about. Daniel Dunstan is the last person in the world I'd be tempted to hook up with again.'

'So perhaps she's just a very good judge of your character then.' Jodie smiled. 'Anyway, it smells as if lunch is nearly ready. In fact it probably *would* be ready, if only James didn't insist upon taking charge of the roasties.' She rolled her eyes ruefully in the direction of the kitchen. 'He takes twice as long over them as I would. Still, he does do a good job, so I

103

hate to discourage him.' She put down her cup and turned back to me. 'But seriously,' she continued, 'why *don't* think about going to Scotland? You wouldn't have to spend all your time together. Take some good books with you or, better still, take your sketch-pad. Going off to do some drawing is a perfect reason for excusing yourself from company.'

'But I haven't sketched for ages,' I protested.

'So what? They won't know that, will they? You could even make it an opportunity to take it up again.'

I smiled reluctantly. 'You have an answer for everything.'

'Just go,' she said. 'Seriously. Go. I can't remember the last time you went away on holiday. And from what you said, it sounds as if Oliver not only thinks it's possible, but is really keen on the idea. You might end up having a great time.'

I waved a dismissive hand. 'No. Absolutely, definitely not. Even if you don't count looking after the shop as a valid objection, there's still my mother to consider. After all, she might not feel up to being left alone for a whole fortnight.' This, I realised, was an argument that I could have used last night, and indeed would have done so, if only I'd thought of it in time. For surely nobody could argue that the welfare of an elderly mother was not a good reason to stay at home?

'Rubbish!' said Jodie robustly. 'You know as well as I do that your mother is more than capable of looking after herself, with or without you on the premises. She's seventy-six, not a hundred and six!

Look where she is right now. Gallivanting around the south coast, probably having a great time, flirting madly with Hector and going out on the razzle with all her friends. I bet she's not sitting in her hotel room wondering whether or not *you're* coping on your own.'

'Well, of course she won't be. But you're forgetting that she's the one who had that nasty virus this spring.'

'And now she's over it,' said Jodie. 'Face it, Tess, she's perfectly fit, both in mind and body. No, I'm sorry, but using your mother as an excuse to get you out of living your own life doesn't do either of you a service.'

Her words stung. 'Well I'm not arguing about it,' I said mutinously. 'The point is, I'm not going, so that's that. End of story. In any case, what about *your* news? You still haven't told me about James.'

'Told her what about me?' said James walking in, and catching the last remark. 'Potatoes are ready, by the way. So what have I done now?'

'You've been a very clever boy,' said Jodie sweetly. 'You've got a new job, haven't you.'

'Haven't you told her anything yet?' asked James.

Jodie smiled. 'Not yet.'

'So tell me,' I demanded.

'James has got promotion. Same firm, but from now on he'll be spending much more time in the office, so there'll no more long journeys all over the country. From next month, he'll be based in Taunton. And once everything's settled down, he may even be able to spend some days working from home.'

'Oh, that's great, James,' I said. 'Well done!'

He smiled smugly. 'Thank you, Tessa. But that's not the really, really big news, is it Jodie? Shall you tell her, or shall I?'

I turned to look at Jodie.

'We're going to be parents,' continued James, before she had the chance to speak. 'Jodie's going to have a baby. She's three months pregnant.'

For a moment I hardly understood what he was saying. Pregnant? Jodie was pregnant? And not just pregnant, but *three months* pregnant – all without having breathed a word of it to me?

I pulled myself together and moved across to hug her. 'Oh, Jodie – I'm so very glad for you - '

She laughed in a small, embarrassed way. 'I wondered if you might have already guessed,' she said. 'I've been so desperate to tell you, but it seemed like tempting fate to actually say anything. We wanted to have the hospital scan first, just to be quite, quite sure. But it's been done now, and I've been thoroughly checked over, and the doctor said that everything's fine, and there's no reason at all to worry.' Again she gave a breathless laugh. 'Tess, I don't know if I'm coming or going. Do you know, we'd got to the point of actually committing to IVF treatment, and then all of a sudden I found out we didn't need to! Even now, I can hardly believe that it's really happened at last!'

'Oh yes it's definitely happened,' grinned James. 'You're a fully paid up member of the pudding club, my dear, and there's no changing your

106

mind about it now.'

'James!' She aimed a playful smack at his head, and he ducked and kissed her, and for a moment I felt like an unwanted outsider, an intruder into her private life. No longer did Jodie feel like my good-old-reliable-friend, but far more like a wife, and now soon-to-be mother.

'Well, that's lovely - the best news ever...' I stood smiling, not quite knowing what to say or do. 'So do you have a date when it's due? Do you know if it's boy or girl?'

James gave a snort of laughter. 'Yes, it's definitely a boy or a girl!'

Jodie smiled serenely. 'No, we don't know what sex it is, and we'd both prefer it to be a surprise. Even if it does mean painting the baby's room yellow or green, rather than blue or pink.'

'But yellow or green can still be nice. You can get some gorgeous wallpaper for nurseries these day, and funny friezes, and musical mobiles...'

I chatted on inanely, while still trying to get my head round her news. But before I could wander too far down the road of interior decorating, James was dashing back into the kitchen and shouting to tell us that the food, and in particular his roast potatoes, was ready to dish up, and we were moving into the dining room to eat.

At the table, James poured me a glass of red wine. None for Jodie. How had I missed such an obvious clue, I wondered, when she had so recently shared supper with me and barely touched her one very small glass? Had there been other signs I'd missed? Were there other things I could have - *should* have noticed? She had obviously thought I might have suspected. But I hadn't. Inexplicably I hadn't guessed and, unbelievably, she hadn't enlightened me.

I sipped my drink. I supposed, if I was being entirely fair, that I did understand. In her shoes, I too would probably have wanted to wait for the official confirmation of a hospital scan. I would have needed to see the image on the screen; to actually hold the photograph of the tiny living embryo.

No, it was not surprising that she'd chosen to share these things only with James. Prospective parenthood was a journey only the two of them could take. A journey on which a friend, however close, could not follow.

Jodie had started yawning almost before we had finished the meal.

'Why don't you go for a lie-down?' suggested James.

She smiled at me apologetically. 'Sorry, Tess, I'm not a very good hostess, am I? It's not that I'm bored, it's just that sometimes I get this feeling of overwhelming tiredness. It sounds silly, but it seems to be a side-effect of this stage of pregnancy.'

'Then while you have the opportunity,' I said, 'go and do what James told you. Off you go, and have an afternoon nap.'

'No – don't worry, I shall feel more awake in a moment. I don't want to go to bed when I've got visitors.'

I smiled at her. 'Come on, Jodie, we're old enough friends for me to boss you about, and I say you must have a snooze. I shall see you soon anyway, I'm sure. And you must let me know if I can do anything. If you need someone to help fetching heavy groceries or whatever…'

She smiled sleepily. 'It's all right, I've got James to do that for me.'

Amid her polite protestations, and James's contradictory insistence that she needed her rest, I said my goodbyes and made my way home.

What a strange and unexpected day it had turned into. And it was still only early afternoon. I had vaguely assumed that I'd be spending several hours with them, but here I was, the social occasion already over.

Almost unconsciously I slowed my steps. So what now? Pass the rest of the time inside my own four walls? No – that would be a real waste of a sunny day. Go into the garden and do some weeding and tidying? I liked gardening, and there was no shortage of jobs that needed doing, but right now I wasn't in the mood. No, I would do something I hadn't done for ages - simply get into the car and go for a drive. And once on the road, I would follow it wherever it chose to take me.

In the end it took me to Bath. Me, and countless other day-trippers. Yet once I'd finally managed to locate a parking place, I found that there was something rather comforting about losing myself in such a throng. Having already been round the famous Roman Baths and admired the Georgian architecture several times before, I felt no guilt at simply wandering aimlessly along the streets, ambling around the shops looking for nothing in particular, and enjoying the cheerful buzz of so many different accents.

But eventually even I grew tired of the crowds, and turned my steps towards the comparative calm of the river. Once on the far side of Pultney Bridge, the banks were quieter than the Parade Gardens opposite, but there was still no shortage of people who had decided to enjoy a sunny Sunday afternoon by the Avon. They wandered across the grass brandishing guidebooks, taking selfies against the background of the weir, eating ice-creams or, like me, simply relaxing in the late afternoon sunshine. I found a quiet space and sat down on the dry grass. The sky was blue, and the few clouds were high and wispy. Beneath me the ground felt warm. Now and then a soft breeze rustled the nearby trees, bringing with it hints of their delicate perfume. Now and then boats slid past almost noiselessly, the colours of their hulls making bright rippling reflections in the dark water.

Sitting on the grass, I watched a toddler as he fed the ducks, his free hand clasped firmly in his mother's as he hurled bread into the river with more zeal than accuracy. How self-sufficient and happy they seemed. Perhaps in two or three years, that would be Jodie standing there with her child. She would make a good mother. She too would keep him from danger, teach him, play with him, encourage him with patience and love. She would take him to nursery and school, go to parents' evenings and join the Young Mums' Club. She would become swept up in the world of toddlers' groups and birthday parties and sleepovers.

And me? I would stay as I was. Boring old Tess, who'd never done anything very exciting, and probably never would. No, not even though things had started out so well, with a good degree and then a job. But things had gone badly wrong when I mistakenly thought I'd found True Love, and somehow they had never quite recovered. So now I was back living in the very house I'd grown up in. Okay, admittedly there was a reason for it. My newly bereaved mother had needed me, and I'd needed somewhere to live. The only trouble was, I'd never left. Never done an awful lot of things.

I sighed, knowing that I was sliding ever deeper into self-pity, yet childishly unwilling to pull myself out. Life seemed to bring change and development for everyone except me. Friends moved on, made good careers for themselves. Jodie's future was blossoming. Even that waste-of-space Daniel Dunstan was now a married man with a child. It was only me who stayed exactly as I was.

I closed my eyes and felt the sunlight on my face. Hadn't I read somewhere that nearly all the high achievers in the world had suffered difficult childhoods? So did that mean I should blame my happily-married parents for the fact I'd accomplished so little? If my responsible and affectionate parents had beaten and neglected me, would I now be a successful entrepreneur running a chain of businesses?

I smiled as I thought of my own humble job helping Oliver with the antiques. Financial tycoon I was not, nor ever would be. Yet surely I wasn't entirely useless? Oliver plainly liked having me in the shop, and I had undoubtedly made my own small mark there over the years. The books were now kept accurately and up-to-date, the shop interior had seen several licks of paint and, though the business wasn't exactly thriving, it still made enough profit to remain viable.

I was also a useful member of my community, albeit in a minor way. I helped to organise the Midsummer Fayre *and* the Christmas bazaar and indeed anything else that Aileen could press-gang me into. I wasn't a complete no-hoper. And I did – yes, in spite of Jodie's assessment – play a positive part in my mother's life. She might not be in her dotage yet, but she still appreciated having me around. Yes, I felt I could honestly claim that I did have a role in life when it came to my mother.

There was a sudden loud splash from the water and I looked up, for a moment half-fearing to see the child had fallen into the water. But it was merely the rest of the contents of the bag that he had thrown in, all in one lump. As the ducks flapped and squabbled, his laughing mother led him away, trying ineffectually to mop the water from his tee-shirt and trousers.

As they passed, I offered her my packet of

tissues. Everybody had a role to play in life, even if it wasn't a big one.

I gave a small offering of thanks when I woke on Monday morning and remembered that Oliver would be out of the shop all day. He had arranged to attend a sale near Bridgwater, and his absence could not have been better timed. For I really did not want to talk about Scotland. I had no intention of going, and I didn't want to be persuaded otherwise. A nice dull day was all I desired, with no unwanted invitations, no challenging conversations, or anything of a troublesome nature whatsoever.

Happily, I was in luck. Unusually for a Monday, there was a slow but steady trickle of customers throughout the day, and during the gaps I was able to catch up with the many small jobs that always needed doing. Shelves got tidied, ornaments got dusted, and faded labels got replaced. I even managed to sell a walnut occasional table which had been taking up floor space for months. All in all, it was a reassuringly quiet day, and I was feeling quite content as I finally swung the door-sign round to CLOSED, locked it behind me and made my way back home.

Until I came within sight of my front door, and saw Fraser outside it, his hand on the doorbell.

'So there you are,' he called, catching sight of me at the same instant. 'No wonder I wasn't getting any answer. I thought you'd have got back from work ages ago.'

'There was a last minute customer…' My voice

tailed away as he swung round fully and I saw that he was supporting himself with a crutch. 'Oh, Fraser - oh dear.'

'No, you see - it wasn't just an excuse, as you probably thought,' he said. 'I really did hurt my ankle.'

It was difficult to tell if it was irritation or amusement in his voice. Perhaps both. I could hardly blame him if he *was* annoyed though. In the confusion of subsequent events I had completely forgotten about him. I hadn't even thought to call in at Hector's and check how he was doing.

'I bought you these,' he said rather ungraciously, pointing to a bottle of wine and a bunch of flowers lying on my doorstep. 'They're by way of an apology for letting you down on Saturday. I was just about to see if I'd got anything to write a note on, explaining, seeing as you weren't in.'

'Oh, Fraser... That was kind. You needn't have done that.'

'No, I know I needn't. In fact I wouldn't have done, if I'd realised just how bloody awkward it is to carry things while trying to walk on a crutch all at the same time. So if the petals are crushed I'm sorry, but at least the bottle made it here in one piece.'

I started to laugh. 'Would you like to come in and recover for a while? You can tell me all about your poor ankle. In fact,' I added, throwing caution completely to the winds, 'if you've nothing more exciting to do, come and eat with me. It won't be as good as the dinner you missed on Saturday, but at least it's a meal.'

114

In the end, and to my embarrassment, it was hardly even a meal.

'It's perfectly all right,' Fraser insisted, as he finished his plateful. 'I *like* beans on toast. It's one of my favourites. And you did it to perfection. It was a magnificent beans on toast.'

'All right, all right, no need to make me feel worse. I really did think I had more in the pantry than that. I'm usually very organised about shopping, but with Mum away, I haven't needed to be. If I'd known in advance you were coming, then I'd have gone to the shop and bought steak or something. Although,' I sighed, 'if I *had* bought steak, then the news that I was expecting a visitor would have been all round the village within the hour.'

'Would it matter?'

I shrugged a little uncomfortably. If my chance first encounter with Fraser had been noticed and commented upon, goodness only knew what the local spies would have made of an invitation into my own home. It might have caused less interest if Fraser had been old and ugly, but he wasn't. Not by any means.

I shrugged apologetically. 'Well, no-one likes to feel that other people are keeping tabs on them.'

He gave me a sideways glance. 'I don't remember that you'd ever have been bothered about that back in the old days.'

I sighed. 'Perhaps I've lived in this village too long.'

He was silent a moment as he toyed with his

115

glass. 'Well – even if it wasn't steak, it was a very enjoyable meal, anyway. I guess if you came to my own place, you'd be lucky to find bread and butter, let alone a tin of baked beans.'

'So where *do* you live' I asked, 'when you're not house-sitting for your uncle?'

'I actually sold my flat a few weeks ago,' he said. 'I've been lodging with my friend Nick as a temporary measure. But I shall be off to Australia shortly.'

'Australia? Really? But oh - not for good, surely? Or are you?'

'No, not for good. At the moment I'm not quite sure how long I'll be out there. But I'm certainly looking forward to it.'

I took a long mouthful. 'So would I be,' I said enviously. 'What will you be doing out there? You know, it's a real pity that you couldn't make it to Erica's dinner party. Did I tell you that she is an Australian? Anyway, she was telling us all about the best places to visit, and they sounded fantastic.'

'So why don't you go?'

I laughed. 'Perhaps I will, one day.'

He looked at me. 'One day?'

'Yes – one day,' I said. 'It's not the kind of thing you do spur of the moment. It doesn't mean I'll never go. And you can give me loads of tips when you get back.'

He shrugged. 'Unfortunately it's not really a holiday,' he said, 'although I certainly hope to pull in as much sight-seeing as I can while I'm there. But I've had a commission to put together a book on

116

industrial archaeology, that type of thing. For such a young country, there's a surprising amount of stuff, and lots of the sites have some really weird and wonderful stories behind them. And better still, there's a big gap in the market when it comes to books documenting their history. Yes, I'm expecting great things from my visit to Australia.'

'Well, they certainly make excellent wine,' I smiled, raising my glass. 'This is lovely.'

He smiled. 'Good. Though if you check the label properly, you'll see it was actually a New Zealand wine. And unfortunately,' he said, looking regretfully at the empty bottle, 'we seem to have killed it completely.'

'Have we? Oh well, never mind - I'm sure I have some more in the cupboard. Even my mother likes a glass with Sunday lunch, these days. You'd be surprised at just how sophisticated we've become in Little Bagford since you left. Why don't you go and make yourself comfortable in the sitting room and I'll see what I can find. Ah, yes, here we are,' I told him, eventually re-emerging to find him sprawled on the sofa. 'I've found two more bottles of red. So we're not changing the grape.'

He laughed. 'Well – we're not changing the colour, at least. Which one do you want to start on? And more importantly, where are they from?'

'Back of the pantry,' I grinned.

'Haha. Come here and let me do it.' He took the nearest bottle from me, opened it expertly, and poured us both a generous measure. Almost without realising it, I found we were sitting surprisingly close.

'Okay?' he said.

'Okay.'

'Good,' he said easily. 'You know, it feels really nice to be back in Little Bagford, even if it isn't going to be for very long. And it's always great to meet up with old friends again, don't you think?'

'Not always,' I observed rather bitterly, without thinking.

He pulled away a little. 'Me?'

'No – oh God, no – not you at all.'

'Who then?'

'Oh – no-one. Just a pain in the backside called Daniel. No-one of any importance.'

'Come on, Tess. Why don't you tell me about him? It's not as if *I'm* going to go round gossiping about it. Ships that pass in the night, etcetera…'

Somehow, with a glass in my hand and leaning back against Fraser's comfortable warmth, it was easy to talk. In the evening shadows, I found myself revealing the full story of my short, sad relationship with Daniel, and of his sudden unexpected reappearance on the scene. As we continued to refill our glasses, so the details slid easily from my tongue. 'And now,' I finished gloomily, 'I've been asked to go to Scotland with them.'

I felt Fraser's arm tighten protectively around my shoulder. 'What an absolute idiot he must be.'

'But there's nothing *wrong* with Scotland,' I said confusedly.

'No, no – I mean about him cheating on you - especially with someone that you thought was a friend. The man's a total moron. And what a horrible

118

way for you to make the discovery. No wonder it hit you so badly, finding him - finding *them* actually in bed together.'

'And not just in any old bed,' I observed with maudlin self-pity. 'It was in our *new* bed, the one that we'd only just chosen together. It was ever so comfortable.'

All at once, the idiocy of that last statement hit me. As if the comfort of the bed had anything to do with anything! In a moment I found I was laughing; laughing about it in a way I could never have imagined, struggling to breathe with hiccups of hilarity. And Fraser too caught the contagion, shaking with amusement as he held me close, convulsed with sympathetic mirth.

At last we shuddered back into some kind of sobriety.

'So you're over him?' grinned Fraser, first to regain control.

'Yes. Yes. I am. Definitely.' I insisted.

'Then why don't you go to Scotland?'

'*What?*'

'Go to Scotland,' he said. 'Why not, if you've always wanted to? It doesn't sound as if you've gone anywhere much else in your life.'

'Not even so much as a gap year before university,' I confirmed sadly.

'And,' he continued, 'if it would please this Oliver that you work with? After all, if you're fond of him…?'

'I'm not,' I exclaimed, taken aback for a second time. 'I mean, I am – but not in a romantic way. I just work for him, and he's such a nice person, and I can perfectly see why he'd like to go on holiday with friends, rather than just all by himself. But - ' I stared into my glass, which strangely appeared to be empty again.

'Then go with him,' said Fraser. 'Go with *them*. Enjoy Scotland. Have a lovely platonic time and come back with a crate of whisky and a herd of haggis.' He picked up the wine bottle and topped up both our glasses.

'But what about Daniel?' I said weakly.

'What about him? You've just told me that he plainly doesn't actually want you to go. So here's a chance to really get up his nose! He'd spend the entire holiday wondering if or when you're actually going to stick the knife in, and tell his wife about what really happened between you. Yes, yes, all right - I know you wouldn't – but *he* doesn't know. It might not be a very dramatic revenge for the way he treated you, but at least it would be better than nothing.'

I was silent, trying to get my head round the suggestion. I had never looked at the matter like that before.

'And it would prove to yourself that you really *are* over him. Which is just as important.'

'I *am* over him,' I insisted. 'I definitely am. But what about Erica? I like Erica. I don't want to ruin her holiday by being there.'

'But why should it? By what you've told me, she'd be disappointed if you *don't* go. And Oliver would get his holiday, as would you. No, the only person who wouldn't be happy is Daniel. He'd be spending every day on tenterhooks, wondering if you had anything dreadful planned for him.'

I giggled. 'You should have been a politician. You're much too devious and cunning to be just a nice normal person.'

'And you should have been out in the world, having a life,' he said. 'Not stuck back in the same village you were born in, doing a nice safe little job and looking after a mother who doesn't appear to need much looking after.'

I drew away, taken aback by this sudden unexpected attack. 'What the hell do you mean by that?'

'Exactly what I said,' he returned. 'When we were at school together, you had ambition. You wanted to go out and do things. You wanted to travel. You wanted a career. So what happened?'

'My dad died!' I responded furiously. 'And my mother needed me. Some of us have a sense of family duty! I couldn't just walk away from her when she was suddenly left all alone and went to pieces.'

'No, of course not. But, as you told me yourself, that was quite a while ago now. From what I saw of her – *and* from what Hector's said – she might be in her mid-seventies, but she isn't helpless. She isn't senile, she's not disabled - '

'No, but she's got used to having me here!'

'And you've got used to being here.'

We stared at each other angrily. Just a few moments ago we had been having such a brilliant evening. And now everything had gone sour. And yet – hadn't Jodie tried to tell me exactly the same thing only yesterday? Which made it even more unforgivable.

'I'm sorry,' he said abruptly. 'It's not my business how you live your life.'

'No, it isn't! It definitely isn't.'

'Shall I go?' He began to rise, and abruptly sat down again. 'Ow! Shit. My sodding ankle.'

My anger evaporated. We'd both had more to drink than we should have done, and now he couldn't even walk properly.

'Does it hurt?' I said.

'Only immensely.'

'Good,' I said cruelly, and suddenly we were both laughing again.

He lolled back on the sofa beside me. 'It really does hurt, you know,' he said. 'Seriously.'

'Have some more wine then. It'll numb the pain.'

He reached for the bottle and once again refilled our glasses. How quickly we seemed to be going through it. In the temporary silence we both drank deep.

He looked at me. 'I'm sorry,' he said. 'I didn't mean to be so rude to you just then.'

'Then why were you?'

He paused. 'Because - ' To my astonishment he leaned towards me and kissed me. 'Because,' he continued at last, 'I hate to see songbirds living in cages. Especially when the door is wide open.'

I stared at him wordlessly. Had that kiss really

just happened? Or had I leapfrogged from tipsiness into having actual delusions? And then, while my mouth was still open, he put his lips to mine and kissed me even more thoroughly.

At last he sat back. He was half-smiling, half quizzical.

'What was that all about?' I asked somewhat breathlessly. 'Did you decide that if you were going to offend me, then you'd better make a proper job of it?'

'Are you offended?'

'I'm not sure,' I said.

'Then we'd better *make* sure.'

This time I knew for certain that I wasn't offended. It was so long since I had been kissed, I'd almost forgotten how it felt. The warmth of his skin, the taste of the wine on his tongue, the touch of his hands on my body - Somehow the mixture of all those sensations combined to create a glorious glowing feeling, a tingle so intense that it reached right to the soles of my feet. Pointless telling myself that it was just the effect of the drink. I didn't care where the effect came from, all I knew was that I wanted it to go on and on.

At last we both drew away. 'Do you think you could actually *get* home?' I enquired inanely. 'I mean, if you actually wanted to?'

He sat back, grinning. 'No. Not really. Not with a crutch.'

'Oh,' I said. 'But you couldn't go *without* your crutch.' There was a pause and we both started laughing again. Why on earth had I drunk so much?

I should obviously do it far more often.

'So then.' The smile was still there, but I could sense he was serious. 'What d' you advise?'

'You wouldn't want me to drive you home,' I said. 'I could, but it would be very, very irresponsible.'

'Absolutely.'

We nodded our heads sagely.

'So do you think your poorly ankle could manage to get you upstairs?'

'Absolutely,' he said. And kissed me again.

Chapter 9

'Tess – are you okay?' At the other end of the phone Oliver sounded alarmed. 'You don't sound at all right.'

I grunted another acknowledgement. 'S'at you, Oliver?'

'Yes, of course it's me - I was just phoning to see if you're all right.' There was a small hesitation while he waited for my non-existent response. 'It's gone ten o'clock.'

'What?'

'Only you're not here. Not that it's a problem. I mean, I can manage the shop. But I was getting worried that you hadn't come in, and it sounds as if I was right to be.'

'I'm all righ'.'

He paused. 'Not by the sound of it. What's the problem? You were fine when I left you on Saturday night.'

'Mm.'

'You haven't got that cold that's been going around?'

'Might have,' I mumbled.

'Well, you sound awful.'

'I *feel* awful.'

'Then you must stay in bed,' he told me with unusual decision. 'If you're feeling rough, then it's the best place for you. Don't even think of coming in

125

until you feel better. Just stay in bed.'

I muttered my acquiescence, and fumbled the phone back in place.

Stay in bed, Oliver had insisted. That was all right then. That's what I would do. Stay in bed. Only... *Shit!*

In a moment of clarity I remembered what had happened last night. Or had it? If it *had* happened, then why was I alone? I could just about remember weaving my way up to bed. Could just about remember pulling off my clothes, then sliding under the bedcovers while I waited. But then - ? I peered around my bedroom, almost as if I expected to see Fraser leap out from the wardrobe, shouting 'Surprise!'.

But where was he? Surely he hadn't changed his mind and gone home after all? Not with his bad ankle, and having to navigate Hector's lane in the dark. It would have been a challenge even doing it dead sober, and neither of us had been that. Definitely not me, anyway.

I groaned again, reached for my dressing gown and stumbled downstairs. There was no sight of Fraser anywhere. If it hadn't been for my sandpaper mouth and throbbing head, I might have wondered if I'd dreamed the whole thing. Then, on the table, I saw a scribbled note.

'Tess –by the time I got upstairs you were so fast asleep I couldn't wake you. But your sofa was comfortable anyway. And thanks for great evening. It's 6.30am now – god knows why I've woken this early, but have just remembered I forgot to feed

Buster last night, so I shall creep (limp?) back without disturbing you. But we'll talk soon - Friday, if not before. Love, Fraser'

I put down the note wondering how I felt about it. It was difficult to know how I felt about anything much with a clog-dance and bagpipes going full blast inside my head. But catching sight of myself in the mirror above the fireplace, I couldn't help but be relieved that he'd gone before I'd emerged from my bed. My hair was as rough as a recently-used floor mop, and there were grey circles under my eyes. I looked very nearly as bad as I felt. He certainly wouldn't have fancied me if he could see me right now.

And yet last night he had. I definitely hadn't imagined that.

And I had fancied him. Very much so.

The phone rang again. Fraser? But when I fumbled it to my ear, it was Aileen on the other end.

'Tessa? I've just been into the shop. Oliver tells me you're under the weather.'

'Well - '

'Only I was going to remind you that it's the meeting tonight,' she said.

'Meeting?'

'The de-briefing,' she reminded me. 'The post-mortem about the Midsummer Fayre. At my house.'

'Oh yes.'

'Do you think you'll be able to get here?'

'Well - '

'Only if you've got anything catching, don't feel you have to come. Probably better if you stayed

127

away, even if it's just a sniffle. Oliver didn't seem to know what you'd got.'

'No, Aileen. Nothing catching.'

'Not that I want you to think I'm unsympathetic,' she reassured me. 'It's just that...'

'Don't worry. I know what you mean.'

'Well, if you're quite sure that you're *not* sickening for something, then it would be really good if you *can* come. I've already had apologies from Jodie, as well as two others. People just don't seem to take these committee meetings seriously.'

I sighed. 'Don't worry,' I said. 'I'll be there.'

Even as I put down the phone I wondered why, with such a ready-made excuse to hand, I had still agreed to go.

I wondered still more as I slumped in Aileen's armchair that evening, gloomily speculating how much longer the meeting would take. Everyone had been very kind, asking me how I was, and whether I felt any better. Aileen had insisted upon giving me the best chair, carefully placing it so that I wouldn't be breathing any potential germs over the rest of the committee. But even with these well-meant ministrations, the hours felt as if they were dragging far more than they usually did at the annual Midsummer Fayre post-mortem.

We'd already had a discussion in minute detail about the best location for the refreshment tent, and the advantages of fairy cakes over doughnuts when it came to keeping them fresh. Maureen had reported

128

on the response to the Photographic Society's display of 'Nature in the Raw', and Brian had read out a long letter from the vicar explaining why he wouldn't be available to judge next year's fancy dress competition. Then Terry had got onto his favourite subject of the Rabbit Club. Even though we had now reached the coffee-before-you-go stage of the night, he still felt compelled to go through all the reasons as to why he felt he'd make a better president than its present incumbent. As both Aileen and Maureen had tried to point out, this actually had very little to do with the Fayre but, once on his favourite hobby-horse, Terry was difficult to dislodge. At last Maureen began to gather up her things and make going-home noises. The rest of us quickly followed suit. Carol, pulling on her coat, leant forward towards me and spoke in what, for her, was a low voice. 'So anyway, Tessa dear, now that we've finished all our official business – do tell me what you've been up to.'

'I haven't been up to anything,' I said, a horrible foreboding looming over me. 'Other than being a bit under the weather, if that's what you mean.'

'No, no, no,' she said. 'Although I was sorry to hear you weren't well earlier, you poor thing, though you look all right now. But no – it was Fraser I was talking about. Your friend Fraser Curtis. A little bird told me that he was seen going into your house yesterday tea-time - but no-one saw him coming out again!'

Unsurprisingly, the rest of the group fell silent.

Carol gave a silly little laugh. 'Oh, goodness. It

wasn't a secret, was it?'

Aileen tutted. 'Carol - '

'Of course it isn't secret,' I said angrily, looking around the other interested faces. 'Why on earth should it be? Next time I have visitors, I'll arrange to have the church bells rung, just so as everyone can see who's coming and going, and make a proper note of it.'

Carol looked put out. 'Sorry, I didn't know I was speaking out of turn. I was just taking a friendly interest.'

'Well just to satisfy everyone's curiosity,' I snapped, 'Fraser called round last night and stayed for a meal. During the evening we had so much to drink that we decided to spend the rest of the night making passionate love, except that we were both so sozzled that we couldn't actually manage it.'

There was a small silence.

'Well,' said Maureen brightly, 'that sounds a *lot* more fun than we've been having here tonight.'

'Tess,' said Oliver. 'Good to see you back again. How are you feeling?'

'Better than I did yesterday morning,' I said. 'Sorry to let you down. I hope it wasn't too busy in here?'

'No, nothing I couldn't deal with. But I'm glad you're back.' He smiled at me. 'It always feels so funny in the shop when you're not here.'

I smiled back, feeling even guiltier.

'So what laid you so low? I do hope it's gone

130

away.'

'Oliver - ' I said.

'What?'

'I had a hangover,' I said. 'And the nicer you are to me, the worse I feel.'

He looked at me with raised brows.

'Fraser came round,' I began to explain heavily. 'Do you remember, he couldn't make Erica's dinner party on Saturday because he'd hurt his ankle? Well, I'm afraid I'd completely forgotten to check up on how he was doing, and when I saw that he'd come all the way round to my house on crutches just to apologise and bring me some wine, I felt so bad that I invited him in, and we ended up drinking far too much, and I really am hugely embarrassed about it...'

Oliver stared at me. 'You had a hangover? *You*?'

'Yes me. And I feel really, really bad about having taken a day off.'

'Oh well. It's not as if you make a habit of it.'

He stared at me in silence, until after a moment I saw his mouth start to twitch. It seemed such a bizarre conversation for us to be having, that even I could see it had a silly sound to it.

'Only I thought you should know,' I said.

He began to laugh. 'Oh poor Tess. Never mind. Just as long as you're feeling better than you did yesterday.'

'Much better,' I assured him. 'Certainly better enough to make you some coffee, if you'd like some?'

'Definitely.' He looked at me again. 'And

feeling well enough to cope with customers if I go and start work on that tallboy?'

'Tessa? Are you busy?'

It was lunchtime when Aileen's head appeared round the shop door. She edged inside, her tone unusually tentative. 'About last night - ' She glanced around to double-check that Oliver was not in sight.

'It's all right,' I said wearily. 'He's gone up to his flat to have a sandwich.'

'Oh good.' She came inside. 'Only I wanted to say – about last night - '

'I should apologise,' I said. 'I know my reaction was way over the top.'

'You were provoked,' she said firmly. 'Sometimes Carol… Well, you know what she's like. She's got no more sense than a butterfly.'

'But I was at fault too. I didn't - '

She put her hand on my arm. 'Everyone understands exactly why you reacted as you did,' she told me earnestly. 'Even though it *was* rather naughty of you to tease Carol like that. But don't worry, we all perfectly realise that you were joking. I mean, *as if* … Well, honestly! But don't worry, we all know you better than to believe you were serious. You're simply not the sort of person who would behave like that.'

'Like what?' asked Oliver.

'Oh – Oliver. Hello.' Aileen looked discomfited by his sudden appearance. 'I thought you were upstairs. I was just talking to Tess about our Midsummer Fayre debriefing. There's always so much that needs sorting out, and there was just a little more unfinished business left over…'

'Well,' said Oliver, 'I'm sure you're right, but this is probably not the best place, not when Tessa's at work. Perhaps you could pick another time.'

I looked at him in surprise as Aileen, rather red-faced, left the shop. It was most unlike Oliver to be so direct, so there had to be something bothering him.

There was. 'While I was eating my sandwich, I had a phone call,' he said without preamble. 'Anita again.'

'Anita? Wow, she must be up early. It can barely be dawn in Chicago. '

'Six-thirty,' he confirmed. 'But apparently she came to a decision last night, and wanted to let me know straight away.'

I waited uneasily.

'She's planning to come home,' he said. 'She says she needs some time away from Todd.'

'Oh dear.'

'I was afraid of this.' Oliver ran his fingers through his hair. 'She's got such a low boredom threshold. She's fine as long as she's got some kind of plan or project to sink her teeth into.'

'But surely she'd be even more bored if she came back to Little Bagford? Unless,' I added, as a hopeful thought struck me, 'she's planning to base herself in London or somewhere?'

'I don't think Anita is a big city kind of person,' said Oliver. He paused, with plainly more to come.

'I told her,' he said at last, 'that I'd been thinking about carrying out some kind of improvements to the shop. She said that she's still got loose ends to sort out in Chicago, but if she's back home in time, she'd like to get involved.' He looked at me worriedly. 'You remember I'd mentioned to you that I thought the place needed a revamp?'

'Yes, of course,' I agreed. 'But I hadn't realised you were quite so serious about it.'

He shrugged. 'It needs doing, Tess. You know yourself just how slow business can be in the shop. We need it to be a space that entices people into it, not somewhere so dark and gloomy that it keeps people out.'

I looked around me. I would have liked to argue that he was imagining the problem, but sadly I knew he was quite right. Viewed with an objective eye, it did have the air of a shop that had been in hibernation for some time. And it was cramped. Furniture was placed wherever it could be squeezed in, the antiquarian books were stacked wherever there was shelf-room, and there were several pieces of really good artwork that could hardly be seen, either because they were in shadow, or because they had other items pushed in front of them.

'I don't think this shop's been given a proper sort-out since well before Margaret died,' he continued. 'And I'm not sure it's had a decent facelift since it opened. I know you do a good job, Tess, in keeping all the stock clean and polished, but we're fighting a losing battle here. The repairs and renovation side of the business is steady enough, but we do need to do something to generate more actual sales, or sooner or later we'll simply go under.'

We looked at each other.

'But the money - ? It's not going to be cheap, Oliver.'

'Well yes, it'll cost, no doubt. But I think I've got enough put by to pay for it. Margaret always insisted we keep something back for emergencies. And actually, when I told Anita about doing a makeover, she did suggest that she might put in some of her own money. I can see you're not keen on all the upheaval, Tess, any more than I am. But I'm beginning to think that if we don't do something soon, it really will be an emergency.'

'I suppose you're right,' I said heavily. 'It does need something to make it look better. But are you sure Anita's the right person for the job?'

He put his hands to his hair once more. 'Actually,' he said, 'if she does come back from The States in time, then yes, I think she'd be the perfect person for the job. Yes, even if we didn't take into account the fact that she'd be driving us both mad if she didn't have a project. Unlike me, Anita's always had a good eye for colour and design. She's always had good business sense too. In fact, it's probably because she's not using her talents in Chicago that she's become so fed up with life out there.'

Reluctant as I felt, I had to agree. Anita had indeed always been good at that sort of thing.

'Yes,' continued Oliver. 'Yes, I'm beginning to feel a bit more positive about it now.' His expression grew more animated as he looked around. 'There's so much room for improvement here, and I'm sure she could come up with better ideas than I could. And also, of course - ' he said pausing suddenly, 'if she *is* here to manage the project and supervise the decorators, then there's no reason why you and I couldn't go to Scotland.' He looked at me wistfully. 'Come on, Tess. Just think, it's a sensibly-priced and ready-organised holiday just waiting for us to say yes to it. I know you've had your problems with Daniel in the past, but you've told me several times that you've long since got over him. And Erica seems a lovely girl, and so keen for us to join them. After all, it's not as if we'd have to spend all our time going round as a foursome. Or should I say 'fivesome'? Mustn't forget Toby. Yes, I'm sure they'll be wanting to do kiddy-type things, not hang around with us.'

I remained silent.

'You did say that you'd always wanted to see Scotland,' he reminded me. 'And we could both do with a holiday.'

I sighed. 'I'll think about it,' I said, knowing myself to be too much of a coward to give him a direct 'No'.

'Oh well,' he said. 'Still, I suppose that at least there is one other very good thing about allowing Anita be in charge of a revamp.'

'Yes?'

He grinned. 'The workmen will be supervised as they've never been supervised before.'

But as the afternoon wore on, my gloom about Anita

136

was joined by another, and rather more urgent consideration. When Jodie had told me the news of her pregnancy, I was guiltily aware that I hadn't felt the surge of unreserved joy that any decent friend ought to have done. Hopefully she hadn't picked up on that, but all the same, *I'd* been aware of it, and I was feeling increasingly bad about it. With her absence from the Midsummer Fayre de-briefing, I hadn't even seen her to reassure her of my delight on her behalf.

'Go ahead,' said Oliver when I asked if he'd mind if I popped out for a few minutes to look for a baby-warming gift. 'It's such good news for her and her husband. What will you get ?'

Of that, I had no idea, I realised, as I wandered along the High Street. Not that I was spoiled for choice. Ideally I'd have bought a little teddy bear or some item of baby clothing – but Little Bagford didn't have a babywear shop, and the only teddy bears for sale were the 'collectible' sort, with labels warning that they were unsuitable for small children. In the end, and conscious of passing time, I hurried into the little mini-mart and chose a large bunch of flowers and a box of chocolates, hoping that morning sickness would not preclude her enjoyment of them. On a last minute whim, I added a bar of Kendal Mint Cake to the basket. If I was shopping for guilt-offerings then I might just as well add Oliver to the list. I couldn't put off much longer telling him that I was never going to change my mind about Scotland.

But when I got back, he was so pleased with the Mint Cake that it seemed a shame to spoil his mood.

I took my offerings to Jodie after supper that evening. I'd rather hoped that James would be out or busy, but it was obvious when I arrived that they were both in the middle of watching something exciting on the television. Jodie was quick to offer to postpone their viewing, but it didn't take a genius to see that James was less keen.

'Stay and watch it with us, if you like,' he called, disappearing back into their sitting room. 'It's just coming up to the important bit.'

'No, it's all right,' I said, unloading the chocolates and flowers onto the kitchen table. 'I won't stay, Jodie, but these are just a little something to say how pleased I am for you.'

Jodie beamed. 'But I always knew you were anyway,' she said, making me feel even worse. 'Hey, why not come over Friday evening? James will be out and we can have a proper gossip.'

I sighed. 'I'd have loved to, but that's the day Mum gets back from holiday, and I'm sure she'll want to spend the whole evening telling me about it. D'you know, she's only phoned me once since she got there, which I take to be a sure sign that she's been too busy enjoying herself to think of it.'

Jodie laughed. 'Well, that's good to hear. And I'm sure you and I will manage to catch up sooner or later anyway. Oh, but there's something I was meaning to tell you before I forget.'

I paused at the open door. 'Yes?'

'I think I've seen your Daniel. Is he tall, dark

138

and handsome? Noticeably handsome, in fact. There was a man like that who came into the Patchwork Pumpkin yesterday, along with a nice-looking girl and a baby. I heard them calling the baby Toby, which made me think that it must be.'

'Sounds likely,' I said cautiously. 'Though he's not 'my' Daniel any more, and hasn't been for a long time. He's Erica's Daniel now.'

She looked at me. 'Well, whoever he currently belongs to, I can see why you fell for him. He's quite something, isn't he! Not necessarily a 'nice' person – but I suspect he wouldn't have to do much talking in order to get a girl into bed.'

'You suspect right,' I said dryly. 'He didn't.'

'Yet I must say he didn't strike me as being particularly your type. I've always thought you tended to play on the safe side when choosing men to go out with. And even in my very brief encounter with him, I didn't get the impression that Daniel was a safe sort of person.'

'Safe'. That word again. As I ambled home, I wondered if I was becoming hooked on 'safe'. Judging by other people's opinions, it appeared that the answer was Yes. Aileen had plainly thought so, when she'd come into the shop to reassure me that my outburst had not been taken seriously. Although this was, in some ways, admittedly a relief, it was also distinctly depressing to realise that she'd so completely dismissed the very idea of me getting drunk or having a sex life.

I sighed. But there again – was playing safe really such a bad thing? Especially if it meant keeping me from getting my heart broken by a good-looking bastard who had only pretended that he actually cared about me.

By the following day summer had returned. Sunshine put me in a far more cheerful frame of mind, and by the time I'd finished work and eaten my meal, it felt like a shame not to make the most of the lovely evening. This, coupled with the fact it was the last one before my mother returned from holiday, made me too restless to stay indoors. And anyway, if I wandered in the direction of Hector's cottage, I might just happen to accidentally bump into Fraser. I knew he'd had a lot of work planned for this week, but the awkwardness of the way we'd parted on Monday had been gently niggling at me ever since. I didn't know if it made things better or worse that I appeared to have passed out before anything could happen. And yet the note he'd left didn't seem to imply that he'd taken my state of unconsciousness personally. Perhaps if I just chanced to be walking past the cottage, and Fraser just happened to see me, then we might get over any initial embarrassment before our enforced meeting when the Fossil Club arrived home.

I ambled onwards, still unsure of quite what I would say if I saw him. If only I had eased up on the alcohol before it overwhelmed me! It really was infuriating that it should have sent me to sleep at exactly the same time it had awoken all sorts of unaccustomed feelings. Feelings that I'd have liked to explore further.

I was so deep in thought that it was a shock to approach Hector's cottage, glance up and find Fraser actually standing at the gate, looking at me as I approached. He waved.

I returned the greeting, hoping he hadn't noticed the sudden pinkness of my cheeks. 'Hi Fraser. How's the ankle?'

He grinned. If he too felt embarrassed, he didn't show it.

'Hi Tess – good to see you. Especially upright and fully awake.'

I cringed. 'I don't usually get like that. Tipsy, I mean.'

'Tipsy? Rat-arsed, you mean.' he said. 'Rat-arsed good and proper.'

'Well I don't think you were any more sober than I was,' I pointed out crossly. 'Anyway, it's certainly not as if I make a habit of it.'

'Then you should,' he said, his smile growing wider. 'It was a terrific evening. Or don't you remember?'

'Most of it,' I said evasively. 'Anyway, I came to see how your ankle is. So how is it?'

'Improving all the time. But it's still stopping me driving, unfortunately.'

'Can I help? Although I'm afraid I could only act as chauffeur outside of shop hours.'

'Thanks. I wouldn't need a chauffeur at all except for the fact that there's still a couple more sites that I need to visit. However - ' He paused as a blue car turned into the lane and started edging its way down the narrow track towards us. 'Ha! This is the person I'd been looking out for. Here's my volunteer driver arriving now. Hi Nick!'

He waved vigorously as the car drew to a stop beside the fence. The door opened and a girl climbed out. Petite, blond, and curvy.

Fraser beamed. 'Nick, you are a total life-saver,' he said. 'Putting your own work on hold to come and look after me.'

She stood looking at him severely. 'And you, Fraser Curtis, are the world's biggest arse-pain,' she told him. 'Only you could manage to injure yourself while standing alone in the middle of a field. You're not fit to be let out unsupervised. Still, I know you need to hit the deadline, so it's lucky for you that I've got time to drive you tomorrow. But I can't spare any longer than that. I'm here for twenty-four hours only.'

'That's all I need,' he said. 'Come on, you, let me give you a hug. It's so good to see you. Hope it wasn't too bad a journey to get here. I know this cottage isn't the easiest place to find. Oh, and this is Tessa,' he added, belatedly remembering to introduce me.

She skimmed a smile at me before reaching into the back of the car to pull out an overnight bag. 'Can you carry this in for me, Fraser – oh no, of course you can't, not with a bad leg. Never mind, I can manage. It's not that heavy, although it does have my lap-top in it. Can't go anywhere without that.' She threw me another brisk nod before striding purposefully towards the cottage door. 'Have you got the kettle on

142

yet? Don't worry, I've brought my own herbal tea, though I'm certainly expecting you to provide the biscuits. Or better still, cake. Where's the kitchen in this place - ?'

She disappeared inside, leaving Fraser still poised on the doorstep. 'Coming in for a cuppa?' he asked me. 'You'd be very welcome. You can come and listen to us talk shop about the book she's helping me with. Just don't expect to get a word in, not when Nick's in full flow.'

'Er, no,' I said. 'No, it's all right, I'm sure you've got a lot to catch up on. And I guess I'll see you tomorrow evening anyway. You are still planning to meet your uncle when the coach gets back?'

'Oh, yes, sure. Talking of which,' he said, suddenly recollecting something, 'Hector rang last night and asked me to book a table at The Dragon's Head for the four of us. That's you and your mother, and me and him. For an evening meal. Said it would make a nice end to their holiday.'

'Oh,' I said, slightly taken aback. 'Yes, I suppose it would be. It would save me having to cook. And the food there is always very good.'

'Excellent.' Fraser looked pleased. 'Oh well then - ' He waited, still holding the door wide open. Are you quite sure you don't want to come in?' He gazed at me rather uncertainly. From within the cottage Nick's voice rang out, demanding to know which room she should carry her bag up to.

I waved a hand and turned quickly away. So in whose room *would* she be sleeping, I wondered. I

was certainly interested to know. I just wasn't sure
that I wanted to hear the answer.

Chapter 10

Despite myself, the question of in which room Nick had spent the night occupied my thoughts well into the following day. I had vaguely recalled Fraser having mentioned someone called Nick who was involved in the book, but I definitely hadn't registered that 'Nick' was a female. And a very attractive one too.

He did say that he'd worked closely with Nick during previous research trips. But how close was 'closely'? I wished I had taken more interest, but by then our conversation had side-tracked down other paths. Not that Fraser's affairs were any concern of mine, I told myself irritably. Even if we *had* got so cosy the other evening, that didn't mean he hadn't already got his own life. So what if Nick *was* a friend with benefits? Fraser was both good looking and unattached. For all it was my business, he might have hundreds of friends with benefits.

But at the thought of hundreds of women all suddenly turning up at Hector's cottage, I smiled in spite of myself. That, if nothing else, would certainly deflect village gossip from my own affairs.

'Tess?' broke in Oliver. 'I'm just putting the kettle on, if you want a drink. You're looking very cheerful. Pleased that your mother will be home tonight?'

'Not particularly,' I said. 'Well, no – I mean yes

– I mean, it will be nice to have her back, but it's also been good to have the chance to do a few things by myself. Like having that meal with you in your flat; that was very pleasant.'

He looked pleased. 'Well, we could certainly do that again. I enjoyed it too. And I don't imagine your mother would mind being left at home alone occasionally. Or would she? I mean,' he added confusedly, 'it's not that she wouldn't actually be welcome to come along as well, but - '

He was getting so tied up with himself that I laughed. 'No, don't worry. She's not that much dependent upon me. She's pretty good for someone of her age.'

'Yes, of course.'

'Anyway,' I said. 'We'll be celebrating her return with a meal out tonight. We're going to The Dragon's Head. That's Mum and me, and Hector and Fraser.'

'That's sounds nice,' said Oliver. 'Would you like to leave work a bit early, if you've any preparations to make?'

'Oh Oliver, you ought to win the Employer of the Year Award,' I told him. 'That's so kind of you. But to be honest, the coach won't be arriving home until around six, so there'll be no mad rush.'

He grinned and disappeared back to the kettle. I sighed, feeling guilty. He was so considerate. He hadn't even said any more about Scotland. The nearest he'd come to it was in pointing out that Anita's arrival would make it possible for us both to be absent from the shop. Even then, he hadn't tried

146

to press the matter, which made me feel even guiltier. Dear Oliver. Damn Oliver.

By six o'clock quite a gathering had assembled on the Green to await the coming of the coach. I was happy to chat with my fellow meet-and-greeters while we waited, but it didn't stop me noticing that Fraser still hadn't rolled up. He was, I presumed, too busy entertaining Nick to have realised the time. In fact it wasn't until the coach was already in sight that I saw him hobbling as fast as he could towards the bus stop.

He arrived, breathless, as the coach drew up.

'You were cutting it rather fine,' I told him. 'Lucky for you that it's a few minutes behind schedule, or you'd have been late.'

'On the contrary, I timed it exactly right,' he said. 'It'll take forever to get this lot off the bus - by which time,' he puffed, 'I shall have got my breath back, and be smiling, relaxed and happy to greet my aged relative. In any case,' he added more honestly, 'it took me longer to walk here than I anticipated. I didn't want to use the crutch, but this ankle is still slowing me down a lot.'

'Hm,' I said unsympathetically. 'Well at least you had your friend Nick to look after you today.'

'Yes, she was brilliant. Took me where I needed to go, and I got all the material needed. A perfect day, in fact. Oh, here's your mum coming down the steps. And Hector right behind her.'

In the confusion of greetings and retrieving the right cases, there was no time to press him further.

My mother appeared, looking tanned, happy, and in far better health than she had done when she departed.

'Bournemouth was good?' I asked. 'Did you enjoy it? You certainly look as if you did.'

'I did,' she beamed. 'I think everyone did. We had lovely weather, and loads of trips out. I'm glad to get home for a rest!'

'Well, I've reserved a table at The Dragon,' smiled Fraser. 'I booked it early, because I thought you'd probably be tired after the journey. So we could go straight there, if you want to.'

We could,' she laughed, 'but what about the cases? We can't take them into the pub with us.'

We all looked at the luggage which, it had to be admitted, would not be welcomed into the snug dining area of The Dragon's Head.

'Then Fraser and I will take all the luggage over to your house now, Pat,' decided Hector. 'If that's okay. It'll be quicker than taking them to my place, and then I can collect mine from your house after we've eaten. You and Tess might as well go straight to the pub and wait for us. Give me your key - we can be there and back in a moment.'

'I don't see Fraser going anywhere at the gallop,' I pointed out. 'I'll go with you instead. I managed to get Mum's case down here in the first place, so I'm sure I can get it home again.'

Hector regarded his nephew with disgust. 'Oh yes, I'd forgotten about your ankle. You're an idiot, lad. Why you decided to walk backwards while looking forwards, beats me. Okay then Tess, if

148

you're sure you can manage…'

While Fraser and my mother ambled their way towards the pub, Hector and I carried the cases back to my house and left them just inside. By the time we returned, they had already been seated at a table for four, and were studying the menu. Being early in the evening, it wasn't busy, yet felt pleasantly cosy after the slightly chill evening air. The smell of food made me realise I was hungry.

'Ah, there you are,' said Fraser, looking up. We haven't ordered any drinks yet, because we weren't sure what you'd want. But if you tell me now, I'll go to the bar and bring them over.'

He made to stand but was forestalled by Hector. 'I'll see to this,' he said. 'If we let you try to carry them, there'll be more liquid on the tray than in the glasses.'

His blunt but accurate assessment of his nephew's current uneven gait made us all laugh. Fraser grinned too and, with a shrug, settled back in his chair. He handed me the menu. 'There are some good choices on it,' he observed. 'Pat and I have already decided what we're having. Do you know what you'd like, Tess?'

I studied the list of dishes, all of which sounded delicious. 'Um, they do look good. Hard to decide. Actually, I'd usually choose my food before the drink to go with it,' I said. 'But Hector was in such a hurry to get them in, that he forgot to ask us - ' I stopped in mid-sentence, suddenly silenced by the sight of Hector himself making his way back to us. And, immediately behind him, a waitress carrying a tray on

149

which was balanced four empty glasses and a bottle of champagne.

She stopped and placed it carefully on the table. 'There you are, sir. Enjoy your celebration.' She smiled at all of us and departed.

'Oh Hector,' said my mother. 'Oh my goodness.' She looked as pink and as girlish as I had ever seen her.

'Yes,' beamed Hector, sitting down. 'Champagne. For a very special occasion. I imagine you've guessed already,' he said looking at me. 'Your mother has done me the great honour of agreeing to marry me. It's quite mad of her of course, but I shan't try to argue her out of it.'

'Wow,' said Fraser. 'Well, that's wonderful. Bournemouth is obviously the place to go. Nothing like the seaside to promote romance. That's great news, isn't it Tess?'

'Yes,' I said. 'Yes. Great news.'

'The very best,' said Fraser. 'We're delighted for you both. Do you want a hand opening that, Hector?'

Hector was doing his best to remove the cork from the bottle. 'The waitress offered to do it,' he told us, 'but I wanted to do it with a bit of ceremony. There's nothing like the sound of - ' He broke off, as the cork did indeed come out with a resounding pop, causing several other customers' heads to turn and glance in our direction.

Hector beamed round. 'I'm an engaged man,' he announced to the room in general, causing a smattering of applause.

'You first, Pat,' he said, pouring my mother a generous quantity. 'Now you, Tess.' I watched the liquid splashing into my glass, foaming over the top a little, running in a clear trickle down the stem and onto the table cloth. A small damp patch appeared around the base.

'A toast,' declared Fraser, raising his own full glass. 'A toast to the happy couple, and may you have many, many good times ahead of you.' I felt his foot nudge my ankle. 'Tess - ?'

I raised my glass. 'Yes,' I said. 'Yes, of course. Lovely news. Congratulations.'

'And now we must eat,' said Hector. 'I'm starving. We only had a sandwich for lunch, didn't we. Pat. Mine tasted like cardboard, although it was supposed to be prawn mayonnaise, or at least so the label said. Now, what's on the menu…?'

As he bent his head to study the choices, I stared blankly down at my own menu. I tried to concentrate on the list, but I was more aware of my mother's gaze upon me than the choice of dishes.

'What's up with you?' hissed Fraser at the end of the meal. We were alone, for my mother had headed off to the loo, and Hector was at the bar, deep in cheerful conversation with the landlord, who had been given the news of the celebration.

Now Fraser leaned closer 'You've sat like a wet weekend since they told us,' he said. 'Surely you're at least a little bit pleased for them?'

'Of course,' I snapped. 'Why wouldn't I be?'

151

'You tell me! Why indeed wouldn't you be? They're two good people who lost their original partners several years ago and who've now got a second chance to be happy.'

'I'm perfectly okay with that,' I insisted. 'I've been smiling, I've been chatty. What more can I do?'

'You can look as if you really mean it. You've been going through the motions all right, but I've seldom seen a less convincing act. Fortunately Hector doesn't seem to have noticed, but I bet your mother has. Surely you're happy for her?'

'I am. I am. It's just been a bit of a shock. You'll forgive me if I take just a few moments to recover, I trust?'

'You can take as long as you like as far as I'm concerned. Only you might try and be a bit more considerate towards your mum.'

'I *am* considerate. She knows that I'm happy for her, deep down. But while you're talking glibly about how lovely it all is, you might try remembering that this news will affect me a damn sight more than it's going to affect you! All you'll be doing is saying 'how nice' and then waltzing off on your adventures again.'

He paused. 'Okay. Okay, I get that. But instead of sitting there thinking nothing but negative thoughts, why don't you try looking at the plus points?'

I looked at him. 'Such as?'

'Such as it opens up a lot more possibilities for you. I know you've always felt that looking after your mum was your first priority. But this lets you off the hook. From now on Hector will look after her. Okay, I know they're both getting on, and it may not be for ever and ever, but at least it'll be for the foreseeable future.'

'But I liked things as they were,' I said childishly. I stared bleakly into my empty coffee cup. 'This is going to mean all sorts of changes.'

'Then try embracing them. Come on, Tess, life is passing you by. You're an adult now, perhaps you should try behaving like one.'

'Oh shut up!' I was aware of the rising volume of my voice, and dropped it to an angry hiss. 'Listen, at the end of the day, the way in which I choose to live my life is absolutely nothing to do with you, so why don't you just push off back to your delightful friend Nick. Her company is obviously more agreeable to you than mine is.'

He glared at me. 'Apart from the fact that she left the village several hours ago, I shall go when I'm good and ready, and not before. And I don't know what that veiled innuendo is supposed to mean anyway. Nick is a good mate, nothing more.'

'Oh yeah?'

'Yeah.' he said. 'Yeah. And just for your information, she already has a partner - a very nice woman called Tanya. Nick's tastes don't run to fellas at all.'

'Oh.' I stared at the tablecloth feeling foolish.

'Anyway,' he said in a quieter voice, 'I can see your mum coming back from the loo. So why don't you stop sulking like a teenager, and try to think of someone other than yourself for a change.'

With a look of pure hatred, I turned away from him to face my mother with a smile that felt more than a little forced. I pushed back my chair. 'Well, if you and Hector are ready to go …?' I said. 'It must have been a long day for both of you.'

'It has,' she confessed, 'although at least I can have a lie-in tomorrow, if I need it. Unlike poor you, who has to get up and go to work. Come on, Tessy,' she smiled, taking my arm. 'We'll let Hector walk us home, and then it'll be bedtime for both of us.'

It was none of Fraser's business, but after Hector had retrieved his luggage and Mum had gone up to bed, I followed her upstairs to reassure her that I was indeed genuinely pleased for her. 'You did take me a bit by surprise,' I admitted. 'But yes, I think it's lovely news, truly I do.'

She put down the mug of hot chocolate I'd made her, and touched my hand. 'Oh darling, I do wish now that I'd given you more of a hint. It was silly of me not to, but I didn't want to tell you over the phone. I wanted to tell you in person, and preferably when it was just the two of us. But then Hector was so keen to announce it - I couldn't stop him.' Her hand tightened over mine. 'You do know, don't you, that it doesn't mean I loved your father any the less. He was such a special man. No-one else could take his place, nor ever will.'

'I know,' I said. I stared down at the carpet, suddenly finding it difficult to speak. I'd have died rather than play the sympathy-card in front of Fraser, but the shock of the announcement *had* at first made me feel as if Hector was somehow proposing to step into my father's shoes. Stupidly, it had never ever occurred to me that Mum might wish to get married again. Was that why I had been so completely blind to their growing relationship?

I continued to stare unseeingly down at the pattern on the carpet. I wondered what my dad would have made of it. He had indeed been a special person - but he had been a generous one as well. A lot more generous than I was being right now. Dad had always wanted my mum to be happy, and even if he couldn't be around himself to make that happen, he would never have begrudged someone else taking on that role.

I chewed my lip, feeling the tears dangerously close. 'Anyway,' I said quickly, turning my head away, 'it's nice to have you home again.'

'It's good to *be* home,' she said, 'even though Bournemouth was lovely. 'I did bring you back a box of cherry fudge but I'll unpack the cases tomorrow. I'm too tired to do it now.'

I smiled. 'And there's no need for you to get up early. If I've gone to work before you come down, I'll see you when I get back afterwards.'

I made to go, but her hand continued to retain mine. 'And Tess, my darling,' she said. 'Just because I'm going to marry Hector, it doesn't mean I love you any the less either. You've been my rock over the past few years, and don't think I haven't been aware of it. I know there will be changes, of course there will be – but nothing major will happen without consulting you.'

I blinked and kissed her cheek. I knew she meant her words, but I also knew that however real her good intentions might be, from now on things would be very different for all of us.

Oliver was in cheerful mood when I arrived at work next morning. 'Could be a good day today, Tess,' he said optimistically. 'What with it being a Saturday, and so nice and sunny too. This weather usually brings out the day- trippers. We might even see a coach party or two, if we're very lucky.'

I smiled. 'If we're lucky,' I echoed. 'And hopefully they'll all be rich and in a spending mood. A nice healthy cash flow would certainly be a good thing.'

'And also good to show Anita. I'm sure she'll want to look at the books when she arrives.'

'Yes, I suppose she will.' I grimaced. The fact that Oliver's daughter felt she had the right to breeze back into Little Bagford and immediately start checking up on shop business was something I'd have to bite my tongue about. And knowing Anita, the first thing she *would* do would be to go through the accounts as if we were children who couldn't be trusted to get our sums right.

'Not that she'll need to worry,' reassured Oliver. 'You look after the financial side of things beautifully. And we're still keeping our heads above water, aren't we?'

'Just about,' I said, 'mainly thanks to all your

restoration work. So it's you who should be patting yourself on the back. No, we won't have anything to feel apologetic about when Anita arrives.'

'Mm. Anyway,' he said, reverting to safer ground, 'did your mother arrive home safely? I hope she had an enjoyable time.'

'She did. In fact she had such an enjoyable time that she's come back engaged to be married to Hector Curtis.'

'Really?' Oliver sounded so completely taken by surprise that I felt quite cheered. Plainly I hadn't been the only person going round the village without noticing the blindingly obvious.

'My goodness,' he continued. 'Well, well, that's a turn-up for the books, isn't it.'

'It certainly was as far as I'm concerned,' I admitted. 'You could, as the good old saying goes, have knocked me down with a feather.'

Oliver laughed. 'Well – yes. Goodness. Certainly a turn-up. Who'd have thought it?'
'Not me,' I said. 'That's for sure.'

He paused and looked at me. 'So - How do you feel about it?'

'Okay,' I said. 'I suppose. Yes, of course, okay. Mum deserves some happiness. Hector too, I guess. And I do *like* Hector. It's not as if Mum's springing a complete stranger on me.'

'Not one of the notorious Gigolos of Bournemouth, then,' said Oliver.

In spite of myself I laughed, and started to feel a bit better. 'No,' I confirmed. 'I did give her strict instructions not to bring home one of those.'

Oliver gave me a completely unexpected hug. 'It'll work out,' he said. He stepped back quickly, as if embarrassed about possibly offending me. 'Yes, it'll work out, Tess, you'll see. Now – a cup of coffee? Or is it too early?'

The morning wore on. Oliver went off to assess some silverware owned by an elderly woman who was too nervous of potential muggers to bring it into the shop herself. A gentle drift of customers wandered through the door, looked around, occasionally bought items, and then went away again. The clock ticked round.

With time to think, I realised that I was already starting to feel a bit more positive. Perhaps it was simply down to Oliver's comforting reaction to the news. Although it might, I reluctantly suspected, have also been assisted by Fraser's revelation last night that Nick was definitely not his girlfriend. Not that I had any real reason to feel cheered by that. It wasn't as if Fraser and I were in any kind of relationship. And even if we were, we certainly wouldn't have been, not after that full and frank exchange of views last night.

And yet... In spite of all this, I *did* feel cheered. However pointless that may be. I sighed. Oh well, I supposed that I would find out for sure next time I saw him. I hoped it wouldn't be too long coming. Whatever happened, I didn't want to leave things on that sour note for any longer than I had to.

Eventually Oliver returned. He was laughing. 'The old lady had brought in her son to supervise matters,' he explained, 'just to make sure I didn't bop her over the head and make off with the loot. But she did have some very nice stuff,' he admitted. 'Most of it the sort of thing that usually sells pretty well. Anyway, I offered her a fair price for them, which both she and her son seemed happy about.'

I smiled. I couldn't really envisage Oliver offering a less than fair price to anyone, which was probably why the shop had never made a huge profit.

'And on my way back,' he went on, still pleased with himself, 'Guess who I bumped into? Erica. She sent you her love, and says she's still hoping that we'll go with them to Scotland. I did tell her,' he said quickly, 'that you hadn't forgotten, and that you were still thinking about it, and that I wasn't going to rush you into a decision. And then,' he continued, 'Erica said that she quite understood, and that there was no hurry for an answer, because she and Daniel will be going there anyway, but that it would be really wonderful to have our company.' He paused for breath. 'She is such a lovely person, you can't help but like her.'

I sighed. This really was the time to seize the moment. I took a deep breath. And then, inevitably, the bell jangled, the door opened, and a customer came in. A customer who was looking for a small table to stand beside her bookcase which was made of rosewood, so of course the table would have to match it really well, but it mustn't be too big because her room wasn't that large in the first place…

I left Oliver to deal with her. It occurred to me that not only was it lunchtime, but that I'd forgotten to pick up my sandwiches before I left home. What a pain. However, the little supermarket did a good line in snacks and drinks, and it would save me having to trot all the way home. I mimed my intentions to Oliver and slipped out.

After the comparative gloom of indoors, the fresh air and bright sunlight was delicious. I ambled slowly down the street, savouring my momentary freedom. The Patchwork Pumpkin was, as usual, doing brisk business, though I did spot Jodie inside, unloading trays of some of her culinary marvels. Had she been less occupied, I'd have been tempted to pause for a gossip, but this was plainly not the time. I realised that I had not yet told my mother about Jodie's pregnancy – nor indeed did Jodie yet know of my mother's plans to marry Hector. I walked even more slowly. These days it felt as if there were so many things changing all around me, that my previous calm existence had been set in a different universe.

I was emerging from the supermarket with a cheese pasty and bag of apples in my hands, when a tall figure moved out in front of me. Daniel.

I stepped back abruptly.

'Tess,' he said. 'There you are! It's taken me ages to track you down. I looked through your shop window and you weren't there, and then I went to see if you were back at your house, but your mother was in the garden - ' He glared at me as if he thought I'd been deliberately hiding from him.

'From which I gather that you're wanting to talk to me?' I asked.

'Yes I am.'

160

'Well?' I said.

'Scotland, of course.'

'Scotland - ?'

'Stop pretending to be stupid, Tess. You know exactly what I want to talk to you about. Erica's just been speaking to me. She says that she saw Oliver this morning, and that you're definitely thinking about coming to Scotland with us.'

'Is that what he said?'

If I had hoped to irritate him further, I was succeeding beautifully.

'Yes he did. And presumably because that's what you told him!'

I fixed a vague smile. 'Yes, I suppose I did.'

'You 'suppose'? Either you did or you didn't.' He stuck his face closer to mine and, even in such circumstances, I couldn't help thinking how good looking he still was. If anything, the passage of several years had only improved things. But, not even for old times' sake, was I ever going to let him bully me again. I smiled even more sweetly. 'Yes, I believe I did tell Oliver I was still thinking about coming to Scotland with you.'

'Then what on earth are you playing at? *Seriously*? You are seriously thinking of joining us for a two week holiday in a cottage in the wilds? Oh come on, get real! Can you imagine just how awkward it would be?! Having to make small talk over the breakfast things – spending the evenings all cosied up together in the sitting room?'

I spoke demurely. 'But Erica said that it was quite a large cottage. Room for us all to have our own

161

space, I'm sure.'

'No space would be large enough! Even if it was a sodding castle, it wouldn't be big enough.'

'And Oliver,' I continued imperviously, 'is really keen to go. I'd feel awfully mean letting down Oliver. Just as in the same way, I'm sure, you'd feel mean about disappointing Erica.'

He paused and took a deep breath. 'Tess. I'm being serious. You've got to get real about this, you absolutely have to. I quite understand that neither of us want to let down other people, but really - For God's sake! It would be impossible. Awkward beyond imagining.'

I gazed at him. But particularly awkward for *you*, I thought. It was clear that he still hadn't told Erica about the reality of our relationship, that we'd once been lovers, living together. Which meant – as Fraser had pointed out to me - that he would spend the entire fortnight just waiting for the cat to leap out of the bag. Not that I would let it, for Erica's sake. But Daniel didn't know that.

I sighed. 'What you forget, Daniel, is that I wouldn't find it awkward at all. You seem to think that I still have feelings for you. But I don't, not in the slightest. I don't even care enough to still feel angry about you deciding to bed Maxine in our own home. Daniel, my dear, I got over you a long, long time ago. So I really don't see why your views on the matter should stand in the way of me having a very happy holiday in Scotland with Erica, Toby and - ' I hesitated. 'And with a man who's never yet let me down - Oliver.'

At which point I swept away, before I could allow myself to wonder what the hell I thought I was doing.

Oliver's reaction, when I told him, was almost enough to compensate for my fears.

'So, we're definitely going then?' he said. 'That's absolutely marvellous, Tess! You know, I really didn't think you'd be up for it – and I did try not to press you – but, oh, this is excellent news. I can start looking forward to it now.' His beam could have rivalled the sunshine, and made me feel quite guilty at my own wet-blanket attitude. But, for Oliver, it was almost as if it was a month in the Bahamas that was being planned, rather than two weeks self-catering in Scotland.

'All the same, I really don't want to spend too much time around Daniel,' I insisted. 'So I'll be relying on you to make sure that we don't spend every day on top of each other - I mean, I don't want to be spending every day going round with them.'

'No, of course. I realise that. I shall make sure that we do our own thing as much as politely possible.'

'And in any case,' I added, 'I doubt if Erica would want to spend all the time with us two hanging round her. She's lovely, but I'm sure she'll want a bit of space for herself, just the same as I do. Just as *we* do.'

'It'll be fine. I'll make quite sure it is.'

'And we'll need to sort out some details, I

suppose. Obviously we'll need to work out how we're travelling there, and of course pay our share of the holiday rental. I don't want to feel beholden to them.'

He looked at me diffidently. 'I don't suppose you'd let me take care of all the expenses, would you? You could regard it as a kind of bonus for all the hard work you've put into the business...'

I laughed. 'Oliver, that is so kind! But I really don't think something like that could be regarded as a mere 'bonus'. And can you imagine what Anita would say if she saw that written down as business expenses?'

He looked thoughtful. 'Mm,' he said. 'Mm, that is a point, I suppose. But there again, it doesn't have to be written down anywhere.'

Chapter 11

Oliver's good mood continued over the next day or two, while I grew increasingly depressed. Was it too late to go back on my word? But after Erica had come into the shop on Monday expressly to voice her own delight, I could see retreat was impossible. Even my mother, when I told her, seemed gratified that I would be going on holiday.

'But do remember that Daniel will be there as well,' I pointed out to her.

'Then it's a good job that you got over him so well,' she said. 'It just shows that you're he bigger person. Not everyone would have been able to forgive him so completely. No, don't you worry, Tess. You'll have a lovely time. Oliver will make sure you do.'

So much for relying upon my mother to throw me a lifeline. In fact, there was only one plus side to the situation that I could see, and that would be in giving me the chance to tell Fraser just how wrong he'd been. I *wasn't* afraid to step out of my comfort zone. Yes, I'd look forward to that.

Except that I wasn't quite sure when I would be seeing Fraser. I'd rather hoped that he might have called in to see me by now. Unless he was still angry. But then if we were going to be petty, I was the one who had more right to be upset. Fair enough that, for Mum and Hector's sake, he might have condemned

165

my immediate lack of enthusiasm – but actually, my relationship with my mother was none of his business. So why should it be me who had to go chasing after *him*?

But by Tuesday, when there had still been no sign of him, I began to feel that things had gone on long enough. Irritated as I had been, I didn't want the quarrel to drift on indefinitely. In every idle moment, the memory of those drunken kisses kept drifting back to mind. I supposed that if I'd been born a woman of an earlier generation, I'd have been relieved that we hadn't quite made it into bed together. But sadly, my own main feeling was of regret for a lost opportunity. Not to mention the underlying worry he might have assumed I'd been deliberately leading him on a road to nowhere. As I dusted an Edwardian crystal decanter, I allowed myself yet again to dwell wistfully on what would have undoubtedly happened if only I hadn't been too tipsy to stay awake.

The inner door creaked, and Oliver emerged to disturb my already-disturbing thoughts.

'Well, I've finished at last,' he announced. 'It took me twice as long as I thought it would, but at least I know I've done a good job on that damn bureau.' He beamed at me. 'Want to come and see it? Before it goes back to Mrs Riley?'

But even as I admired the splendid job he'd done on the restoration, my mind was still not entirely on the subject. If I did want to see Fraser again, I'd simply have to go and call on him. I just wished he had lent me a book or something that I could return, so that I'd have a good face-saving excuse. As it was, I'd just have to build on my mother's words that I was the 'bigger person', and set off armed with nothing more than a desire to settle our differences and go back to being friends.

Having made up my mind, I decided I might as well do it as soon as I finished work that afternoon. Before I could chicken out, I rang my mother to tell her not to wait dinner for me, giving vague excuses about Oliver wanting me to stay late. There had been no point in telling her of my quarrel with Fraser, nor did I want to, especially as she been the innocent cause of it.

Thus, when it was time to shut shop for the day, I headed off in the opposite direction to my usual one. The air was still warm and pleasant, making it all too easy to drag my feet. There were shop windows to be gazed into, and front gardens to be admired. I dawdled reluctantly along in the direction of Hector's cottage until I was suddenly halted by the sound of a voice from behind me.

'Tessa! Just the person I wanted to see.'

I turned to find Aileen close on my heels. 'Well, this is fortunate,' she said. 'It's saved me having to phone you.'

I waited, both relieved and irritated to have my mission brought to a pause. 'Something important, Aileen?'

'Yes. Yes, I do need to talk to you. And it's plainly not a good idea trying to chat to you when you're at work.'

I remembered her recent brush with Oliver, and said diplomatically, 'Well, some times are definitely better than others. If you want my undivided attention, then it's probably best to speak to me when I'm not in the shop.'

'Hmm. Anyway, the reason I want to talk to you is that Jodie tells me that she's expecting a baby.'

'Yes,' I said. 'Yes, it's lovely news, isn't it? She's so thrilled.'

'Yes,' agreed Aileen. 'But as you can see, it's left me in a bit of a quandary.'

I looked at her in surprise.

'Well, it must have occurred to you that the birth will take place around next February time.'

'Yes, I suppose it will.'

'Well then - ' she said, seeing that I still looked blank. 'It's much too close to Easter, Tess! What about the Easter Gala?'

'Er - ?'

'Tessa,' she said. 'You are being very slow. Who's going to organise the Easter Egg Hunt if Jodie is busy looking after a brand new baby?'

I remembered belatedly that over the last few years the annual Easter Egg Hunt had indeed been organised by Jodie who, after much trial and error, had now got it down to a fine art; maximising the fun, and minimising the opportunities for cheating.

'Um, I suppose that does leave you with a bit of a problem?'

'Yes,' she said. 'Yes it does indeed. And it's amazing how these problems always seem to come

168

back to rest upon *my* shoulders. Do you know, Jodie hadn't given the Egg Hunt the slightest thought when I pointed that out to her?'

This time I couldn't help but laugh. 'I think you'll have to forgive her that one,' I said. 'I don't imagine that she planned it deliberately. And even if she can't do the egg hunt herself, I'm sure she'll be more than willing to pass on her expertise to whoever you get to take her place.'

Aileen looked triumphant, and I realised what I had just let myself in for.

'No,' I protested. 'No – I'm happy to run the Easter Bonnet parade as usual, but I can't take on the egg hunt as well.'

'But you said yourself that Jodie would give tips on what needs doing.'

'But I don't have the time.'

'We'll all help you. That's the thing about being part of a committee. It means we all muck in and work together.'

I sighed. I knew that if push came to shove, Aileen could go on arguing for far longer than I could go on resisting. Nor did I have the time to.

'I'll think about it,' I said mutinously. 'But right now I have to get on.'

Before she could say any more, I hurried onwards down the lane and towards my target. Without giving myself any chance to waver, I walked up Hector's garden path, pressed hard on the doorbell, and waited for Fraser to open it.

Except it was not Fraser but Hector himself who opened the door.

'Tess! This is a nice surprise. Come on in.'

He led the way into his little sitting-room and ushered me towards an armchair. Ejecting Buster from the other one, he sat down opposite me.

'Has Pat sent you for something? Or is this just a social call? Would you like a cup of tea – or a drop of something more exciting?'

It was impossible not to smile back at him, but I did want to get the business over. 'I'm actually here,' I admitted, 'to see Fraser, if he's around.'

He looked disconcerted. ' Fraser? I'm sorry, my dear. I'm afraid he's gone.'

'Oh.' I looked down at Buster who, I noticed, was now seated comfortably upon my knee. 'Any idea when he'll be back?'

'No, Tess – he really has gone. Properly gone. Gone to Australia.'

'What?'

'I'm afraid so.'

'Oh.'

'Such a shame you missed him – he only left about half-an-hour ago.'

'Oh no.' I stroked Buster's warm fur mechanically. 'Oh. I didn't know. He didn't tell me he was going so soon.'

'Well, the trip was brought forward in the end,' explained Hector. 'I think there was a one-off chance to have a trip down a copper mine if he could get there in time. Something like that. But the whole thing was all very last minute. I'm sure he'd have mentioned it to you otherwise.'

'Did he say anything before he left?' I asked. 'I

170

mean – did he leave any message, or anything?'

'Hmm…' Hector stood up. 'Here - shall I take Buster? No? You're sure? I know not everyone likes cats climbing all over them, whatever this one chooses to think.'

'A message?' I repeated helplessly.

'Oh yes – sorry, Tess. I'm getting distracted, aren't I.'

'No, it's all right – it's just – I wondered - did he happen to say anything before he left?'

'Um… I don't remember any specific message, I'm afraid. Nothing other than passing on general goodbyes to anyone he might have missed. Was it important? To be honest, I was more bothered about him driving all that way back to Nick's place to pick up his stuff. It's quite a distance, after all. Didn't know if his ankle would hold out, but he seemed to think that it would be okay. Not that he had a lot of choice really,' he continued, 'not if he wanted to get himself and his car back to base. Are you sure you wouldn't like anything to drink? You do look disappointed. I'm sorry you missed him, and by such a narrow margin too. If you'd only come a little earlier, you'd have caught him on his way out.'

I thought back to how Aileen had delayed me, and cursed her heartily. If it hadn't been for her… But what was worse was the fact that Fraser hadn't even deemed me worthy of a proper farewell.

I said, fruitlessly, 'But he's definitely gone, and there was definitely no message?'

'No, I'm sorry, my dear. He was in such a rush, getting his stuff together, and phoning around to

171

revise all his arrangements. I suppose everything else just went straight out of his head. I hope it wasn't anything urgent you wanted? You might try him on his mobile, but I know he always keeps it turned off when he's driving. Doesn't always remember to turn it on again, either.'

'Oh. Oh well. Thanks, Hector. It wasn't anything really important, I suppose.' I stood up, Buster leaping from my lap as I did so.

Hector stood in the doorway watching me go. 'Give my love to Pat,' he called. 'Tell her I'll see her on Thursday.'

Despite the pleasantness of the evening air, there was no pleasure in the walk back home through the village. So Fraser had gone. I still felt completely thrown by the news. I would never have believed he would just up and leave without so much as a goodbye. For there was no getting round the fact that if Fraser couldn't even be bothered to scribble a farewell note, he was plainly not bothered about clearing the air between us. So much for what I had once thought of as a friendship.

Lost in my gloomy reverie, I was oblivious to my proximity to Oliver's shop until suddenly jolted to a halt by his voice hailing me.

'Tess! Hey, Tess!'

I stopped abruptly, peering around, unsure of where the voice was coming from. Then it came again and I looked up and saw Oliver at his upstairs window, leaning out and waving to me. 'Tess? I just noticed you walking past. What very good timing - I've got some excellent news for you. Hang on – I'm coming down.'

He disappeared, and within moments was opening the side door to let me in. 'Sorry, Tess. Goodness, isn't that weird, there I was just picking up the phone to give you a ring, and lo and behold, I glance out the window and there you are, walking by! Talk about a coincidence. But anyway, that's even better. Now I can tell you in person. Anita's just rung me. She was on the line for ages, but the most important part is that she's booked her ticket home. She'll be back just before we go off on holiday, which is perfect. It'll give me time to talk her through all the refurbishment plans.'

'Oh,' I said. 'Well – that's lovely.'

'Isn't it just,' he beamed.

'And Todd?'

His face clouded. 'Apparently nothing is settled. In fact, I suspect that's the reason she picked a date and booked her ticket. A sort of ultimatum, to show him she's serious. 'Either you come with me, or you stay behind and we're finished' - that sort of thing.'

I sighed. From my brief acquaintanceship with Todd, I'd rather liked him. And he had seemed to have a distinctly softening effect on Anita's abrasiveness.

'Anyway,' said Oliver. 'Whatever happens, this does mean that when we go to Scotland, we need have no worries about how the refurb is going. Anita will see that it's done properly.'

173

'Yes,' I said. 'With her on the case, there'll be no doubt about that, I'm sure.'

He looked at me more closely. 'Poor Tess, you're looking tired. Have you been home for your meal yet? If you've got the time, why don't you come in for a while? I could put the kettle on.'

For the second time in the last half hour, I refused the offer of a hot drink, plastered a smile on my lips and turned towards home. I just wished I could have shared Oliver's pleasure, but my spirits were too low for that. As if Fraser's unexpected desertion hadn't been bad enough, I now had the delightful prospect that after my two weeks' purgatory in Scotland, I'd have to return to the shop with Anita installed on the premises. *And* having carried out God-knows-what changes to its interior while we were away. That she would have it done to perfection, I hardly doubted. It was just a case of wondering to whose idea of perfection. Because to me, the shop was perfect as it was, and in my current state of self-pity I didn't know if I could stand any more major changes in my life.

'Ah, there you are,' called my mother from the kitchen, as she heard me come into the house. 'Your meal's ready whenever you want it. It's only salad, so nothing's got spoiled by waiting.' She put her head round the door and smiled at me. 'Just as well I did do salad in the end. You took even longer than I thought you might. Oliver certainly kept you late, didn't he?'

174

I remembered that I had not told her about my attempt to see Fraser, and hoped Hector wouldn't think to mention it to her. '*Oh what a tangled web we weave, when first we practise to deceive.*' Well that was true enough. However, I could mitigate my sins a little. 'Oliver wanted to tell me about Anita,' I said truthfully. 'It seems she's booked her flight home now. She'll be back in a fortnight. Though whether or not Todd will be with her has yet to be decided. Anyway, Oliver's pleased she's definitely coming, because it means she'll be back in time to take charge of the shop alterations when we go away next month.'

'Ah, no wonder he's happy,' she said. 'Lucky man – first he gets to go on holiday with you, and now he'll have someone capable on hand while he's gone. There'll be no mice playing if Anita's there to keep an eye on things. Anyway, are you ready to eat yet? There's some cheese flan to go with the salad – do you want me to warm it up for you or will you have it cold?'

She was setting out the plates when I came downstairs again, now more comfortably clad in old jeans and a tee shirt.

'I was going to eat earlier on,' she said, 'but I didn't in the end, so now we can eat together.'

'You didn't have to wait for me,' I protested. 'Any salad dressing?'

'Already on the table.' She pushed it towards me. 'No, I wasn't going to wait,' she said, 'but I had

175

a visitor.'

'Oh yes? Nice potatoes. Are they our own?'

'The very last of the new ones. They did well this year, didn't they.'

'So who was your visitor?' I asked. Now that the food was in front of me, I found I was hungry after all.

'Fraser,' she said. 'He called in on his way back to his friend Nick's house. It's a good job he's feeling up to driving again. Did you know that he's off to Australia? Hector had told me he was going, but I don't think even he had realised it would be quite so soon. But anyway, he called in just to say goodbye to both of us. Wasn't that nice of him? Very thoughtful.'

I had stopped in mid-mouthful. 'Fraser? He called here?'

'Yes, I just said. He seemed a bit disappointed that you weren't around.'

'He did?'

'Yes, but don't worry, I explained that you were with Oliver.' She took another mouthful. 'These radishes are ours too. It's been a good year. Yes, Fraser seemed quite put out when I said you were still at work. But then I told him that you'd decided to go on holiday with Oliver, so that the two of you would have a lot to talk about.'

'But - How long was he here for?'

'Long enough to have a nice chat. He did hang on for quite a while waiting for you, but of course you didn't appear.'

It was a bitter pill. 'If only I'd known,' I

lamented, 'I'd have certainly come straight home. Oh, I do wish I had known.'

'Oh well,' she smiled. 'I shouldn't worry about it. I'm sure that he didn't take it personally.'

'No, but I'd have still liked to see him before he went.'

'Don't worry, I did wish him a *bon voyage* on your behalf,' she reassured. 'I knew you'd want me to. Come on Tess, eat up. That flan will be going cold again if you leave it too long.'

I stared down at my plate, no longer hungry.

'Anyway,' she continued, 'it sounds as if he's going to have a wonderful time out there, seeing all sorts of interesting places. He's doing a book about Australia's industrial heritage, did you know? Well, I'm sure you did, but how nice to have a job that takes you all over the world like that. Must be absolutely fascinating.'

I nodded mutely.

'He told me he's going to Coober Pedy, among other places,' said mother. 'That's in the south of Australia, isn't it? It's where they find all those diamonds, so Fraser says. No, not diamonds. Opals. Am I right?'

I nodded.

'Well, whatever it is – let's hope he brings us back a big bag of them,' chuckled my mother. 'You never know.'

But the most important thing that I didn't know, I reflected, was exactly when Fraser would be coming back. Or even *if*.

The only ray of cheer during the following day was an invitation from Jodie to come and have dinner with her on Thursday evening.

'So, where's James gone this time?' I asked, after we'd finished the first course.

'Oh, the usual monthly meeting in Birmingham,' she said. 'Not that there will be many more of them to go to, not once he's started his new job. So he'll have no more long boring car journeys just in order to sit through long boring meetings. Meanwhile,' she grinned, 'I shall make the most of our girlie evenings, while I still can.'

'Yes, we should. And in any case,' I added unthinkingly, 'you'll have no time for anything once the baby's arrived.'

'Oh, Tess - ' She looked horrified. 'Oh, Tess, don't say that. I'll always have time for you, you know that.'

'Sorry.' I realised what I'd said, and felt remorseful. 'Yes, I know you will.'

'I *will*,' she insisted. 'I'll make sure I do.'

'Sorry,' I repeated. 'I've got the glooms today. No, it will be wonderful once the baby's here. Different, of course, but wonderful.'

'Good. And hopefully not *too* different.'

I sighed. 'But it will be different. In all sorts of ways. Just in case you hadn't already heard, my Mum's getting married.'

She goggled. 'Wow! No, I hadn't heard that. Wow. Married. So I'm guessing it's to Hector?'

'There, you see. Even you had an inkling. I

appear to be the only one who had no idea. I knew they were good friends of course, but I honestly thought it was just a flirtation. Hector's always seemed so popular with all the ladies, I never realised that with Mum it was more than just...' I shrugged. 'Well, that it was anything more.'

'Hmm,' said Jodie thoughtfully. 'Obviously I've never had the chance to observe them as closely as you but, when I think about it, there always does seem to have been a definite spark between them.'

'There you are then,' I said slightly bitterly. 'Proof. I was obviously the only person blithely unaware of it.'

'Oh poor Tess.' She touched my arm. 'So it must have come as quite a shock.'

'No, it's not 'poor Tess'. It's Tess the mean-spirited. Tess the selfish. Tess the nasty.'

Jodie started to laugh. 'Tess the Terrible,' she giggled. 'Or, as you might put it, Tess the normal human being. Come on, I know that you love your mum and want her to be happy, but it is going to mean some pretty big changes for you, isn't it.'

I nodded glumly.

'Where are they intending to live when they get hitched?'

'That,' I said, 'is the question. In fact, that is the question I haven't yet brought myself to ask her. You see why I call myself nasty? That's probably the last consideration that would be going through any nice person's mind.'

She shrugged. 'I think it would be the first consideration in most people's. For goodness sake, you're only human, Tess.'

I said, slightly comforted, 'To give them their due, I'm not sure they've actually decided themselves yet. I know Mum wouldn't keep me in the dark for no good reason.'

'That's true.'

'But the thing is,' I went on, 'Hector's cottage is smaller than ours. Yes, they're both attractive properties, and handy for the shops and bus stop and things. But at the end of the day, neither house is perfect. They've each only got two bedrooms, one sitting room, and one bathroom.'

'So if they should choose to live at your place, then you're going to feel a bit in the way?'

I nodded. 'Totally. Not fair on them. Not fair on me.'

'And if they move to Hector's, and leave you living in your mum's place?'

'But that's it,' I said. 'It *is* my mum's place. Yes, I pay my way, but it's still Mum's property. If she'd prefer to sell it, I don't want to be the obstacle stopping her. And a bit of spare cash would spark up her life a lot. She and Hector could go on some decent holidays – or whatever else they fancied doing. She might even need money for health care one day. You don't know what's round the corner. Anything could happen. I'm quite sure she'd never actually demand that I move out, but I certainly don't want to be the one preventing her enjoying the use of her own money.'

'She's looking pretty healthy at the moment,' comforted Jodie.

'I know. But one does need to think about worst case scenarios.'

She grinned. 'I rather thought you were doing that already.'

'Oh, not by a long way,' I said. 'I haven't yet got to the bit where I'm lying homeless in a gutter while the wind howls and the snow falls all around me.'

At that she laughed aloud. 'Well, don't worry, I promise that I won't step on you as I walk straight past.'

As I raised my glass in mock gratitude, Jodie stood up and went to extract a plum crumble from the oven.

'Jodie,' I said. 'You must be the best friend ever. You've no idea how nice it is just to be able to come here, sit down and unload all my grumbles on you. I know I'm being horrible, moaning on like this. And despite everything, I *am* happy for my mum, I really am.'

She put the warm dishes on the table and pushed a jug of cream towards me. 'Tess,' she said, 'When I first came to live here, your mother was still in pieces after the death of your dad. She's a much stronger person now, but I don't know how she'd have coped if you hadn't come home to look after her. You put your mother's interests first without even thinking about it. And she knows that as well as anyone. But she's been better for a long time now. It could be that this change of circumstance is exactly what you need to make you start considering your own interests for a change.'

181

This time it was she who solemnly raised her glass to me. 'Here's to a new future, Tess. Perhaps this is your chance to claim back your own life.'

Chapter 12

September and Scotland. How on earth had the time gone so quickly, I wondered. Now, as I sat in the passenger seat of Oliver's car, it seemed only a couple of weeks since I'd finally agreed to go. It was ironic that one of my fears had been that our destination might be too remote for easy escape. Now the remoteness felt quite attractive. Anita had arrived back in Little Bagford several days ago, and had already been making her presence felt as only she could. At least Scotland provided a legitimate excuse to get away from her. And if things *did* go pear-shaped on holiday, then I'd simply stay in my room. I'd feign illness if necessary. Something contagious, but which still allowed me to be fed regularly by meals left outside my door. Even for the sake of avoiding Daniel, I did not fancy going without food for a fortnight.

Oliver glanced across at me. 'That was a big sigh. You okay?' he asked. It's been a heck of a long journey, despite the early start. Want another break? I could stop at the next place we see.'

I glanced at my watch. 'No, I'm okay. But what about you? It's you who's probably most in need of a break. You've been the one doing the majority of the driving.'

'No problem as far as I'm concerned. I may not be keen on motorways, but they do make it easy.

However, I suppose we'd better not be too late in actually getting there.'

'Well there's one thing for sure, we shouldn't get lost,' I comforted. 'I've never seen such detailed instructions as the ones Erica gave us. Apparently she even phoned the holiday house key-holder to get a blow by blow description of the road, and what landmarks we need to look out for.'

Oliver grinned. 'It's nice to know she's so keen on us arriving there safely.'

'Yes, isn't it just.' But despite the tartness of my reply, I had to admit I was feeling a bit easier about the holiday now, and not just as an excuse to avoid Anita, or even to take my mind off the still unresolved question of where my mother and Hector would be living. No, my new found acceptance was thanks to a visit that Oliver and I had paid to Erica and Daniel only a few days earlier for a pre-departure planning meeting. I had gone expecting the worst but, in the end, Daniel had been a distant but perfectly polite host. Erica had been her usual ebullient self, but it had been Toby who made everything easy. It was impossible to stay reserved with a small child crawling around the floor, wobbling to his feet, handing us a succession of rather sticky toy animals and plainly expecting us to play with him.

'If only Toby's paraphernalia didn't take up so much room,' Erica had observed regretfully, 'we could have all travelled together in our car.'

But even with our new-found truce, I was glad practicalities would make it impossible. It was much more comfortable to be just me and Oliver.

184

I peered again at the road map in front of me. Even with a sat-nav in the car, I liked to follow the route, although by now it was almost too dark to see it properly. It had been raining on and off for most of the journey, and the sky seemed gloomier than ever.

'Anyway,' said Oliver, 'It shouldn't be much further now. By the way, don't let me forget to ring Anita when we do get there. I did tell her I would.'

'Has she had any more ideas about the refurb?' Even as I asked the question I regretted it, for I was trying to keep out of things as much as possible. Anita had already made it clear that my input was not required. Indeed, even my attendance had not been required for the last few days, for the shop had been closed while the stock was either removed to safety or comprehensively draped with dust sheets and polythene.

'She's already changed the workforce,' admitted Oliver. 'Apparently she spoke to the firm I'd been intending to use, and decided that she didn't think they were up to it. Not enough vision, she told me.'

'Oh dear.' Hearing the note of depression in his voice, I couldn't help but feel sorry for him. His initial elation at the thought of having Anita home again was fast fading now that he was faced with the actual reality.

'Oh well,' I said, feebly. 'I'm sure it will be all right in the end.'

'Anyway,' he continued, 'at least it's good news about Todd. Seems that when he saw she was serious about leaving Chicago, he finally grasped the fact he either had to follow her, or lose her.'

'When's he arriving?' I asked. 'Any idea?'

'It's all rather vague at the minute. Anita's left him to wind up all the various loose ends, and then he'll be flying over here to join her.'

'Well, whenever it is, I'm glad he's coming.' My words were genuine, for Todd's presence would hopefully deflect her attention from trying to run Oliver's life for him. With any luck, and with both of them needing to find some kind of paid employment, it would be most unlikely that they'd be able to stay too near to Little Bagford.

'Oh, look - That's the first time I've seen Aberfeldy on the signposts,' said Oliver with satisfaction, and we swept on towards our destination.

'Come in, come in – this place is lovely!' Erica had plainly been looking out for us, for she was already waiting at the open door as we pulled into the drive. 'How was your journey? Did you manage to leave as early as you planned – or is Oliver a secret boy racer?' She beamed at him and gave him a hug. 'How about you, Tessa?' she asked, giving me an equally enthusiastic embrace. 'You must be so glad to have got here at last. What a long way it is - but worth it! Come in and see what you think. I'm really pleased with this place. It's just as good as the photos showed it, thank goodness. I bet you'll like it too.'

I had to say that so far, she was right. We had driven right through the town of Aberfeldy wondering where on earth we were going to end up, but only a mile beyond its grey streets and houses we started to recognise the landmarks Erica had described. The sight of the actual house cheered us even further, for it was a handsome-looking building with plenty of parking space in front, and what appeared to be a generous sized garden wrapped around it.

'It does look nice,' I admitted. 'And bigger than I imagined it might be.'

'I think it must have been an old farmhouse,' Erica laughed. 'But it's been beautifully done up. Come in, come and see. And I'll make you a drink, I'm sure you must be desperate for one. We've bought some booze with us of course, but you might prefer a cup of tea first...?'

I was glad that Erica had arrived before us, for she had obviously already familiarised herself with the kitchen and the kettle. She, Daniel and Toby had left Little Bagford the day before, breaking the long journey north with an overnight stop. 'It's too far to travel in one day with a small child,' she had told us. 'In any case, it makes the holiday seem longer if we can add on an extra day at the beginning and end of it.'

Now Oliver and I followed her through a wide hall and into a family-sized kitchen.

'I'm glad we brought a few groceries with us,' she said. 'There's a starter pack here, but not enough for what we'll need, and the nearest shop is back in the town. It's not miles and miles away, but I was still glad that we could settle in without having to rush out again and look for supplies.'

'And we've got plenty more things in the car,' I confirmed. 'We'll fetch everything in, in a minute. And I can see we won't have to worry about where to store the stuff. So many cupboards – and look at the size of that fridge. It's twice the size of the one I've got at home.'

I was aware of a shadow in the doorway, and looked up to see Daniel standing there, holding Toby in his arms, and observing me with a rather cynical smile. 'So glad you approve of the place.'

'Yes, I do,' I said rather defiantly. 'It looks as if Erica did a very good job when she found it.'

'Didn't I just,' she grinned. 'Though I do think that luck comes into these things. I booked it online of course, so you never quite know if something's going to live up to its photographs. Not until you actually see it for yourself.'

'Well, it's a very good first impression,' said Oliver. 'And thank you for inviting us to share it, Erica. Now, let's have a cup of tea and then you can show us around.'

The first moment of awkwardness awaited upstairs.

'There are four bedrooms,' said Erica, as we reached the landing. 'Big ones too, they are – three double, and one single. We've put Toby's cot in the single, of course, and thought we'd better go in the room next to him, if it's okay with you. It's possible that, in a strange bedroom, Toby might wake up in the night. Even if he does sleep through, he always wakes up really early. So I thought you'd prefer to

188

be across the corridor. That way you should get an undisturbed rest.'

She flung open the doors of the two rooms facing the back of the house. 'So you two have got a choice of the other bedrooms. They both have great views.' She grinned at the pair of us. 'Which one would you like?'

I suddenly felt so embarrassed that I couldn't even look at Oliver. There was a horrible pause.

'I tend to sleep alone,' I said. 'I don't always sleep well, so I like to be able to put on the light and read a book. It helps me to drop off. So probably best if we have separate rooms.'

I still couldn't look at Oliver, but stepped quickly through the nearest door. 'This one will do perfectly.'

Actually, looking around, it would indeed do perfectly. The bed looked comfy, and the view over hills, as far as I could see in the dusk, was simply beautiful. And as if to make the most of the panorama, a little table and an armchair had been placed in front of the window. If I did end up spending most of the fortnight in here then I'd certainly be able to do it in style.

Oliver had already taken himself into the room next door. 'This is very nice,' I could hear him telling Erica. He called to me through the wall. 'What about yours, Tess? I'm happy with my room, if you are with yours?'

'I am.' I popped my head round his door and saw that the space was more or less identical to mine. Relieved to have the difficulty resolved, I came in and plonked myself down on the bed. 'Oh this is so comfy - you'll have some lovely nights on this, Oliver.' And I immediately felt awkward again.

Fortunately Erica seemed to be accepting things without question. 'That's sorted then. I'll leave you to get unpacked. I thought I'd do a chicken curry for our meal tonight – I brought all the ingredients with me, so it won't take long. I hope that's all right with you guys?' She flashed us a grin before disappearing back down the stairs. 'It'll be your turn to do the cooking tomorrow!'

Oliver and I looked at each other, our awkwardness still not entirely dispelled.

'Sorry about that,' he said.

'Don't worry,' I reassured. 'Not your fault. I guess Erica just assumes that…' I shrugged. 'Well, you know… Ridiculous, of course,' I added with more vehemence than I'd intended.

He stood with his back to me, looking out of the window.

Even down in my hole, I couldn't stop digging. 'No, I didn't mean ridiculous, I meant…'

Oliver spoke expressionlessly. 'Would you like me to explain to them that we don't have that sort of relationship?'

I bit my lip, unsure of how much my words had hurt him – or even *if* I had hurt him. I said, 'No. No, it's not a problem, Oliver. Our relationship is none of their business anyway.'

'No.' He spoke quietly, still without looking at me.

'Anyway,' I said, 'it might even be a good thing.

190

Don't you think? I mean, what with the me-and-Daniel situation – us having lived together – I don't want Erica to have any doubts that there might be anything to worry about. I'm sure she believes – because it's quite true of course - that I've moved on now, same as Daniel obviously has. Long since. So if we let her – them - continue to think that you and me – that we're some sort of item, perhaps…' At last, thank God, I ran out of words, grinding to a miserable halt.

Oliver turned round. 'It's okay,' he said. 'It's quite okay, Tess. Now, let's go down and see if there's anything we can do to help get that meal ready.'

Happily, if the first few moments of moving in had proved awkward, the morning found me in a far more upbeat frame of mind. Yesterday, once we had finally got our luggage into the house, the bustle of dealing with practicalities had forestalled any further opportunities for embarrassment. In the kitchen, Erica had been fully occupied with working out how to operate the oven and microwave, and by the time Toby had been fed his own chicken-and-vegetables dinner, our main meal was very nearly ready. After that, while Toby's parents settled him into his new room, Oliver and I had searched out the dishwasher tablets and stacked the machine. The evening had been just chilly enough to warrant lighting the wood-burner, but by the time it was fully going we were all half asleep. When I eventually got to my room, the

191

bed proved as comfortable as it had promised, and I slept well. On waking, my cheerfulness was further increased by the discovery that my little en-suite bathroom boasted a wonderfully efficient shower, and thick fluffy towels. Feeling much refreshed, I ambled over to the window to take stock of what was outside. Now that it was full daylight, I could see that it was beautiful. The garden, with its daisy-dappled lawn and flowering shrubs was pretty enough in itself, but it was the scenery beyond which commanded attention. A range of high hills, stippled in shades of green and gold, purple and amber, glowed in the tentative morning sunlight. I opened the window and leaned right out, breathing in deep lungfuls of cool fresh air, still soft with yesterday's rain, but now infused with hints of heather and honey.

Leaving the window open a little, I went to get dressed. I hadn't bothered unpacking my case properly last night, but now I thought with pleasure of the positive glut of new clothes inside. I had wrestled with myself about splashing out on these, for I was determined that I was absolutely *not* going to dress to impress Daniel. No way. But then I'd remembered my first encounter with him at the fete, when I'd been clad in my oldest things, hair untidy, and no make-up. Even later on, at Erica's dinner party, I'd worn that frilly blouse, which had been a definite mistake. And after all, if even the antiques shop was deemed worthy of a revamp, surely I was too? So I had taken myself off to Bristol for the day, credit card at the ready. I might not be able to compete with Erica, but I was not going to allow

Daniel the satisfaction of looking at me and congratulating himself on his lucky escape.

Now the results of my shopping spree gave me renewed pleasure. Three tee-shirts, which unlike my usual ones, were expensive and well fitting. Two pairs of jeans, again well-cut and not cheap. New shoes, smart but comfortable. A scarlet cashmere jumper, in case it was cold, and a floaty dress in case it was warm.

I couldn't remember ever spending quite so much money on clothes all in one go. But my decision not to stint myself had made it seductively easy, and started me wondering why I didn't do it more often. It wasn't as if I frittered much money on other things, so I could certainly afford it. Or at least I could for the moment.

But I swept aside any thoughts of my possible future homelessness. I was not, simply not, going to let myself dwell upon it. Even if I'd wanted to, I couldn't make plans until I knew what my mother had in mind. So I would take the sensible route and ignore the problem completely.

Oliver was already in the kitchen when I went downstairs. 'You look nice,' he said, handing me a mug of freshly-made tea. He frowned at me as if he couldn't work out why.

I was just explaining that I was wearing a new tee-shirt when we were joined by Daniel, who ambled downstairs clad in his bath-robe. It was annoying to see that even when rumpled and unshaven he still looked like an upmarket advertisement for aftershave.

193

I turned away. 'Toast, anyone?' I offered. 'Unless you'd prefer porridge, seeing as we're in Scotland?'

'Toast,' said Daniel. 'If you're making some. Toast will be fine.' He looked at me under his brows, and I remembered that it had always been his breakfast of choice. And I remembered too just how often we had shared that meal together.

'Toast it is, then,' I said brusquely, stabbing two slices of bread into the toaster. 'Shall I do some for Erica?'

'She won't be down yet,' said Daniel. 'Even Toby was still fast asleep when I looked in on him. He was awake a lot in the night. Teething.'

'Ah.' And no doubt it was Erica who had been the one getting up to see to him.

'Marmalade?' said Oliver hopefully.

'Have a look in that box of groceries we bought,' I instructed. 'And the butter should be in the fridge.'

We sat down to a rather silent meal. Daniel had never been a morning person, and I wasn't much better. It was left to Oliver to lead the conversation, which he did by opening one of the guidebooks that he'd brought with him.

'Where do you fancy going today, Tess?' he asked, adding with a glance at Daniel, 'I'm guessing you and Erica will have your own plans?'

'I'm sure they will,' I said.

'Yes,' said Daniel. 'Erica picked up a load of leaflets from the Tourist Information place, and there were even more in the house when we arrived. I'm sure she'll have no shortage of ideas.' He gave me

194

another oblique look. 'So it's possible we might end up visiting the same place, but equally possible that we might not. In any case,' he added rather gloomily, 'our time-table will be dictated by Toby, no doubt.'

'Yes,' said Oliver, 'having to cope with the needs of a small child can be rather limiting. I remember what it was like when Anita was little…' His voice tailed away rather vaguely, and I wondered if Anita as a small child could have possibly been more annoying than she was as a grown adult.

But that was another topic I didn't want to dwell upon, so I pulled myself up sharply, and smiled at Oliver. 'Anyway,' I said, 'as you and I can be as fancy free as we like, what about exploring the town itself? We've got the whole day at our disposal, so let's make the most of it.'

He smiled. 'Definitely,' he said, and started spreading butter thickly upon his toast.

With so many other concerns on my mind, it hadn't occurred to me until we'd actually arrived to wonder just how well Oliver and I would get on together. I knew I was happy working with him of course, but once we were away from our normal environment, and without the common ground of antiques and irritating customers, would we find enough to talk about? Without transport of my own we would be thrown together a lot. Would we soon be bored rigid with each other?

My concerns were needless. Oliver was undemanding and enjoyable company, and together we chatted happily through most of the day. And there were plenty of things to provide interest. A morning spent wandering round a distillery was followed by a light lunch at a café where we sat in the sunshine, eating food that could have rivalled the Patchwork Pumpkin's for excellence. Then a visit to a restored water mill, before belatedly realising that we were supposed to be in charge of providing the evening meal.

'I suppose we should have asked if there was anything special that Daniel and Erica would like to eat,' said Oliver worriedly, as we headed quickly back to the shops in the town centre. 'What do you think we should give them? Cooking isn't really my thing, you know.'

'Well, you do a perfectly respectable sausage and mash,' I laughed. 'In any case, whatever we choose to do, we'll be cooking it together. Hang on, I can see a butcher's just over the road. Let's see if we can get some inspiration from there.'

So it was a locally-made pie and mash on the menu that evening which, despite Oliver's fears, went down very well with everyone. Like us, Daniel and Erica had spent a busy day exploring the nearby area, and were glad to get back to the house and relax. Toby, well-fed on a mashed-up version of our own food, went to bed without complaint, leaving us to sit cosily beside the log-burner. A large television stood in the corner but, with nothing that we wanted to watch, we amused ourselves with books and crosswords, while Oliver went into the kitchen to phone Anita for the latest progress report.

Erica yawned copiously. 'Too much fresh air,' she smiled apologetically. 'It's been making me feel tired all day long. I know it's early, but I think I'll turn in now.'

Daniel glanced at his watch.

'Yes, I know,' she said. 'I do know it's awfully early, but I *am* on my holidays, Danny. That means I can do what I like.'

He too stood up. 'Well, if you're going up, then I suppose I better had too.' He gave me an abrupt nod and followed her from the room. Whether his departure was due to an eagerness to be in bed with his wife, or an unwillingness to find himself alone with me, I simply couldn't guess.

Next morning our leisurely breakfast was interrupted by an unexpected knock at the door. We looked at each other in bemusement, until Daniel had the wit to get up and open it.

A plump cheerful-looking woman stood there. 'I'm the housekeeper,' she announced. 'Key-holder and housekeeper. I've just come to check that everything is all okay for you. Should have come yesterday I know, but my youngest came down with a tummy bug, so I couldn't get over here. Sorry about that – but I hope you found everything you needed?'

Even if we'd had any complaints, it would have been difficult to air them in the face of such sunny confidence.

'Yes, everything's fine,' said Daniel.

'And I'm guessing that you must be Mr

Dunstan?'

'Yes,' said Daniel. 'I know it was my wife who you dealt with over the phone. I'm afraid she's not down yet.'

'No problem. It's just that I was rather expecting you to be Australians, judging by her accent.'

'Sorry to let you down,' smiled Daniel. 'It's just my wife who's Australian. Not me. I'm just boring old English.'

'Like me.' The woman dimpled. 'I don't mean boring, of course. I mean English. It's my husband who's the Scot. I'm a Londoner, but when I got married I had to follow him up north. Now I'm the only one in my family who doesn't have a Scottish accent.' She suddenly seemed to become aware of that fact that there were two more people in the room, and broke her gaze from Daniel's face to encompass Oliver and me. 'Anyway, that's enough of me rambling on. So you're sure you found everything, and discovered how everything works....? Did you find all the guide-books in the cupboard?'

'We did,' confirmed Daniel. 'A very good selection, thank you.'

'Good.' She hesitated a moment. 'Well, you make sure you call me if you need anything. My name's Rosie, by the way.'

'And I'm Danny.'

She retreated, still smiling at him as she backed away down the path. Daniel shut the door, and returned to his seat at the breakfast table looking slightly amused. I buttered my toast fiercely. Oliver sipped his tea.

'Don't you think,' I asked Daniel at last, 'that you should take a hot drink up to Erica? I imagine she'd appreciate it.'

'No,' he said, a half-smile still playing around his mouth. 'No, she'll be all right. I'm quite sure that if she wants a hot drink then she'll come down and get it for herself.'

'What about Pitlochry?' asked Oliver suddenly, who had been looking at the map again.

'Pitlochry?'

'Yes, it's not that far away from here. It looks as if there's quite a lot to see there. Fancy it, Tess?'

I slid a glance towards Daniel. 'Yes,' I said. 'Yes, that sounds lovely.'

Chapter 13

Slowly, hour by hour, day by day, the fortnight that I had so dreaded started to slip by pleasantly. Even before the end of the first week a comfortable routine had been established in which Oliver and I would depart soon after breakfast, leaving Erica and Daniel to do their own thing for the rest of the day. With Toby's needs to be considered, their expeditions were seldom as wide ranging as ours, but certainly enough to tire out both Toby and Erica. And if Daniel felt frustrated about not being able to explore further afield, then he certainly didn't grumble about it in my hearing.

In fact, now that we were becoming more accustomed to our enforced proximity, I found we were both more at ease with it. I had forgotten he was a competent cook when he chose to be, which meant that on my own cooking-duty days, if Oliver got side-tracked chatting to Erica, then Daniel would silently take his place beside me. I didn't begrudge Oliver his chats with Erica, for she was a far more patient listener than I was when it came to sitting through a blow-by-blow account of the shop's refurbishment. Oliver was still phoning Anita each evening, despite my suggestion that he might have more peace of mind if he left it all as a surprise to return home to.

'But I do feel I need to know,' he told me. 'I need to keep my eye on the budget, if nothing else.'

200

'So does she talk about the budget?'

'Not in detail,' he admitted. 'In fact no, not really at all. She just keeps telling me that it will be worth every penny spent upon it.'

'Does she actually tell you *anything*?'

'Oh yes. She tells me where the various shelves will be going. And where the new counter will be, except that it won't be a proper counter, she wants it to be a nice old fashioned desk and a wing-backed chair. And she always tells me the various colours of paint we can choose from, and then she lets me know which ones she's decided upon.'

He gave a wryly amused smile, but I found it harder to share the joke. What on earth would be awaiting us when we did finally get back to the shop?

Now Daniel glanced at me. 'Had enough of chopping all those onions? You can swap with me if you like. Courgettes aren't so eye-watering. Or you could do the peppers?'

'No, I'm fine.' I nodded towards Oliver and Erica, who were currently perched on the sofa, peering at Erica's phone and looking at the photos of where they had been that day. 'I just hope those two appreciate all the work that's going into this ratatouille.'

'They won't, of course,' he said. 'Still, we can certainly make them do all the clearing up afterwards.'

We suddenly found ourselves smiling at each other, and I looked down hurriedly. Busily chopping again, I said, 'As you and I seem to have become chief caterers, I think we should demand to dine out one evening. What do you think? Sounds reasonable? Or would it interfere with Toby's time-table?'

'No,' he said decisively. 'It's a great idea. We can't allow all our time to be dictated by Toby's schedule. A meal out would give you and me a well-deserved break, so I think we should do it.'

'Day after tomorrow? I know you've already got the ingredients for tomorrow's dinner, so if we go out the following evening, then that would be good. And it would give us time to find out the best place to eat. Rosie might know. She's local. She should be able to recommend somewhere that's child-friendly, but still does good food.'

From across the room, Erica looked up at us and grinned. 'Now what are you two plotting? I couldn't hear everything, but it sounds as if you've definitely got something up your sleeves.'

'A meal out,' said Daniel. 'Tess and I have decided.'

'Oh,' said Erica. She glanced towards Toby who, around his face, was still bearing traces of his tomato-and-pasta tea.

'He'll be fine,' said Daniel.

'It does sound tempting,' smiled Oliver. 'I think we all deserve a treat, whether we be the head cooks or merely the chief bottle-washers.'

'Just as long as we're not too late back,' said Erica.

'Good,' pronounced Daniel. 'That's settled then.'

At breakfast on the day of our proposed treat, Oliver, unusually for him, was plainly abstracted.

I put some more bread in the toaster. 'Have you had second thoughts about doing the walk?' I asked, as I opened a jar of thick white local honey. We had made plans to explore the Birks of Aberfeldy which, the guide book said, was a well-known trail renowned for its picturesque setting. 'I've heard it's pretty steep in parts, so we could always do something less strenuous.'

'No,' he said, 'I'd definitely like to do it, if you do. I don't think it's too long and if it's as beautiful as they say, then it would be a shame not to see it before we go home. After all, the guide book does describe it as 'unmissable'. Apart from anything else, the weather forecast says that today is likely to be the last of the nice weather. It's going to rain tomorrow.'

I was glad he hadn't changed his mind, for I did think that the expedition might help to take his mind off whatever was preoccupying him. I had selfishly made a point of *not* asking about the latest bulletin from Anita, but had little doubt it was that which was making him seem so distracted.

'Bring your boots then,' I said cheerfully. 'And the last one to reach the top has to pay for coffee and cake when we get back down again.'

It was good that we did have our walking boots, for although the start point was easy to find, the path certainly had its challenging moments. Yet despite the uneven terrain and loose stones, it was unquestionably worth the effort. Meandering its way ever upwards and crossing a boisterously foaming burn, the route led us on past trees and rocks. Occasionally a small waterfall danced down the rock face, sending fine droplets to glisten against the moss-covered stones.

'This is so lovely,' I exclaimed. 'And so quiet. It's just you and me and the scenery. I only wish I could spend more time looking at it, and less time looking down to see where I put my feet.'

'There's a handrail on this bit,' reassured Oliver. 'Keep tight hold and it won't matter if you do stumble. If it runs all the way to the top, we should be fine.'

The trail was getting steeper by the minute, and I was glad to find a natural rock shelf on which to perch and catch my breath.

'This is Burns' Seat,' said Oliver, reading aloud from an adjacent notice. 'This rock is where Robert Burns is said to have once sat and admired the view. It also says that he liked it so much that he wrote a poem called 'The Birks of Aberfeldy'.'

'Well, I can share his admiration,' I said, 'even if I don't end up writing a poem about it. I just hope he was fitter than I am. If the gradient gets any worse, I shall be asking for a rope and crampons.'

Oliver looked at me worriedly. 'Are you all right? Have you had enough? We could always turn round and go down again.'

'No, of course not,' I said, surprised that he had taken me so seriously. 'Now we've come this far, I certainly want to get to the top.'

I got up quickly, and started to lead the way up the increasingly zig-zagging trail, made green and slippery by the windblown spray of several more waterfalls. Ferns peeked out from every stony crevice and, with still no other walkers in sight, I had a feeling of being alone in a primeval world. 'Romantic,' I murmured aloud.

Behind me, Oliver's footsteps paused abruptly. 'What?'

'Romantic, I said. I turned to grin at him. 'Like those pictures by what's-his-name – that German artist,' I elaborated. 'The one who painted those spectacular landscapes. All craggy mountains and far vistas.'

'Caspar David Friedrich?' said Oliver. 'Yes, I suppose so.'

'That's the one. He'd have made a great job of painting this place.'

'Mm.'

I paused to drink it all in and he moved on ahead of me. I was glad to see, not too far away now, a wooden footbridge spanning what appeared to be the top of the falls. 'Is that the highest point?' I called. 'I think it must be. But if you've overtaken me just to avoid buying the coffee and cakes, there's still no way I'm racing you to the summit.'

Oliver paused and looked at me over his shoulder. 'Take my hand,' he said. 'That way we'll reach it together.'

At last we stood on the little bridge, leaning on the rail and getting our breath back. It had been a hard climb, but worth every puff. Although, glancing at Oliver, I did wonder if he had felt the effort more than I'd realised, for he stared out into the gorge as if he hardly saw it.

I gazed into the water beneath me, losing my own thoughts in its ever-changing form and colours as it tumbled and bounced its way over the black rocks, a foaming flood which streamed endlessly down and down, until the last diamond drops disappeared from sight. I was so glad that I hadn't missed this. So glad that I had finally been persuaded to come on the holiday. It hadn't been anything like the ordeal I'd feared. If the inevitable ghost of my long-ago relationship with Daniel had hovered, then it had now been exorcised for good. Or almost. For I knew I would always find Daniel physically attractive. He *was* attractive, and one had to accept it. I smiled wryly, remembering the housekeeper's reaction to meeting him. She hadn't quite blushed, but she had plainly been smitten. And there was no doubt he could be charming when he wanted to. With the gradual thaw between us, it was all too easy to remember just why I had once fallen for him. And to remember the many good times that we'd shared. And why it had taken me such a very long time to get over him.

Beneath me the water whirled and glittered on its never-ending journey.

I felt a touch on my hand and looked up to see Oliver gazing at me. 'Tess?'

'I was just thinking,' I said. 'I was watching the water and thinking that I owe you an apology. All that fuss I made about coming to on holiday. It's worked out well. I'm really glad that you didn't give up trying to persuade me.'

He gave a half smile.

'Yes,' I said. 'The scenery is just glorious. Even better than I thought it would be. And I've enjoyed all the places we've been to, and exploring all those little towns and villages. I've even enjoyed the craft centres,' I laughed, for it had become a running joke just how many of our destinations had boasted that particular amenity.

'Good.'

'After all,' I rattled on, rather unnerved by his continuing abstraction, 'where else would I have bought my souvenirs from if it wasn't for the craft centres? And they do have some lovely things, you must admit. Did you see what I got from the last place? I bought a Harris tweed purse for my mother, a lovely soft plaid scarf for Jodie – not to mention those sweet little tartan bootees I got for the Bump. Jodie will love them. She's getting really excited now that her pregnancy is beginning to show.'

'Yes,' he said. 'Yes.'

In the ongoing silence I decided I would have to bite the bullet. 'Oliver,' I said. 'I can see there's something bothering you. Would you like to talk about it?'

He took a deep breath. 'You're right. Yes, there is something I need to say.'

I looked at him, slightly alarmed.

'You see, I've been wondering….'

'Yes?'

'In fact I'd been a bit afraid…' He paused, and

again I waited.

'I did wonder if you might find – if you *have* found – that spending so much time with me has been a bit of a bore?'

I turned towards him, horrified. 'Oh, Oliver! No, of course not. It was only Daniel I was worried about spending time with. Not you. You've been great company. In fact,' I laughed, 'you were probably far more at risk of *me* boring *you*.'

Instead of smiling as I had expected, he stared back out over the gorge. He said, addressing the air, 'You're very special to me, you know, Tessa. Very special.'

'Thank you,' I said uncertainly.

'I mean – *very* special.'

I caught my breath.

'I was wondering – I mean – this holiday has been a success, hasn't it? You've just said that you'd enjoyed it.'

'Yes.'

'Then - I wonder if you'd consider - perhaps - putting things on a more permanent basis?'

'How do you mean?' I croaked. This was *not,* I assumed, going to be a request for me to work extra hours at the shop, but all the same it wasn't the moment for misunderstandings.

For the first time he turned and looked directly at me. 'How would you feel about hooking up with me? Sorry, that's not the right way to put it, is it? Not at all romantic. It's just that I don't know how things are arranged these days. All those years ago when Margaret and I got together, it was marriage that was

208

the order of the day. I'd still prefer marriage really, but nowadays it seems more usual to just live together. But whatever way you chose, I'd be happy to go along with it. If you understand what I'm trying to say, Tess?'

'Yes,' I said faintly. 'I mean, yes, I understand you. But…' I bit my lip. 'I don't quite know what to say, Oliver. I had no idea…'

'I'm sorry,' he said. 'I should have led up to it with more warning.'

'No, no. It's not you. Anyway,' I added with an edge of hysteria, 'I'm not quite sure how you *could* lead up to it with more warning - not without actually telling me.'

'No,' he agreed. But his eyes remained on mine.

'Oliver,' I said. 'I'm honoured.'

'But ?'

'There is no 'but'. Well, I suppose there is. The 'but' is that you really have taken me by surprise. Even now…' My voice tailed away, for I was still too shell-shocked to think or speak properly. 'I *am* honoured,' I repeated at last. 'Truly. But I don't know what to say. I just hadn't…' I shrugged unhappily.

'If you need time to think,' said Oliver. 'There's no expiry date on the question. Take as long as you like.'

I swallowed. How could anyone *not* love Oliver. If only I could be sure that I loved him in the right way. 'Thank you,' I said. 'I do need time. It's not a yes, and it's not a no. But I promise I'll give you an answer as soon as I can. But when I say that I'm honoured, I do mean it.'

He gave a faint smile and then, in a formal gesture, took my hand and kissed it. It should have felt ridiculous, yet it brought a lump to my throat in a way which nothing else could have done.

To my relief, our walk back to the carpark was almost relaxed. Now that Oliver had said what he needed to, it was as if a weight had lifted, and he chatted far more easily than he had done on the way up. In a plain attempt to dispel any awkwardness, he read bits from the guide book, and paused to point out various flora and fauna on the way. Not that I took in any of it. I answered Oliver as normally as I could, but my attention was far away.

I should have known. I should have been more prepared. Why on earth hadn't I? If only I'd taken notice of my mother's and Jodie's suspicions, at least it would have forewarned me. But now that I did know... My brain hit a brick wall. Now that I did know - what?

'Coffee and cake?' said Oliver. 'What about that little café we passed on the way here? Unless,' he added, consulting his watch, 'you'd rather make it lunch? Technically it's already afternoon.'

'Oh. Is it?'

'Lunch then,' he said. 'Though I suppose we'd better make it a light one. What with going out tonight.'

'Oh yes, of course,' I said, remembering. 'Yes,

210

we're going out, aren't we?'

'Always assuming,' he smiled, 'that Daniel and Erica were able to make a booking.'

They had indeed made a booking. On Rosie's recommendation, we had chosen a restaurant which, she assured us, served the best food for miles. Moreover, it had terrific views over the river. We just had to make sure that we asked for a table by the window.

So it was that at just before eight o-clock that evening we climbed into Daniel's large four-wheel-drive, and set off to find Skerrymore Lodge. Although it was later than we might have chosen to eat, Rosie had made the offer that if Toby was safely in bed, she would be happy to babysit. For Daniel it was too good a suggestion to turn down, so with Erica's strict proviso that Rosie ring them if there was any kind of problem, it was agreed.

'I like this place already,' said Daniel, as we sat down to eat. 'It's a shame it's nearly too dark to enjoy the view, but the menu looks terrific, and the wine list looks even better. You won't mind being the designated driver, will you, Erica?'

'Oh,' said Oliver contritely. 'I hadn't thought of that. I suppose we could easily have come in my car. It wouldn't have bothered me to do without alcohol.'

'And it won't bother Erica, either,' said Daniel smoothly. 'Will it, my darling?'

Was there an edge of malice in his voice? If there had been, she chose to ignore it, which meant

211

that I had probably imagined it. 'It won't bother me at all,' she said. 'I shall have some good Scottish mineral water. And some good Scottish food to go with it.'

She examined the menu, as did the rest of us. Daniel had been right that it offered some excellent choices.

'Grouse,' decided Oliver. 'That's a good traditional dish of the country. I don't know about everyone else, but I'm definitely ready to eat.'

It didn't take long to order our various choices; a mixed grill for Daniel, and steak pie for both Erica and me – the chef's speciality, so the brisk waitress assured us.

It arrived promptly and looked delicious, and I only wished that I could do it justice. But I still felt only half connected with anything around me. The rest of my thoughts were still on the bridge over the waterfall. From time to time I caught Oliver's steady gaze resting upon me, and was occasionally aware of Erica's quizzical glance.

'Tess, what's up with you tonight?' demanded Daniel at last, putting down his glass. 'You've not been right since you got back from your walk this morning.' He looked at Oliver, frowning.

'She's a million miles away,' smiled Erica. 'But I suppose we all will be, the day after tomorrow. Well, not quite a million miles, but far enough. It'll be nice to get back home again, but it's been such a lovely holiday I'm sad it's nearly over.' She took a sip from her glass. 'Anyway, I've just had a great idea,' she continued. 'Danny and I have really enjoyed you guys' company, but do you realise we've never yet gone out for the day all together? Tomorrow let's have a proper day out. Let's do something, all of us together. It would be such a nice way to finish off our time here.'

'There's always the castle,' suggested Oliver. 'I keep seeing leaflets advertising it, and it looks interesting. What do you think?'

'If you like,' said Daniel. 'Tess?'

'Yes, if you like,' I agreed.

Erica sat back with satisfaction. 'That's all sorted then.'

But, as it turned out, all was *not* sorted. I was late going down for breakfast next morning, but even so I was plainly the first one to rise. I wasn't too bothered about Daniel's non-appearance, nor yet Erica's who, I had come to realise, was most definitely not an early riser. But Oliver had been the first one up each morning for the past fortnight.

I went back upstairs and tapped on his door. 'Oliver? You okay?'

For a moment there was silence, then came the slow sounds of movement. Oliver, still pyjama-clad, appeared in the doorway.

'Oh – oh wow – whatever's wrong?'

Oliver was not looking good. His face was pale, his eyes deeply shadowed. 'Migraine,' he said hollowly. 'Soon as I woke up, I knew. Could have been something in the food triggered it. Don't know.'

'Oh poor you! Can I do anything?'

'No. Just happens sometimes. Not often. Best thing to do, sleep it off. Sorry, Tess. Really sorry.'

'Right then,' I said rather helplessly. 'Back to bed with you. Are you sure I can't get you anything?'

He gave a weak smile. 'No. Bed's the best cure. Be better soon. Sorry.'

I watched him get back under the duvet, made sure the room was as dark as it could be, and tiptoed out. I had occasionally heard him mention migraines before, but so infrequently that I'd almost forgotten he ever suffered from them. It was certainly bad timing for him, and yet - I bit my lip guiltily. At least it would buy me a little more thinking time.

As I slipped quietly from Oliver's bedroom, the sight of Daniel emerging from his own room made me jump.

'Tess?' He eyed me unsmilingly. 'I'm going down to get a hot drink for Erica. Do you want anything? Or have you and Oliver already indulged?' he added, with a curt nod towards the door I'd just quietly pulled shut.

'Er, okay. Don't worry, I'll come with you.' I followed him back down to the kitchen. 'Coffee for me, but not for Oliver. He's in bed and he doesn't want anything.'

'Really.'

'He's not feeling good,' I explained.

'Oh.' Daniel's mood seemed to lighten. 'I suppose he can't take his wine, by the sound of it.'

'No,' I said indignantly. 'Poor thing has a migraine. That's much worse. I'm lucky, I've never suffered from them myself, but I do know people say that they're awful.'

'Mm.' Daniel concentrated on filling the kettle. 'Okay. Sounds like he won't be going on any outings this morning then. Nor will Erica either, by the way. She's under the weather too.'

'Well, I know that's not a question of *her* not being able to take her wine,' I said. 'She didn't have any.'

He shrugged. 'Pass the mugs, they're just over there. You can have one of Erica's foul herb teas, if you prefer. She's got plenty.'

'Lemon and ginger,' I observed, reading from the packet. 'Probably a lot better for you than coffee. Still, I think I shall stick to my usual.'

He filled the other two mugs with coffee, and pushed one across to me. To my surprise he raised his own mug in a toast, to chink against mine. 'Anyway, now that it's just you and me, I think we deserve to congratulate each other, don't you?'

'Do we?'

'We do. Over this past fortnight we've been models of good behaviour. Despite everything, we've made this holiday work. We've played nicely together, and we've been good.'

'Oh.'

'Well don't you think so?' He was looking at me intently. That old, familiar smile. The hint of wickedness. That unspoken invitation to side with him against the outside world.

I looked down into the dark depths of my coffee. I had almost forgotten that look. Forgotten the effect it had on me. But I was thirteen years older now. *And*

215

thirteen years wiser. Determined not to be drawn in, I stared fixedly at my mug.

At last my silence seemed to penetrate, and he turned away. 'Oh well, I suppose I'd better take this drink up to her before it gets cold.'

'Yes, perhaps you had,' I said. 'And tell Erica I hope she'll be feeling better very soon.'

But with both Oliver and Erica out of action, it did leave me with the question of just how I'd fill the day. If I was to avoid spending any length of time alone with Daniel, the question had some urgency. Even if he was supposed to be looking after Toby, there was only so much diversion that a small child could be relied upon to provide. No, I certainly didn't want an intimate morning with Daniel, heavy with sideways glances and loaded silences.

With sudden inspiration I remembered my sketch pad. The sketch pad that Jodie had so helpfully recommended as an excuse for solitude. I had unpacked it on the first day, and never looked at it since. But now I blessed the brainwave that had made her suggest it. Within minutes I had retrieved my drawing materials and, by the time Daniel came back downstairs carrying Toby, I had my rucksack packed and was almost ready to depart.

He looked at me in surprise.

'I'm off to draw some of the scenery,' I said. 'I've made myself a sandwich and filled a flask. So, if Oliver should recover from his migraine and come downstairs - '

216

'Then I shall tell him where you've gone,' he said. 'By the way, where *are* you going? Just in case we need to call out Mountain Rescue or anything.'

'I'm going to explore that little path that runs up behind the house. It looks a bit of a climb, but I'm sure I shall find some good views along the way. If you've looked at the cottage Visitor's Book, you'll see there are several comments saying that it's well worth the effort.'

'Oh.' Daniel sounded distinctly put out.

'It's a shame,' I said blandly, as I headed for the door, 'that you can't come with me, but I'm afraid it would be much too steep for a pushchair.'

Chapter 14

My sudden urge to go sketching might have been an excuse but, as it turned out, it was an excellent one. The path that led beyond the back garden soon took me into dark and scrubby woodland, but after a steady plod upwards, I eventually found myself in open countryside, rewarded with views that would have inspired even the most reluctant artist. And, as I quickly realised, I wasn't actually reluctant at all. In younger days I'd always loved drawing and painting and now, having found a comfortable rock overlooking a perfect panorama, was soon absorbed in my work. The dramatic cloud formations made a perfect backdrop to the hills, but were frustratingly quick to change and mutate, affecting light and shadows. As my pencil skimmed over the paper in an effort to keep up, I became so engrossed that it wasn't until I'd finished that I remembered this was not the only reason I was here. I was not just trying to avoid Daniel, I was also supposed to be coming to a decision about Oliver's proposal.

Feeling suddenly depressed again, I put away my things and continued up the path. So what was my response to be? I still didn't know. I kicked at a stray pebble, its sudden clatter disturbing a distant rabbit which immediately scampered out of sight. I wondered if it would be worth trying to put a rabbit in the foreground of my next sketch. It might be useful in giving an idea of scale that I didn't feel I'd captured earlier. But would a rabbit sit still enough for me to draw it accurately? Not a hope, of course, but perhaps if I managed to sneak up on a rabbit, get a few lines on paper before it even noticed my presence…?

I realised I was giving in to distractions, but by now I was higher still, a turn in the path giving me yet another tempting view. There was even a few shafts of sunlight on the far slopes, making a pleasing contrast with the darkness of the valleys and black ribbon of pine trees. A glance at the sky behind me showed that although the sunlight might not last much longer I ought still have enough time to make a good stab at it. Soon I was lost in my work again, dashing lines down on the paper, making shapes, shading and blending, and generally doing my best to capture the vista in front of me. I might not be creating a masterpiece, but the satisfaction of rediscovering old skills was far exceeding my expectations. I vowed that once back to normality, I would definitely make time to keep up with my old hobby.

But there it was again. *Once back to normality.* So what was going to be my future normality? I couldn't keep going on avoiding the issue. Oliver's question needed and deserved my full attention. Reluctantly I returned my pad and pencils to my rucksack. If only I'd been more prepared for his question. But every time I tried to work out what I really wanted, my mind went blank. I might just as well have stared at the ground to try to see how many blades of grass I could count. My brain just refused to co-operate.

I took out my sandwich and flask. It was no good, I would have to resort to the classic advice so often given to the terminally indecisive. Make a list of pros and cons. Not an exactly romantic approach, admittedly, but…

I took a sheet from my sketchbook, and wrote at the top:

Pro:

1)   Oliver is good company.

2)   Oliver is kind.

3)   Oliver is generous.

4)   We have a lot in common.

I pondered a little over number four. *Did* we have a lot in common? Apart from the welfare of the shop, that is? But the fact we'd got on so amicably during the holiday must mean something.

5)   It would solve the problem of my future homelessness.

It was a shameful reason, but it had to be included as a <u>Pro</u>. If my mother could be reassured that my future was with Oliver, then it would leave her a free hand to do whatever she wanted with the house. But did I want to live in Oliver's flat? As flats went, it was a nice one, and certainly conveniently situated. It even had a garden behind Oliver's workroom. But in my mind it was still Anita's home, still the place in which she and her mother Margaret had ruled the roost. I couldn't imagine ever thinking of it as *my* home. But neither could I ask Oliver to find a new place where we could start our new life together. It wouldn't be

220

fair, and it probably wasn't even practical.

And yet - Was I putting the cart before the horse? Surely in this sort of case the practicalities ought to take second place to emotions. The question was, *did I actually want to marry Oliver?*

A cold breeze whispered across the hillside, rippling the grass into a sea of silver. I returned my unfinished sandwich to the rucksack. The clouds were definitely greyer now, but I knew that if I stood up and walked away I'd only be postponing the dilemma. Instead I stared at the view below me and tried to imagine what it would be like to live with Oliver.

What would it be like to go to bed with him? How would we get on? How would he feel about babies? How did *I* feel about babies? I'd enjoyed having Toby around, but I wasn't going to kid myself that enjoying someone else's child was anything like having a child of my own. Although, with Jodie expecting her own new arrival in the spring, at least I'd have her to show me the ropes of new motherhood. That would be fun. Not to mention, I thought rather hysterically, that it would provide me too with an excuse to get out of organising the Easter Egg Hunt.

But even as I bit back a giggle, reality kicked in again. Even if I did decide I wanted a family, I doubted if Oliver would feel the same. After all, he already had Anita.

I sobered immediately. Perhaps it was time to concentrate on filling in my list of *Cons*.

1) Is Oliver too old for me?

Oliver had turned fifty last year. It was a bit of an

age-gap certainly, but not unworkable. I knew several other couples with similar or even bigger discrepancies, and it didn't seem a problem to them. I decided I'd better remove that one from the Cons list, for it wasn't even as if he'd been a bachelor all his life, and unused to considering anyone but himself. I smiled again at that thought. No. No-one who had been married to Margaret could have possibly remained unschooled in the art of considering his wife's needs.

Staring at the paper in front of me, I suddenly realised that it was getting wet. Moreover, so was I. The first fine mist of rain had been so gentle that I had hardly registered it. Now I discovered that I was feeling cold as well as damp. The hills I had so recently drawn had become obscured by cloud, and it was getting greyer by the moment.

I opened my rucksack to retrieve my raincoat, rummaging fruitlessly past the sketching materials, the bag with the remains of the sandwich, the flask, the banana, the half-eaten tube of peppermints... Hell! I clearly remembered placing my jacket over the back of a kitchen chair, ready to gather up as I left the house. Which was presumably where it still was. And with the rain becoming heavier by the minute, I was now shivering in earnest.

I shoved everything back again and got to my feet. It would take me at least an hour to get back to the house, and I was already wet and chilled. The sooner I started, the better.

It was impossible to move at speed on a rough path of loose stone. Slithering and sliding, hopping and balancing, I picked my way downwards as quickly as I could, rain plastering my hair to my face and dripping down my neck. Half-numbed with cold and absorbed in effort, I'd been going a while before suddenly becoming aware that I was no longer alone on the hillside. Below me I could see a figure making its way up the path towards me. With his head down, and clad in sturdy rainwear, it took me a moment to realise who it was.

'Daniel?' I called in bewilderment.

He looked up, saw me, and raised a hand in response. 'At last! For God's sake, I thought I'd find you long before this. I hadn't expected to walk halfway to John O' Groats. It's sodding steep too.'

I skidded down to meet him. 'You were looking for me? Is there something wrong?' My stomach clenched as I wondered if there had been some kind of accident, or if Oliver had perhaps got worse and been rushed to hospital.

'Not what *I'd* call an emergency,' he said sourly. He stood still, recovering his breath. 'However, the others seemed to think it was.' He stopped, pulled something out of his bag, and held it out to me. 'Your coat, madam. Erica noticed you hadn't taken it with you, and when Oliver came downstairs and saw how hard it was raining, they both insisted that someone ought to take it to you. To be fair, Oliver was all set to do the job, but Erica stepped in and said that he still looked far too rough to be hiking up hillsides. And then we tried to phone you, just to see just how far away you actually were. And *then* we realised that the ringing was coming from your jacket pocket.

Very clever, Tess. And so - finally discovering that you'd taken no basic precautions whatsoever - I got handed the short straw and sent out to find you.'

'Thank you,' I said stiffly. 'But you needn't have bothered on my account.'

'No, I needn't. But I did anyway. Although,' he added, eyeing me, 'you look so wet already that it was probably a wasted effort.'

'Well - thanks anyway.' Clumsily I pulled the jacket over my wet jumper.

'You're shivering,' he said. 'Really shivering. For God's sake, Tess – why on earth didn't you think of taking shelter somewhere?'

'Like where?' I asked. 'Care to point out just where?'

'It's no good getting ratty with me,' he said. 'You're the one who chose to leave the house without a coat or a phone.'

Since this was so palpably true, I marched on in silence. Or tried to march, which wasn't that easy on a path that now appeared to have a small river running down it.

'Careful,' said Daniel, grasping my arm as I stumbled and started to slide. 'Listen, on the way up here I saw some kind of shepherd's hut just off the path. If I can find it again, we can wait inside until the worst of this is over. Keep looking.'

I stumbled sulkily after him until at last we were nearing the beginning of the wooded area. Here he suddenly stopped and pointed. 'There - I knew it was somewhere around here.'

His powers of observation were more acute than

mine, for even now it took me several moments to realise that the grey stone just visible behind a tangle of saplings and brambles was actually part of a man-made building.

'In there?'

'Unless you prefer drowning?'

Despite my reluctance, there was sense in his words, for by now the rain was hurtling down with torrential vigour. Following him, I squelched my way across the rough ground to an open doorway. The interior, though dim, was blessedly spacious, and kept almost dry by a rusty corrugated iron roof.

'Dear God,' said Daniel, shouting to be heard above the noise of rain on the roof. 'That's a fucking relief. I knew it could rain in Scotland, but I wasn't expecting monsoon conditions.' He threw down his rucksack. 'Are you all right?'

I nodded mutely, unable to speak for the chattering of my teeth.

He looked at me, then pulled off my coat, and then my jumper. 'Stupid of you to put on your mac over a sopping wet jumper. Now they're both wet. You should have taken it off first if you'd had any sense. Yes – all right – I know you didn't want to do a striptease standing out in the elements. Have you got a spare jumper, or *any* spare dry clothes in your bag?'

I shook my head, and he frowned. 'No, of course not. That would have been far too intelligent. Go on then, you're going to have to wear my coat. At least it's dry on the inside.' Before I could protest, he was taking it off and draping it round my bare shoulders. 'Better?'

I nodded again. It *was* better, although I grudged having to admit it.

'Well, at least there are worse places in which to shelter,' he said, looking around him. 'I don't know what this was ever used for, but I'm glad I saw it. It's a damn sight better than being out in the deluge.'

'But now *you'll* get cold without your coat,' I mumbled.

'Not as cold as you were,' he said. 'I was still hot from having to climb so far to find you.'

'You didn't have to,' I pointed out again.

'Well, either way, I did.' He drew back and looked at me seriously. '*Are* you all right? Really? You're still shivering.'

Before I knew it, or had a chance to protest, he had put his arms round me. 'Shut up,' he said. 'This isn't a seduction. I'm trying to get you warm again. As much as you might like the thought of developing hypothermia, I'm the one who'll end up having to lug your body back to the house.'

'But now you'll get wet too,' I objected, 'from off the outside of your coat.'

'Oh - for God's sake.' He stepped back, pulled the garment from off my shoulders, and wrapped his arms round me once more. Almost at once I could feel the heat of his body spreading warmth into my own. 'There – happy now?' he demanded.

I nodded, unsure whether I wanted to giggle or to cry. For several long minutes he stood holding me, until at last I broke away. 'Thanks, Daniel. That *is* better – a lot better,' I admitted.

226

'Good. At least your skin has lost some of that blue tinge now. You almost had me worried for a moment. Look, there's an old bit of polythene on the floor over there. If we sit down close, I can wrap my coat around both of us. There's not a lot of warmth in it, but it's better than nothing.'

Huddled together, I could feel myself slowly thawing. A few trickles of cold water still ran from my hair down my back, but at least my face and fingers felt as if they were getting some sensation back into them. I shivered again, and felt Daniel press closer.

'We seem to make a habit of meeting in rainstorms, don't we?' he said.

'Do we?'

'The Midsummer Fayre,' he said. 'In that marquee, where Erica first bumped into you.'

'I suppose so.'

'Definitely so. In fact, looking right back, I think the very first time we ever met was when you bashed an open umbrella into me. Remember?'

I sat very still. Even I had almost forgotten that very first meeting. That Daniel should have recalled it, took my breath away.

'There, that shook you, didn't it,' he said. 'You didn't think for a minute I'd remember that. But I do. I'm sure you always knew that you hadn't really hurt me with that stupid great brolly. But it gave me a bloody good excuse to chat you up.'

I sat silently. There was nothing I could think of to say. Despite Daniel's protestation that he wasn't out to seduce me, I had a disturbing feeling that this

227

was turning into one of those corny ravishment scenes so favoured in old-fashioned movies. But its effectiveness was worryingly real.

'You know,' he said, after a while, 'I'm sorry, really sorry that it all ended like it did.'

'Your fault,' I said. 'Not mine.'

He sighed. 'If it's any consolation, it didn't take me long to realise what a total twat I'd been.'

'Good,' I said nastily. 'Still at least you had the delightful Maxine to take your mind off your sorrow.'

'I didn't. Maxine could never hold a candle to you. It's just that she made herself very available, and I was young, greedy and stupid. You don't have to believe me, but after that time you caught us, I never went with her again.'

I shrugged. 'It hardly matters now anyway, does it?'

For a while we sat in silence until, unable to stop myself, I said, 'Anyway, what did you mean when you called me Little Miss Perfect? That time when you came to pick up Toby, when Erica had rushed off to the dentist.'

'Oh, I don't know. I was just in a temper, I suppose.'

'But it's a weird thing to say if you didn't mean anything by it.'

He took his time to answer, and all the while I was aware of his closeness, his solidity and warmth. How long was it since we had last sat like that? It was as if the years in between had never happened.

Eventually he said, 'I always felt that you were a better person than I was, Tess. No, I *knew* you were

228

a better person. More likely to do the 'right thing' than ever I was. Better about commitment. More mature, more responsible, more loyal.'

'Oh. Well, I can't argue with you about the 'loyal' bit.'

Daniel said nothing.

I sighed. 'Okay, let's just agree now that it's water under the bridge. What was done was done. I won't pretend it didn't hurt like hell at the time, but at least you seem to have grown up enough to realise just how badly you behaved. That's something, I suppose.'

'Thank you.' He tightened his arm around me, and pulled the coat even closer around the two of us. 'You're still shivering,' he said. 'What does that mean?'

'Probably that I'm cold.'

'Perhaps. All the same…' He drew me even closer and. before I knew it, his lips were on mine, softly and gently.

'What - ?' I drew back abruptly and stared at him.

'Just a thank-you kiss,' he said. 'For being far nicer than most people would have been. And also,' he added, 'for old times' sake. We did have some good times, didn't we?'

His eyes met mine, and I breathed in the old familiar nearness of him, felt the warmth of his breath on my skin. Then suddenly his kiss was no longer gentle, but hard and purposeful. And I was responding.

It lasted far longer than it should have done. At

229

last I pulled away, more shocked at my own behaviour than at his.

He smiled lazily at me, and gently pushed back a strand of wet hair from my face. 'You look like a timid water-sprite. There's no need to worry, Tessy. No-one's going to walk in on us, and you know you want it every bit as much as I do. We could easily....'

'No, we couldn't,' I snapped. 'Of course we couldn't! Dear God, Daniel! Even if I did - what about Erica? I already know how much it hurts to be cheated on by you. I'd never do that to her. And *you* shouldn't even be thinking of it!'

'No,' he agreed. 'I shouldn't.' But he held my gaze, and his eyes were still questioning. 'But then, she doesn't have to find out.'

I took a deep breath, waited for my heart to stop pounding in my ears. 'No, no, no. And that 'no' is for *my* sake, not just Erica's.'

'And what about Oliver's sake, Tess?' asked Daniel. 'What sort of relationship are you in with him?'

'Mind your own bloody business!'

Daniel grinned.

'And in any case, whatever may or not exist between me and Oliver,' I carried on angrily, 'it's the relationship between you and Erica that you ought to be concerned about. Not only are you married to her, you also have a small child to think about.'

'And,' he said casually, 'another one on the way. You did realise that she's pregnant again?'

I stared at him. 'Pregnant?'

'I thought you would have guessed. All those

spells of being tired, and spending half the morning in bed because she feels so sick.'

'She didn't say anything,' I said wonderingly.

'No, she wants her parents to be the first to know. She wants to get it all properly confirmed before she rings them. So perhaps you'd better not mention that I've already told you.'

'I won't.' I stood up abruptly, went to the doorway, and stared out. The lessening of the noise on the roof should have already told me that the rain was easing, but that was the last thing I'd been thinking about.

I turned. 'You can stay or you can go,' I said coldly. 'Either way, I'm going back to the house.' I wriggled my sodden jumper back over my head, and yanked my damp jacket on top.

'Hang on - No need to get so arsy with me. Wait a sec - '

But I was not waiting, and went skidding on down the path until his long legs enabled him to catch up with me.

He grabbed my hand and swung it as if we were best of pals. 'Friends again?' he said, smiling.

I looked at him and shrugged. For just a brief while we nearly had been, but now I didn't even care what he thought we were.

Chapter 15

'Well, I'm relieved to see that you don't look as if you've suffered any ill-effects,' observed Oliver as we sat down to a very early breakfast next morning. 'That was quite a rainstorm you got caught in yesterday. If we didn't have to go home today, I'd have insisted you have a lie-in. It's a shame it's such a long journey back to the West Country. It's all right for those sluggards upstairs,' he said, raising his eyes to the ceiling. 'I know they've booked an overnight stop again, but you and I really need to be heading off soon.'

'I'm fine,' I said. 'You're the one who had the migraine yesterday. Are you sure you're up to such a long drive? I suppose we could always sort out a stop for ourselves, if you'd rather.'

'No problem,' he said. 'I'd rather get back today if I can. I still don't know what caused that migraine, but I'm well over it now. I'm just sorry that I wasn't much company for you, especially it being our last day. I wish I could have come with you on your walk.'

'But I wouldn't have been much company for *you*,' I smiled. 'You know, I really enjoyed getting back into doing some drawing, but it's definitely not a sociable occupation. You'd have been bored stiff, not to mention ending up getting as wet as I did.'

'But *I* wouldn't have forgotten to take my

raincoat,' he said smugly. 'And I'd have reminded you to take yours as well. If I'd have been there, you'd never have got so wet in the first place.' He surveyed me more seriously. 'But you are okay now, aren't you Tess? You were so quiet when you and Daniel got back to the house.'

I shrugged. 'I was cold.'

'But you stayed quiet all evening.'

'The warm bath made me sleepy. And then the whisky and honey hot-toddy that you brought me afterwards made me even sleepier.'

'Just as long as that's all?'

'Well,' I said, searching for a reassuring answer, 'I suppose I'm a bit sad that the holiday is all over.'

He looked relieved. 'Right. I'd just wondered if…' His voice trailed away, and he stood up and took his empty plate to the sink. 'Still, it will be nice to get home again, won't it.'

'It will,' I said. 'Especially for you. You must be desperate to see how the refurb is going?'

Oliver pulled a face. 'Yes, I suppose. But to be honest, I actually forgot to phone Anita the last two days. I don't know if that's a good thing or a bad. But it has been rather restful not to have to keep thinking about it.'

Yes, it must have been. What had started off as a vague plan to give the shop a bit of a face-lift had, with Anita's involvement, quickly turned into a major project both inside and out. I had to admit to some feelings of trepidation at what it might look like on our return. I'd always been fond of the shop's peaceful interior and its slightly eccentric layout. I'd

233

liked its calmness, the faint smell of beeswax and books, and the soft tick-tock of the grandfather clock that Oliver had never yet had the heart to sell. I'd liked the exterior too, the pleasant brown and gold livery that blended in so well with the warm stonework of the buildings around it. How much of that would still be there on our return? Not that any of it was really my business. But when it came to it, I wasn't convinced that Oliver would appreciate radical change any more than I would.

'I'm sure Anita would have let you know if there was anything she was unsure about,' I comforted. 'You'd agreed all the main things with her before you left home - hadn't you?'

'Yes,' he said. 'Yes, we did. I'm sure she would have rung me if she was intending to go too far off plan.'

'And talking of phone calls,' I said, suddenly reminded, 'I ought to call Jodie. She asked me ages ago if I'd like to come for lunch once I got back. I need to ring and confirm I'm still up for it. She'll be keen to hear all about our holiday.'

He looked at me a little anxiously. 'And shall you tell her *everything*?' he asked.

I shook my head. 'No, not everything. The question you asked me on our walk will remain strictly private between you and me. But I have been thinking about it, I promise. I just need to be quite, quite sure before I give you my answer.'

All the same, even with that particular topic off-limits, I had to admit that I was looking forward to having a good face-to-face chat with Jodie. So much seemed to have happened during the past two weeks. Indeed, I had been very tempted to phone her earlier, but then decided I'd much prefer to tell her in person. So I had contented myself with merely sending her brief messages and photos, and reassurances that Daniel and I had not yet come to blows. And now, since yesterday, there would be even more to tell her. Jodie was a great listener, and exactly the sort of person to see things in their proper proportions and make sensible comments.

While Oliver went off to start putting our luggage in the car, I found my mobile and rang her number. With any luck, I would catch her before she left for work at the Patchwork Pumpkin.

To my vague surprise, my call was picked up almost before the first ring had finished.

'Who's that?' shouted James.

'Er – me. Tessa.'

'Tessa?' For a moment it sounded as if James had never heard of me. Then, 'Tess – this is not a good time!'

'What? Oh. Sorry.' I drew back a little. What on earth was going on? Were they in the middle of a massive row or something?

'Oh, it's all right,' he said angrily. 'But this is definitely not a good time. Jodie's been having cramps, and now a bit of a bleed, and they're sending an ambulance for her. I thought you were them, saying they were almost here.'

'Oh. God, James - Oh – I'm so sorry. I'll get off the line. But give her my love, won't you? Do give her my love - and to you too. I'll be thinking of you. And let me know how things go, won't you? Please. If you get the chance.'

'Yes, I will,' he said, and the line went dead. I sat staring at my phone, feeling sick.

Oliver came in and saw my face. 'Tess? Tess, what's up?'

'Jodie's not good,' I said. 'That was James. He said they're taking her into hospital.' I looked at him. 'Oh, Oliver - Oliver, whatever will she do if something happens to the baby? Whatever will she do? She's waited so long for this…'

I found I was crying. Oliver hurried over and put his arms round me.

'Come on, my love. It hasn't happened yet – has it? What did James actually say?'

'Not a lot,' I sniffed. 'But I could tell he was really worried. He just said that Jodie had been having cramps, and now some bleeding. That can't possibly be good. I don't know. But they wouldn't send an ambulance if they didn't think it was really necessary.'

Oliver held me close. 'Then we can only hope for the very best. Perhaps we could try ringing James back later.'

'Yes,' I said. 'Yes, we will. I did ask James if he'd let me know. But I bet he won't. He might be too upset anyway.' I could feel tears threatening once more. 'Oh Oliver - '

For a second he continued to hold me, then gently let me go. 'Come on,' he said. 'I'm sure I heard Erica and Daniel moving about, so if we go up now and explain things, then we can head straight off.

236

Once we're home, you can go directly to Jodie's house. With any luck, you'll find you've spent the whole journey worrying over nothing.'

We made steady progress, only stopping for any length of time to take a hurried lunch break. Even the weather seemed to echo our glum mood.

'It's just like it was on our journey north,' observed Oliver, as we continued down the motorway. 'Rain all the way. Let's hope it stops soon, just as it did when we arrived in Aberfeldy.'

It was strange how the holiday house in Scotland already seemed like a different world. One good thing about our hurried departure was that it had forestalled any protracted farewells. I knew I would miss being around Toby, and it was impossible not to like Erica. Now that I was aware of her own pregnancy, I felt distinctly awkward about explaining to her the reason for our extra-speedy departure. But if she felt any unease on her own behalf she hid it well, contenting herself with giving affectionate hugs and extracting promises that we would let her know how things worked out. With Daniel I had exchanged nothing more than an air-kiss – although even then I felt I detected a faint hint of smugness in his fleeting embrace. Had he really managed to persuade himself that I'd be up for some future dalliance with him? If so, I thought rather distractedly, he was in for a nasty shock.

'Not much longer now,' said Oliver at last, speaking over the steady swish of the windscreen wipers. 'At least this horrible weather has kept the roads nice and empty. For a Saturday, that is. Anyway, we've made better time that I thought we might.'

I made no answer. To me, it felt as if we had taken forever. During my own turns at the wheel I'd done my best to keep my foot down hard, but as Oliver had gently pointed out, any accident would only serve to delay us more. Perhaps it was just as well, I admitted to myself, that he had taken on the lion's share of the driving.

'Shall I take you to your own house first, or to Jodie's?' asked Oliver.

'Um...' I had rung my mother earlier, to give her a rough idea of when I'd get back. But I hadn't yet made any mention of Jodie, for I knew the news would upset her, and there was plainly nothing practical she could do.

'Jodie's, then?' suggested Oliver. 'I don't imagine you'll rest until you've made some kind of contact with them.'

'Yes please,' I said, grateful that he'd made the decision for me. Now that I was so close to hearing the latest update, I wasn't sure that I actually wanted to know. Not if the news should prove to be bad.

But Jodie's house, when we stopped outside it, showed no sign of life. Although it was now dusk, the curtains were still open, and there were no reassuring lights gleaming. Leaving Oliver in the car, I walked up the front path and rang the bell. I could hear it echoing in their hall with the kind of dead resonance that empty houses always have. I rang again, and then again, but there was plainly no-one at home. Once again I checked my mobile, but there was still no sign of any missed call, or even a text message.

Oliver got out of the car and wordlessly put an arm round me. 'An empty house doesn't necessarily mean that it's bad news.'

'But it doesn't mean that it's good news either,' I said despondently. 'Do you think I should try ringing James?'

'You could certainly try,' he said.

But even as I went to my phone again, I realised that I didn't actually possess James' mobile number. I had their land-line number and I had Jodie's number, but I didn't have his.

'What about ringing the hospital?' suggested Oliver. 'I presume she would have been taken into our nearest. Would it be worth a try, do you think?'

'Even if she is in there, I bet they won't tell me anything.' I sighed. 'No, it looks as if I'm just going to have to wait until James remembers to get in touch. I do hope he will. Oh, Oliver. I'm sorry this has been such a miserable end to our holiday. But would you mind taking me home now? I think I've had enough of this horrible day.'

Thankfully, the warmth of welcome provided by my mother was just what I needed. As soon as Oliver had dropped me off, I sat down and told her of the bad news about Jodie.

To my relief she took it seriously, but didn't go all doom and gloom about it. 'I've known plenty of women who've been through a bit of a scare during

239

their pregnancies,' she comforted me. 'And nearly all of them have ended with a perfectly healthy baby at the end of it.'

I hugged her. Even if I wasn't going to ask her for the exact statistics, it was the sort of sensible reassurance that I wanted to hear. Cheered by her response, and with a meal of hot tomato soup and fresh bread inside me, the tension of the last few hours began to leave me at last.

'Spiced apple cake?' asked my mother as I put down my spoon. 'I made it this morning, just so that it would be ready for you when you got home. And after that, if you're not too tired, you can tell me more about your holiday. What was the accommodation like? How did you get on with Erica? I hope Daniel made himself pleasant. Did you have to go round with them every day, or was it just you and Oliver for most of the time?'

Thanks to an evening spent recounting all the best bits of my holiday, when I finally got to bed I felt calmer than I had all day. Too tired to do any serious unpacking, I opened my case merely to retrieve my nightwear and toiletries. But there, just beneath my sponge bag, I saw a flash of bright colour. It was the tartan bootees that I had bought for Jodie's baby. I lifted them out and placed them carefully on top of my chest-of-drawers. In the shop, they had seemed so funny and sweet that they'd made me laugh. But now, as I gazed at them, the two tiny bootees appeared unbearably poignant.

'So you had a lovely time in the end,' said Hector the following day, as he arrived at our house in time for elevenses. 'Pat said that you would, once you'd finally made up your mind to go.'

I smiled. 'She isn't always right about everything, you know. You'll find that out just as soon as you're married to her.'

He laughed, sat back in his chair and took another slice of yesterday's spiced apple cake. 'Well, I know she's very good at cooking, so I'm quite happy to settle for that.'

'Settle for what?' asked Mum, arriving with a tray of coffee mugs.

'Settle for you not always being right,' grinned Hector. 'Tess tells me that it doesn't always happen.'

I helped myself to a mug hoping that, all the same, she had been right last night. She had been so matter-of-fact about the frequency of problems in pregnancy that I had accepted she knew what she was talking about. But now in the cold light of day, I was not so sure. I had still not heard from James.

As if reading my mind, Hector smiled at me. 'Pat was telling me about your friend. I'm sure her husband will ring you soon. And modern treatments can work wonders these days.'

'Yes,' I said. 'Yes, the logical part of me knows that. It's just that…' I let my words trail away.

Mum looked at me sympathetically. 'Anyway,' she said, 'I didn't tell you last night, but at least Hector and I have some news for you. We've set our wedding date.'

'That's lovely,' I said. 'Good for you. So when

will it be?'

'Well,' said Hector, 'at our age, there's no point shilly-shallying, so we thought we might as well make it as soon as we can.'

'It will be in six weeks' time,' clarified my mother. 'That still gives us time to sort things out.'

'Wow,' I said. 'That's not long to go, is it? Will you have time to organise everything? Is there any help you'd like from me?'

'No, it's all falling into place, thank you. It will be a very simple registrar's office do. We're not inviting that many people, and none of them will have to travel far. And after the ceremony, we'll come back to Little Bagford and have a small reception at The Dragon. We've fixed that up already, and it should work out very nicely.'

'Good.' I sat back and looked at the table. Despite my smile, I couldn't help but feel deflated. Having a definite date made it suddenly much more real.

Which led, with equal urgency, to the next question. 'So where,' I asked, 'are you going to live? Have you made a choice yet?'

They looked at each other. 'We've been talking about it a lot,' said my mother, 'and I think we've finally come to a decision.'

'We have indeed,' confirmed Hector.

'Yes?'

'We've decided,' he continued, putting down his cup, 'we've decided to sell my cottage and - '

'And sell this one as well,' said my mother.

'Oh.'

'It just seemed that the best thing we could do was to pool our resources and buy a place that will provide a brand new start for both of us,' she went on. 'Now, before you say anything - we obviously have *no* intention of making you homeless.'

'No,' I agreed rather blankly.

'Absolutely not,' said Hector.

'And so,' went on my mother, 'although Hector's place will go up for sale immediately, we won't be doing anything about this cottage, until we've all had a proper talk and see how you feel about things. As we see it, there are several options that you could take.'

I nodded.

'First of all, I could sell this cottage and split the money with you.'

'But it's *your* cottage,' I said automatically. 'Dad left it to you. There's no onus upon you to give me any of the money.'

Mum leaned across and took my hand. 'Your dad would have never expected me to sell up and keep all the proceeds to myself. And even if he hadn't, I still wouldn't. It may not be a legal obligation, but it's certainly a moral one. You gave up your career in Bristol to look after me when I needed it. I haven't forgotten. I won't ever forget.'

I blinked and nodded. 'It wasn't that much of a sacrifice,' I mumbled.

'Anyway, it's your home,' she carried on unheeding. 'Whatever happens, there will be no question of kicking you out before you're quite ready to go.'

'And if you decide you want to stay here for ever,' said Hector, 'then we go to Plan B.'

I looked at him.

'Plan B,' he elaborated, 'is the possibility of you either buying or renting the property from your mum. At a very reduced price, of course.'

'But then you'd be losing out.'

'We're not trying to make a profit,' he said. 'Just as long as we have enough to buy the house we want, then that's fine.'

'You've already got somewhere in mind?'

'We do have somewhere that we've seen and liked the look of,' admitted my mother cautiously. 'It was almost by accident. We hadn't even intended to start looking until we'd talked things over with you. But while you were away Hector and I went for a walk, and happened to pass a house that both of us thought looked exactly the sort of place we'd like to end up in.'

'Yes?'

'It's actually on the Windmill Hill development,' she continued. 'After we'd seen it, we thought we might as well pick up the details from the agent. I'll show you in a minute. It's got three bedrooms, a separate shower as well as a bath, and a garden that's just the right size to be manageable. And the inside layout is so well planned. It would give me room in the kitchen for a dishwasher *and* a decent-sized fridge. In fact, all the things that would make life easy, but which we wouldn't have room for here. There's even a downstairs toilet. And the biggest attraction of all is how much less maintenance it would need than either this place or Hector's.'

'It sounds as if you've fallen in love with it already,' I said.

'No – don't worry. It just opened our eyes as to what's out there on the market. If we don't get that one, then there are bound to be other places coming up. So there's no hurry for you to make up your mind as to what you want to do.' She paused and regarded me, half-quizzically, half-smiling. 'And of course you may have quite different plans of your own that you haven't yet told us about. Just have a think about things and let us know in your own time. It's obviously going to be a big decision for you.'

Yes, it would indeed be a big decision for me, I thought as I carried the empty mugs back to the kitchen and started running hot water into the bowl. And if Mum did but know it, that was the second big decision I'd been asked to make within the space of just four days. And as yet I was barely beginning to make up my mind on the first one.

Hector had been invited to stay on for Sunday lunch, and so after we had eaten I decided to take myself off for some fresh air, leaving them to dawdle over cups of tea. There was nothing like a walk, I told myself, for helping one to see things with fresh eyes. Not for the first time I missed my father. He'd never been a great talker, but he had always been a great listener, and very good at working out the different ramifications of any scenario. He'd been brilliant at helping me choose which university to opt for. Now,

245

even if he couldn't have helped me decide about Oliver, I'm sure he'd have had sensible thoughts about the cottage. I sighed, aware of the irony of wishing him here to help me make choices which would never have arisen if he *had* been here.

Oh well. Perhaps I ought to start up a regular rambling group; a properly organised event for anyone who happened to be wrestling with their own dilemmas. It could be a kind self-help thing, in which we talked over each other's problems before making a group decision about the best resolution. I could visualise us already; everyone setting off with downcast faces and dragging feet, before eventually returning home with beaming smiles and a new sense of purpose in life.

With these rather wild schemes rattling round my brain, I left the cottage and took myself off down the road. Inevitably my steps led me towards Jodie and James' house, but there was still no outward sign of occupation. I rang the doorbell with no great hopes, and was unsurprised when nobody answered it.

I walked on, still lost in thought. To marry. or not to marry? To move, or not to move? These were the questions. Whether t'was nobler in the mind to suffer the slings and arrows of -   I pulled myself up sharply. Once again I was seizing distractions rather than concentrating on actual solutions. I needed to focus.

I was aware that I was still heading down the road that led away from the village. If I turned round, then I could go and look at the outside of Oliver's shop and see what had been done to it. Yet it seemed a bit mean to sneak a preview without him being aware of it. He'd want to show me himself all the changes that had been made. No, I would wait until tomorrow when I was due back at work. Assuming that there was work for me to do. I did hope that the shop would be in a fit state to open. Keeping it closed was costing us customers, and we were already relying on the revamp to bring in enough of them to have made it worthwhile.

I plodded onwards aimlessly. As far as the weather went, it wasn't as bad as yesterday when we had driven home through the endless rain. Today it was merely overcast, with a sky that resembled the colour of an indigestion remedy. Wet leaves lined the path and gutter, and occasionally drifted down from the trees, as if too listless to even attempt a twirl or a flutter. I felt much the same myself.

I was on the very edge of the village by now. It wasn't particularly pleasant walking alongside the main road, yet still I kept going. How tempting it would be just to keep walking away from it all, and yet… No. Running away *from* things was a stupid move. It was running away *to* things that was important. Running away to somewhere like Australia.

I had not, during the past nine weeks, forgotten Fraser. I still felt upset about the way we had parted, with our quarrel hanging between us. So much so, that before heading off to Scotland I had decided to take the bull by the horns and try to contact him – until I realised that I didn't have his details. The only time he'd ever rung me was from Hector's land-line. Hector might know, but I was reluctant to ask, nor was I even sure he'd possess the information. A tentative questioning of Hector had only elicited the fact that although affectionate, their relationship was not one based on regular contact. It had been a blow. For a while I'd cheered myself that at least Fraser had cared enough to try to see me before he left the country. And yet he hadn't cared enough to try getting in touch again. Perhaps, I reflected sadly, it was simply a case of 'out of sight, out of mind'. I'd certainly known other people like that. Yet somehow I had felt he would be different.

I stopped walking, aware that the afternoon was turning greyer and colder, and that I really was much too old to run away from home. It was time to go back.

The real renewal of my gloom, I knew, had been sparked by that casual remark made by my mother earlier, when talking about the wedding. 'None of our guests will have to travel far', she had said. And with those words she had removed any vague hope I'd held that Fraser might be back to attend it. Oh well. Good job I hadn't been counting on it. Not really. No, not at all. In fact, sod him, I thought defiantly. It hardly mattered, did it. For even if he *had* been coming, what was I expecting would happen? Even I didn't know the answer to that one.

With these imponderables to keep me company, I made my way back home. So much for my theory that a walk might clear my mind. The only thing that had become plain was that exercise did *not* relieve worry, and that dilemmas might be more easily resolved by simply throwing a dice. At least that way a decision would actually get made.

Chapter 16

'Tess?' said my mother next morning, peering around my bedroom door. 'You awake? You're running a bit late, you know. Shall I put some toast on for you?'

I stirred myself to rise, although I had actually been awake for some time, unsuccessfully willing myself to get up. Yesterday evening had crept by with still no news about Jodie. I veered between gloom and optimism as to whether this was a good thing or not. Did it mean that everything was fine? Or did it mean the news was so bad that James was too upset to talk to me?

Downstairs, my mother had already scrambled some eggs to go with the toast. 'You might as well go back to work on a proper breakfast,' she said. 'I expect you're looking forward to seeing what's been going on in the shop. I've walked past it several times since you've been away, but you can't get any proper idea what's going on inside. They've put up sheets of brown paper behind the glass, so you can't see a thing. And I did try.'

'What about the front of the shop? Surely that must be visible? That was supposed to be having a face-lift as well.'

'Well, the paintwork has been rubbed down and undercoated,' said my mother doubtfully. 'You can see that it's being worked on, but it certainly wasn't finished last time I walked by.'

'Wasn't it?' I frowned. 'Well, let's just hope that the workmen have got a move on since then. Oliver can't afford to keep the shop closed any longer than he has to.' I finished the last morsels of egg. 'I do hope he's happy with it.'

But despite my fears, I had to admit I was curious. My steps quickened as I grew nearer, and I was relieved to see that the exterior had now been completed. It was no longer the friendly brown and gold that I had always liked, but a smart slate-grey and white, with the name 'Pilgrim's Antiques' picked out in purple. I wasn't sure if I liked it, but supposed I would get used to it before long.

However, the interior was plainly not yet finished, for not only was the paper still up behind the windows, but the door-sign read an uncompromising 'SHUT.'

I pushed open the door and was immediately greeted by a sharp female voice saying, 'I'm afraid we're not open. Didn't you see the sign?'

Anita was looking at me crossly, and for a moment didn't even appear to recognise me, for she said again, 'We're closed.'

'But not closed to Tessa,' said Oliver, emerging from the shadows. He hurried forward to greet me. 'How are you? I thought I'd give you all Sunday to get over the journey before I dragged you in to see what's been going on here.'

'Oh, it's you,' said Anita without noticeable warmth. 'Sorry. I'd forgotten you were coming in. And it was too dark for me to see you properly.'

'It is dark,' agreed Oliver. 'I can't wait for the

moment we're able to tear down all that brown paper from the windows. It's like being inside a cave at the moment.'

'Well we don't want to take it off before it's all finished,' said Anita. 'We want it to be a grand reveal, otherwise people won't bother to stop and look inside when we *are* open.'

'Yes, I see the logic,' said Oliver, 'but that doesn't mean we can't have the light on either.'

He flicked the switch, and immediately the interior sprang into clear sight. It had certainly undergone some major changes, and yet it took me a moment to comprehend the biggest one.

'It's larger than it was,' I said. 'Much larger. So how - ?' I turned round slowly, trying to take it all in. 'You've had a wall removed,' I said in amazement. 'What's happened to the workroom?'

'Gone,' said Anita. 'It was only a stud wall. Easy to take down. And now we've incorporated that area into the shop floor, it's almost doubled the amount of usable space. Such an improvement.'

'But,' I said, confused, 'where will Oliver do all the workshop stuff?'

'Oh, that can be done outside. In the shed. There's plenty of room.'

'But surely it'll be cold in that shed. And if I'm seeing to customers in here and he's out there, I won't be able to talk to him very easily.'

'Do you actually *need* to talk to him?' asked Anita.

'Well, yes. If anyone asks a question that I can't answer, then I certainly need to talk to him. After all, it's your father who's the antiques expert. I know quite a lot, but I'm nothing like as knowledgeable as he is.'

'You are pretty good,' reassured Oliver quickly.

I smiled at him. 'But the other thing, Oliver, is that you'll get terribly cold out there in that shed. It might not be too bad at this time of year, but once we're heading properly into winter, you'll notice it. And even if *you* don't mind it, I can't imagine it'll do much good to the pieces you're restoring. Varnish isn't going to dry very well, or even glue set properly if it's bitter cold.'

'The shed can be insulated,' said Anita. 'It'll have to do for now, but obviously we'll be thinking about sorting out something better in the long run.'

I glanced at her and wondered if she realised just how much time Oliver actually spent working on the restorations and repairs.

'And the other thing we have to remember,' she carried on, 'is that once the shop really comes into its own, we can forget about that side of the business completely.'

'What? Stop doing all the workshop stuff?' asked Oliver. 'I didn't realise that was what you had in mind.'

'Ultimately,' she confirmed. 'Not immediately.'

'But I *like* doing the renovations. To me, that's the most interesting part of the business - taking something that's old, or mistreated, and bringing it back to life again. It's very satisfying.'

She looked at him in some exasperation. 'Okay then, we'll keep it. But there's no alternative to the shed, I'm afraid. Not unless it gets very cold,' she conceded. 'In which case you can use the box-room in the flat. If you're only working on one piece at a time, I can't see a problem.' She frowned. 'Anyway, let's stop concentrating on what you both seem to see as negatives. Let's think about the positives for a change. There must be something you approve of, Tessa?'

I tried to quell my misgivings about just how Oliver was expected to manoeuvre large or fragile items of furniture up a narrow set of stairs, and made myself take time to give a fair opinion. 'Well, it *is* larger,' I said. 'And, once we've got daylight coming in through the windows, I think it will feel a lot more spacious. The fresh paintwork helps. And I can see you've had a lot of new shelving put up.' I added, nodding towards the empty area that had once been Oliver's workspace.

'Yes,' she said. 'I've decided to have a proper dedicated book section over there. The antiquarian sort, of course. Collectors' editions too. And I shall squeeze a couple of small armchairs into the corners. It'll give just the sort of ambience that I want to achieve. You see, I'm aiming to make the whole shop look much more upmarket. I want to encourage people to feel that this is the sort of thing they could aspire to in their own homes.'

I had to allow that it did sound sensible. That space could indeed be made to look inviting, and perhaps even attract the sort of customers who wouldn't have lingered otherwise.

'Yes,' I conceded. 'Yes - but don't forget that at

the moment we don't have anything like enough books to fill all those shelves.'

She shrugged impatiently. 'Then we'll build up our stock of course. I shall put up a notice saying that we're looking to buy them. People are always wanting to get shot of their old books. So as long as we make it clear that we're not interested in their tatty old paperbacks, then I'm sure we'll be able to pick up all sorts of decent stuff for peanuts.'

'We've always tried to play fair with people about prices,' I said.

'And we still will do. But we're not running a charity, you know, Tessa. The whole point of being in business is to make money. Anyway,' she continued, 'more to the point, Dad's very pleased with everything, aren't you?'

He nodded, though not, I felt, with unreserved conviction.

Anita smiled at me triumphantly. 'There, you see. All good, all happy. Now, what about you? I can quite understand that you wanted to come in and check out the refurb for yourself, but now that you have done, you can see that we shan't need anyone acting as shop assistant today.'

'But we can certainly do with someone to help get the shop straight again,' said Oliver. 'And if Tess doesn't mind, I for one could do with an extra pair of hands. There are so many things that still need to be put back in the right place.'

'Yes, you could be doing that,' allowed Anita. 'But be careful. We don't want to have the stock damaged.'

'Or people,' I said. 'Some of those heavier items will certainly need more than one person to lift them. None of us wants a bad back.'

She sighed. 'As you like. I'll leave you to get on with it then. I'm sure you know far better than I do just where it all goes. And in any case, I need to be getting on with the more urgent stuff.'

Left to ourselves, Oliver and I looked at each other.

'So - ' I said. 'Are you okay with all this?' I waved a hand around the empty interior. 'Is this how you visualised it?'

He gave a slight grimace. 'It's certainly not how I thought we'd agreed it would be,' he admitted. 'I rather thought that Anita and I had settled all the basic changes, and that it was only the finer details she'd be sorting.'

'So the loss of your workshop was a complete surprise?'

'You could say that.'

'Will you be able to manage?'

He shrugged. 'I shall have to,' he said. 'I'm just glad that I'd managed to complete all the outstanding jobs before we went away. All the same, I did promise Mrs Stewart that I'd sort out her gate-legged table as soon as I got back. And next week someone else is meant to be bringing in a set of chairs for me to look at.'

'Will you use the shed?'

'I suppose so. There isn't anywhere else. Fortunately, it's big enough to store several pieces at once. But you're right about it being too cold out there over the winter months. Something better will have to be sorted out soon. And worse than that, I shall miss having you in the next room.'

'I suppose we could always set up some kind of simple intercom. So if I get a customer with questions I can't answer, I could give you a buzz.'

'Mm.' Oliver didn't look convinced.

'Or we could just use our mobiles. Then, if you fancy a hot drink, you could ring me, and ask me to put the kettle on.'

I was finding it difficult to sound positive when I myself felt so lukewarm. Indeed, I would have much preferred to ask him what the hell Anita had been thinking of when she made such sweeping changes without first consulting, or even bothering to mention them to him. But it would have been not only tactless, but pointless. Anita's decisions were now done-deeds and besides, if Oliver was unhappy with his daughter's actions, it wasn't up to me to stir the pot.

Seeing him looking increasingly despondent, I gave him a small hug. 'Well, I suppose Anita's right in thinking that an antiquarian book section could work well. And if it turns out not to be, you could always have it made back into a workspace. So it's win-win, really.'

I looked at the space again, wondering just how expensive it might be to replace a wall. 'By the way,' I said, as a thought struck me. 'Surely all the extra changes must have taken you over budget?'

'Oh absolutely,' he agreed. 'Way, way over budget. But you see, Anita's paid for all the extras herself.' He glanced at me. 'I think I mentioned some time ago that she said she'd like to put some of her own money into the refurb? I just didn't appreciate quite how much. It was certainly more than I thought we'd agreed she would.'

For a moment we stood in silence.

'Oh well,' he said at last. 'Shall we make a start on things? Or would you like a coffee first? And I've just realised – I've not asked you how your friend Jodie has been getting on? Sorry, I meant to do that straight away. I do hope that everything turned out all right?'

By the time we'd had coffee and I had explained that I was still none the wiser about Jodie, we both felt more in the mood to begin working. When all was said and done, there was something reassuring about bringing order to chaos, and it would be good to see the place really beginning to look like a shop once again.

'I've fixed you some sandwiches,' announced Anita sauntering in just as our stomachs were reminding us that we hadn't yet had lunch. She looked round for a space on which to deposit the cling-filmed plate.

'Oh,' said Oliver. 'Tess and I were thinking that we might nip over to The Dragon for a quick lite-bite. I feel we deserve it.'

'Well, sandwiches will save you the trouble,' said Anita. 'I can see there's still lots to be done. Never mind, I'm sure you'll manage it all. Anyway, I've decided we're sufficiently up to speed to have our official reopening on Thursday. I'd already tentatively arranged things, so now I just need to confirm. I've already rung the local rag, and they're going to send round a photographer, which is great. And now I'm going to post it on all the local social media.'

Without waiting for any kind of answer, she swept upstairs again.

Oliver smiled rather wryly. 'Sandwich, Tess?'

'I suppose she's right,' I said, as I debated the choice between tuna or cheese. 'There is a lot left to do if we're to have it in a good enough state for Thursday.'

'And it would certainly be sensible to reopen as soon as we can,' sighed Oliver. 'But it's a shame about lunch. I was going to treat you.'

I laughed. 'It's me who should be treating you, after all that driving you did on Saturday. Well, if we can't go out for lunch today, I shall treat you tomorrow.'

Wrangling gently over who would be treating who, we sat and ate our sandwiches until Anita appeared again, this time bearing a tray containing three cups of tea and half a packet of digestive biscuits. 'There you go,' she smiled. 'Don't say I don't look after you. I thought I'd join you for a little break myself, just in case there were any details that you want to check with me. Now, where can I sit?'

Oliver rose from his perch and she took his place. 'Oh, and I've heard from Todd,' she went on. 'His flight's on Wednesday. He won't actually get to Little Bagford until the evening, but at least he won't

259

miss the grand reopening on Thursday. I do feel it's important that he should be here for it.'

'Todd's definitely coming?' I said. 'Well, that's very nice.'

She looked at me, frowning.

'Nice for you,' I added reassuringly, just in case she thought I might have designs upon her husband. 'You must have missed him a lot.'

She was about to answer when the shop doorbell jangled, and we all looked up as my mother walked in.

'Yes, I know I shouldn't be here,' she said interrupting Anita in mid-reprimand. 'I can see very well that you're not open to the public. But I do need to speak to my daughter.'

I stood up, alarmed, but she beamed at me. 'I've got news of Jodie. Good news. Everything is fine. She's all right, and the baby is all right. It's only James who's in danger right now – and that's from me. I could kill him, keeping us on tenterhooks all this time.'

In my relief, I started laughing. 'But how - '

'I was on my way out to buy a cauliflower when I saw James coming up the path. He'd only just remembered that he hadn't got back to us. Apparently all was okay and stabilized by Saturday evening, but they decided to keep Jodie in hospital for a couple of nights, just to be quite certain.'

'But why didn't he go home once he knew all was well?'

'He's been stopping over with his parents. They live near the hospital, so it did make sense. But I do wish he'd remembered to pick up the phone and let us know!'

'Well,' I said, gladness making me generous, 'I can see how he'd have had other things on his mind. I'm just so pleased that all's well. Oh, it would have been absolutely unthinkable if...'

'Well, we won't think about it then,' broke in Oliver cheerfully. 'All's well that ends well, as they say. So when will she be back home?'

'She's home now,' said my mother. 'James brought her back this morning. And he says she's definitely allowed visitors, just as long as they don't stay too long and tire her out . So you could pop round this evening, if you want to.'

'Or you could go this afternoon, if you like,' suggested Oliver. 'I'm sure you must be longing to catch up with her, and see how she's doing. I can carry on perfectly well by myself for a while.'

'No, it's all right,' I smiled. 'Thanks for the offer, but now that I know she's okay, I can wait a few more hours to see her.'

'Yes,' said Anita, 'and we really do have plenty of things here that still need doing this afternoon.'

She stood up as my mother waved me a jaunty goodbye and disappeared back to the high street.

'Oh - such a relief!' I said, beaming at Oliver.

'Good,' said Anita. 'And now, if there are no more friends or relatives dropping in, we can all press on again.'

The knowledge that both Jodie and her baby were

fine transformed the afternoon for me. I was even able to start calming my reservations about the changes and, as Anita had instructed, look for the positives. I couldn't quibble with how she had arranged the new pay desk, with its elegant table and chair, which was not only more comfortable but also looked far better than the old counter had ever done. And with more space in which to move around, I could see that the shop-floor did have a more inviting air to it now.

Oliver and I continued to arrange and rearrange the stock in a pleasantly companionable atmosphere.

'Are we allowed another tea-break, do you think?' grinned Oliver as the afternoon wore on. 'It's a good job Anita didn't decide to reclaim the little scullery, as well as my workshop. At least we can still make ourselves a hot drink without having to sneak upstairs to do it.'

'By the way,' I said, as we enjoyed our mugs of tea, 'I forgot to tell you – my mother has set a wedding date. It's to be at the end of this month.'

'Not long then,' observed Oliver. 'Still, I suppose there's no reason to delay. Have they decided where they're going to live?'

'Yes.' Telling him of their decision, and of the house they had seen and liked, I did my best to skim over the dilemma this would cause me but, as I had half-feared, Oliver was all too quick to see it for himself.

'Hmm,' he frowned. 'So you have decisions to make. Well, don't forget,' he continued rather diffidently, 'the offer I made when we were in

262

Aberfeldy. I'm not saying it's the best reason for coming to live with me, but any reason is better than none.'

He looked so wistful that I felt like hugging him. But not wanting to make a gesture that he might misconstrue, I restrained myself. 'By the way,' I said, as a welcome change of subject struck me, 'What will happen when Todd arrives? Will there be room for all three of you in the flat? Do you know how long they're intending to stay with you? Has Anita said anything?'

Oliver gave a small grimace. 'That's a talk that we haven't yet had,' he confessed. 'So far, we seem to have skirted round anything to do with her long term plans. Anita isn't giving anything away. That might mean that she herself isn't sure - or it might mean that she *is* sure, but doesn't want to tell me yet. Or it might simply mean that she's waiting for Todd to arrive before making any kind of announcement.'

I stood back to survey an arrangement of china plates. 'Do these look okay here, do you think? Or would they be safer on the shelf above? Anyway, if Anita and Todd *are* both planning to come back to England to live,' I said, returning to the subject, 'I'd have thought they must have something definite in mind. Now that the shop's pretty well sorted, surely they'll want to be heading off somewhere more exciting than Little Bagford.'

'The only hints that I've managed to pick up,' he said, 'seem to indicate that they could be around for some weeks yet.' He paused. 'She's already suggested that it would make sense for me to swap bedrooms with her and Todd while they're staying here. Her old room would be quite small for two people, you see. And mine is bigger.'

'And will you swap?'

'I suppose I will.' He sighed. 'After all, I presume it won't be for long, and I can't really come up with a good reason as to why I shouldn't. Well - not unless... Not unless my circumstances change.' He looked at me with a wry smile. 'Which again, is a very poor reason for hoping that you'll decide to marry me.'

'No, not the best,' I agreed, smiling to soften my words. 'But I shan't let that affect my decision one way or the other, don't worry. Whatever Anita and Todd finally choose to do with their lives need not affect us. And I *will* let you know soon, Oliver, I promise.'

All the same, even as I spoke, I realised that my good intentions were not enough. I had to make good that promise, and soon.

It felt odd, when I called in at Jodie's house that evening, to be walking up the stairs to her bedroom rather than into the kitchen. But propped up in bed, surrounded by pillows, she looked the same as ever, and was obviously pleased to see me.

'I do feel a fraud,' she smiled, apologetically. 'I don't actually feel ill at all. But the medics have told me to get as much bed-rest as I can, so I shall do as they say.'

'Definitely,' I said. 'It would be silly not to take

264

their advice.'

'I'm not even tempted to risk it,' she admitted. 'Oh Tessa – I was just so scared. I don't think I've ever been that scared in my life before.'

I squeezed her hand. 'Well, you're all right now,' I said tritely, longing to be able to say something more profound and comforting, but unable to think of anything. 'I'm sure the hospital wouldn't have let you come home if they still had concerns.'

'No. That's what James keeps telling me,' she said a little uncertainly.

'And he's right.' I smiled at her, wishing I could clear the shadow from her expression, but guessing that only time would do that. 'Anyway,' I said firmly, 'all you have to do is exactly as you've been told. And that is to stay put, and take everything very easy until the baby's born.'

She looked more cheerful. 'Yes. Yes, I'm already counting down the weeks until then.'

'Have you thought of any baby names yet? That must be hard, when you want the sex kept secret. Aren't you tempted to let them tell you?'

'No. Not at all. Not knowing makes it all the more fun. Anyway, we think we have a name for a boy, but can't settle on a girl's name yet. And in any case, whatever we choose, it's going to be a secret until the baby arrives!'

As our talk turned to all the weird and wonderful names that might be given, she was already beginning to look better. I produced the small gifts that I had brought back from Scotland, and enjoyed the laughter with which she received the tartan bootees, thankful that she would never know the pit-of-the-stomach feeling they had so recently caused me. As she lay back among the pillows, I was soon deep in descriptions of the holiday house, the places we had visited, and the antics of Toby.

'He's such a little love,' I said. 'I don't know if I envy you about to have your own little one – or pity you for all the hard work that's involved in looking after them.'

She grinned. 'Right now, I wouldn't change anything!'

'I wonder,' I mused aloud, 'if your child and Toby will end up playing together – although of course they won't quite be of the same age.'

I debated whether or not to mention that Erica had already started another baby, who would be even closer in age, but remembered in time that she'd wanted to keep the news private for now.

'Anyway,' continued Jodie. 'Enough about what you saw and what you did on this holiday. How did you and Daniel get on? Was it better or worse than you expected?'

I should have foreseen that question. But having had so much else in the interim to occupy my mind, I hadn't.

'Well?' she pressed.

'Um. Yes and no.'

She looked at me in exasperation. '*Tessa*!'

I chewed my lip uncertainly. I hadn't the slightest qualm about betraying Daniel's behaviour, but there was Erica to consider. Even though Jodie knew her only by sight, I didn't want any report of the incident getting back to her. On the other hand, I found that I did very much want to talk about it. Swearing Jodie to secrecy, I told her all. 'What's so depressing,' I finished, 'is that I'd just got to the point where I thought he and I might yet end up as friends.' I sighed. 'For most of the holiday, he seemed to be a reformed character. He was perfectly pleasant to me, and good company too, until - '

'Until he could see that he'd softened you up enough, and got the chance to pounce,' said Jodie angrily.

'Perhaps it was partly my fault. If I'd been better prepared, then I wouldn't have come across as easy prey,' I said. 'At least, not quite so easy.' Absently, I took an edge of the bedspread in my fingers, starting to fold and unfold it. 'Jodie,' I said, 'I kissed him back. Kissed him properly, I mean. I could so easily have let him go further.'

'But you didn't,' she said. 'Even though you could have done, and even though no-one else would have ever known.'

'But I wanted him to,' I insisted. 'I really wanted him to, and that's almost as bad. Even though I knew he was behaving appallingly. Even though I stopped loving him years ago, I still felt - I just wanted to have sex with him. Am I unnatural?'

Jodie reached out a sympathetic hand. 'Loads of women fancy bastards,' she reassured. 'It's a classic syndrome. And from what I saw when he came into the cafe, he *is* extremely fanciable.'

'Perhaps I'm a repressed nymphomaniac,' I said gloomily.

Jodie burst out laughing. 'Oh Tess, we aren't living a hundred years ago! These days, women are allowed to fancy a spot of sex. It's perfectly healthy and natural, and no-one goes round beating themselves up about it. Your problem is that you need to find someone you actually like, as well as just lust after. Anyway, if you want to qualify as a nymphomaniac, I'm afraid you'll need a lot more notches on your bedpost than you've ever told me about.'

'I pass them off as woodworm,' I grinned, grateful as ever for her reassuringly common-sense attitudes. I might have arrived at her house expecting me to be the one dispensing comfort and cheer, but it seemed she had given it back to me in spades.

And yet I still couldn't help but feel that the encounter with Daniel had told me more about myself than I'd wanted to acknowledge. For if I could feel that aroused by someone I didn't like, then why did I remain so unmoved by someone that I *did* like?

'Incidentally,' said Jodie, almost as if she knew what I was thinking of, 'Did you say anything to Oliver about Daniel coming on to you like that?'

'No,' I said. 'No way. It would only upset him, and there's nothing he could do about it.'

'Horsewhip?' she suggested mischievously. 'Pistols at dawn?'

'No. Not Oliver's style, thank goodness. In any case, I'm not his property to defend.'

Jodie looked at me sideways. 'Aren't you?'

But she was edging too near the truth for my comfort, and when I turned the talk to Aileen's attempt to rope me into running the next Easter Egg Hunt, I was relieved to find the subject mercifully dropped.

Chapter 17

When I had finished work on Monday, the grand reopening planned for Thursday morning had seemed a safe distance away. Yet by halfway through Tuesday it was becoming increasingly obvious that almost everything was taking longer than expected. By Wednesday I was wondering if there was any hope at all that we'd be ready in time.

'It's nice that we now have a lot more space to put things,' I grumbled to Oliver, 'but in some ways it makes things worse. There are so many decisions to make about what should go where, and all of them have a knock-on effect on the next thing we put out. If you see what I mean.'

'I do,' confirmed Oliver, with equal gloom. 'I'd just arranged all those Toby jugs in the new cabinet when I realised that if I left them there, then there wouldn't be room for the jewellery. So I've had to take them all out again and find somewhere else. I just hope,' he added on a tangent, 'that your mother's wedding arrangements are going more smoothly than things are in here.'

'I think so.' I gazed at the porcelain mantel clock I had just placed on a shelf, and wondered if I had given it a prominent enough position. 'Hector seems to be taking charge of all the more practical things, thank goodness. So Mum's quite relaxed at the moment. She's even going over to see Jodie this afternoon, just to keep her company. It must be so boring for Jodie at the moment. She knows she has to be sensible and keep resting, but I think she's missing doing all the baking for the Patchwork Pumpkin.'

'And they'll be missing her baking even more, I suspect,' observed Oliver. 'I wonder how they'll manage without Jodie's cakes and scones and shortbread.'

'She says that fortunately they'd already arranged with various other people to cover for her maternity leave, so they've been calling on their services earlier than expected.'

'I hope that they're all just as good as Jodie,' smiled Oliver. 'Though I bet they aren't. Anyway, talking of food, I need to find a place for this dinner service. Preferably somewhere visible, but not vulnerable to knocks and bumps. Any ideas?'

We looked around despondently.

'Of course,' Oliver admitted, 'I should have made a proper plan. Anita has pointed out that to me several times. But I wasn't expecting to come home from holiday and find everything so different to what we *had* planned. If she'd stuck to doing just a few changes, most of the stuff could have gone back where it came from in the first place.'

'In which case,' said Anita coming in, and catching the last part of this speech, 'it would have been hardly worth doing.' She looked around with satisfaction. 'Now, it's like a brand new shop. It's transformed.'

We nodded mutely.

271

'Oh - anyway,' she said. 'The reason I came down. Dad, you promised to swap bedrooms with me and Todd, and so far very little has happened. You haven't forgotten that he's arriving this evening, have you?'

'No.'

'So if you could come up and do something about it, then that would be good. If you do it now, I can spare a few minutes to give you a hand.'

She whisked off again, and Oliver and I exchanged glances. 'Will you be okay working by yourself for a while? Sorry to leave you in it, but I actually *had* forgotten about Todd,' he confessed. 'I suppose,' he added doubtfully, 'if he doesn't arrive too late, he might be able to give us a hand getting everything ship-shape down here.'

'We'll be finished by then,' I said with a confidence I didn't feel. 'No, off you go Oliver.'

'It shouldn't take very long,' he said. 'I don't have that many possessions to move across.'

I waved him away. 'I'll manage, don't worry. Just as long as you don't mind trusting my judgement as to where the other stuff goes.'

He gave a wry grin. 'Dear girl, I trust your judgement more than my own.'

He disappeared upstairs, leaving me to continue by myself. There was still a lot to do, boxes to be unpacked, shelves to be filled. I looked round at the remaining stock, and tried to reassure myself that everything would indeed get done in time. Oh well. Hopefully, it would. And at least it was a good excuse to put more weighty problems on hold.

Amazingly, Thursday morning did in fact find Pilgrim's Antiques looking splendidly smart and ready for business, and the rest of us looking equally ready for the Grand Opening. It helped that it was rather later than our usual opening hour, as Anita felt there would be few customers before eleven o-clock, and besides, the photographer could not arrive any earlier. Anita had done well with the publicity; posters had been put up, flyers distributed, and social media alerted. She had even, by some miraculous means, managed to get hold of a minor local celebrity – a pundit from a television antiques show, whom she had persuaded to drop by for long enough to cut a ribbon and declare the shop officially open.

By the appointed hour a small crowd had already collected and, as soon as the pundit's brief speech was over, Anita was handing out glasses of wine and fruit juice. Todd was also on hand, wandering round with a dish of champagne truffles in hand, beamingly offering them to all and sundry. Happily, the photographer was in perfect time to take pictures of both the pundit and the crowd, a circumstance which pleased everybody, especially those local residents who were looking forward to seeing themselves in the paper.

With the immediate rush finally over, and Oliver temporarily free, I smiled at him. 'It's going very well,' I observed.

He nodded. 'Yes.'

Was there a hint of reserve in that single syllable,

I wondered? For although the shop was indisputably looking attractive, and the number of customers very satisfactory, it didn't really feel like Oliver's domain any more. The old interior had been quiet and rather dim, and smelled of dust and varnish and years of history. The new shop-floor was larger and lighter and smelled faintly of new paint and scented candles. It should have felt like a vast improvement, yet somehow I regretted the passing of the old order.

But I felt it important to be positive. 'The book corner is a real success, don't you think? Or it will be, as soon as we have a few more books in.'

'He nodded. 'Yes, I can see now that it was a good idea of Anita's. She's got more vision than I have. Inherited it from Margaret, I suppose.'

From the nearby tray of wine glasses I helped myself to two of them. 'Here's to you, Oliver,' I said, handing him one, and raising my own in salute. 'Here's to you, and also here's to finding an even better place for your workshop. It's your hard work that's kept this place going for so long, and I think you should be proud of yourself. All these changes are just another step on its journey.' I hoped he would not question whether or not a shop could be said to have 'a journey', but I also hoped my words would cheer him, and they appeared to.

He raised his glass to me in return, his eyes on mine. 'We've been a good team, haven't we.'

Observing my mother and Hector making their way towards us, I stepped quickly away to greet them. 'There you are! Glad you could make it. Have some wine, Anita's ordered in loads of bottles. What do you think of it all, then?'

Mum smiled. 'Oh, we wouldn't have missed it! And I must say, it does look like a proper shop now. I was worried when I came in on Monday, and saw the mess. Now it looks very different, doesn't it? And there are so many people here!'

'Half the village have turned up, I think. Aileen and Brian have been in, and Carol, and most of the others on the Fayre Committee. Even Erica popped in with Toby to wish us well, but it was too crowded to bring the pushchair inside, so she couldn't stay very long. Daniel was off working somewhere, of course.' I didn't add the mental 'thank goodness' that I felt. 'And do you know,' I continued, 'that Erica is expecting another baby?' Earlier, I'd needed to feign surprise when she told me, but she was so plainly thrilled about it that I didn't have to fake any of my good wishes. I just hoped that Daniel had enough intelligence not to jeopardise her happiness.

But my mother was already back to extolling the merits of the newly refurbished shop. She beamed at Oliver. 'You must be so pleased. And your son-in-law's a nice chap, isn't he? Those chocolate truffles he's handing round are delicious.'

She looked across to where Todd was still doing sterling work, chatting to customers and making them feel welcome. Not only was he a natural at it, he had the advantage of novelty. Over the past few days several of our usual customers had noted that although Anita had returned to Little Bagford, her husband had not. And now here he was, large as life, handsome and charming, and with the most attractive

American accent. Sensing my glance, he caught my eye, grinned at me, and pointed to the dish of truffles. 'Want one?' he mouthed.

I smiled my refusal, and reflected how very much nicer he was than Anita. It was mean of me, I knew, because stationed at the sales desk, she appeared to be doing more business than Oliver and I had done over the last three months put together. I looked across to catch Oliver's eye, but he was now deep in earnest conversation with my mother. I wondered what they could be talking about.

'Perhaps she's sounding him out about my book collection,' said Hector reappearing at my side. 'I've got quite a few local history volumes - some of them quite old and a lot of them with beautiful colour plates. And I believe that Oliver is wanting to increase his stock?'

'He is,' I confirmed, 'but I hope you're not letting my mother steam-roller you into getting rid of anything that you want to hang on to. I'm sure there will be plenty of room in your new house for you to keep whatever you like.'

He laughed. 'I don't let Pat steam-roller me into anything, trust me. But now that my place is on the market, I've started to see that I do need a clear out. D'you know, I must have dozens of books sitting on my shelves that I haven't looked at in years. So it will be quite handy for me if Oliver *is* interested in them.'

'Good,' I said. I glanced back to my mother who was now taking her leave of Oliver. She certainly looked pleased about something. I just hoped she wasn't persuading him to take any more of Hector's stuff than he had intended to part with.

I had assumed that Friday would see a return to more normal numbers of customers, but was agreeably surprised to find the shop was still noticeably busier. At least three people, prompted by the notice put up by Anita, had decided to strike while the iron was hot, and brought in collections of books that they hoped to sell. Stashing them safely to one side, I continued to deal with those people who had actually come in to buy things. I had my work cut out, for at this inopportune time Oliver, Anita and Todd had deserted me, having gone outside to consider where there might be space to locate a new workshop. It had taken Anita a while to realise it, but after receiving several anxious customer enquiries, even she had begun to see that the repair part of the business was a significant one. Not only did it bring in the steadiest income, it also brought in people who otherwise might not even have stepped through the door.

However, with the shop still so unusually busy, I was not at all sorry when Todd and Anita eventually reappeared. As Todd was immediately waylaid by a customer, Anita headed straight towards me. 'What are these?' she demanded, looking behind the desk at the boxes of various volumes that had been brought in for inspection.

'Books,' I said briefly, being in the middle of persuading a woman that a little writing desk would be the perfect present for her niece.

Anita bent to examine them. 'Oh, God - half this pile is entirely unsuitable. Do tell me you haven't promised anyone that we'll buy them.'

'No of course I haven't,' I said irritably, having now lost the attention of my potential customer. 'I've told them that we'll need time to look at them properly, and we'll let them know later. As yet, I haven't even had a chance to glance at them myself.'

'But surely you've given everyone a proper receipt, itemising all the titles?'

'I've given them a receipt listing simply the number of books they brought in. There was no way I had time to sit down and write out every detail.'

'But what if they try to pull a fast one?' She frowned. 'Without titles, what if someone comes in and claims that they left something really valuable here, and that you've lost it? Really, Tessa, you should have known better.'

I took a deep breath. 'Firstly,' I said, 'as I've already told you, I didn't have time to list everything they brought in. Secondly, I happen to know, and would trust, every one of these people. Thirdly, they know and trust *us*. Pilgrim's Antiques, as run by Oliver – and me – has always had an excellent reputation for *not* cheating people.'

She backed away a little. 'Oh, very well. Only do try to manage it a bit better in future, won't you? I'll come down again when it's quieter, and have a proper look to see if there's anything that's at all suitable.'

Yes, you do that, I thought angrily, watching her disappear again. Her apparent belief that I was as much use as an unusually stupid Saturday-girl was infuriating. Did she seriously think that I wouldn't be capable of knowing in which sort of books Oliver would be interested? With difficulty, I restrained myself from kicking the desk, and instead smiled nicely at Janice, the proprietor of the Patchwork Pumpkin, who I now found standing in front of me.

'I've just popped over to have a look at your new interior,' she said. 'Very impressive. And so different from how it used to be. I'd intended to come over yesterday, but the café was busy all day. I think the boost to your customer numbers meant a boost to our own as well! Anyway - better late than never - ' She thrust a large cake box towards me. 'It's a sort of 'Congratulations on your Revamp' cake. Not baked by Jodie, of course. This is one of Linda's, but she's almost as good. Coffee and walnut – I hope you like it.'

She had gone before I could thank her properly, but at least she had restored my temper back to manageable proportions. I waved Todd over. 'Look,' I said. 'Look what Janice has brought for us. A present from the cafe. So kind of her. D'you want to take it upstairs and see if the others would like some?'

He grinned at me. 'I've a better idea. You're the one who's been working while we were idling outside. You go out the back and fix yourself a good big mug of coffee, a good big slice of cake, and sit down and eat it slowly. Then, and only then, you can take it up to see if the others want any.'

I opened my mouth to point out that the shop

279

was still too busy to leave him alone, but realised that at last there was now a lull.

'Go on,' he shooed me. 'Away you go. Kettle on, coffee in mug, cake in mouth.'

I laughed and decided to do just as I was told.

'And mind that there's a piece left for me,' his voice floated after me. 'Coffee and walnut's my favourite.'

I headed into the little downstairs scullery, looking forward to a few minutes of respite. Todd seemed to be managing well, so with mug of coffee in hand, I cut a generous slice of cake. Its rich coffee-soaked sweetness was exactly what I needed at that moment, and I made the most of my breathing space. Until, inevitably, Anita marched in.

'I came to see if you wanted a lunch break yet,' she said. 'Only I see that you're already taking one.' She eyed my mug and my half-eaten slice of cake with disapproval. 'I hadn't expected you to leave Todd all alone in the shop.'

'It was Todd's idea,' I told her. 'And if he needs any help, then he can give me a shout. And if he gets a question that I can't help with, then I can always nip upstairs and ask Oliver.'

'Dad's gone out,' she said.

'Oh. Well, in that case, I can take the details of the enquiry and ask Oliver when he gets back.'

All the same, I was surprised that he had gone out without telling me. Even if he was just going down the road, he usually mentioned it first.

Anita looked again at the cake.

'It's just been brought in,' I said. 'It's a present from Janice at the Patchwork Pumpkin. A gift for our reopening, and very thoughtful of her.'

She continued to stare at me silently.

'Yes,' I went on, 'I was going to sit here and scoff the whole cake entirely by myself.'

She sighed, as if she wouldn't have put it past me. 'Anyway,' she said, 'I'm here now, so if you want a proper break, or to go out, or whatever? Just as long as you don't take too long, of course.'

'Yes, miss.' I didn't quite say it aloud, but put down my plate and mug. Grabbing my jacket, I pulled it on and walked out of the door, just managing to restrain myself from banging it behind me. With no particular plan in mind, I stood for a moment, certain of only one thing. If I didn't take myself beyond smacking range of Anita, then I would not be responsible for my actions.

Oliver, to my surprise, was not far away at all. I could see him sitting at the far end of the Green, on the bench overlooking the small duck-pond. I wondered if Anita had sent him out too. Really, this was ridiculous. I thought we had long since passed the stage of being sent out by the school prefect, yet here we seemed to be all the same.

I sat down heavily beside him, and he looked up with a start.

'Oh, Tess. It's you.'

'Sorry,' I said. 'I didn't mean to startle you. If

you're not in the mood for company - '

'I'm always happy with *your* company.' He placed a hand over mine, but his smile had a forced quality. 'It's just that I was thinking.'

'It's not a very nice day for sitting outside and thinking,' I said. 'Looks as if it could start raining any minute.'

He nodded absently, but was plainly not listening.

'Things on your mind?' I asked lightly. 'I really won't take it personally if you'd rather I went away again.'

'No,' he interrupted. 'No, you stay here. I could do with talking things over with somebody, especially with you.'

I waited for him to begin, but he remained silent, staring absently at the ducks as they paddled around the reeds.

'Well,' I said eventually. 'It's certainly been a busy few days, hasn't it?'

He nodded rather glumly.

'I imagine that you'll miss Anita, when she eventually moves on.'

If he noticed my unsubtle angling for information on that point, he didn't show it. 'Hmm,' he agreed.

'Has she said anything?' I pressed on rather desperately. 'About her future plans, I mean.'

'Yes,' he said.

For several more silent moments we stared at the ducks.

'It's what she and I and Todd were talking about

this morning,' he said at last. 'Well, she was talking and I was listening.' He sighed. 'It's all come as a bit of a surprise.'

'Yes - ?'

'It seems she and Todd want to stay on here, living in Little Bagford. In fact, to put it bluntly, they want to take over the running of the shop.'

'What?!' I gaped at him. 'But - ?'

He shrugged. 'Yes, that was my reaction when she told me. Which is why I need to think about it.'

'But what about *you?*' I said. 'It's not just your shop – it's your whole *life*.'

He smiled faintly. 'Well, I think that's putting it a little strongly, but it's certainly been - *is* - a major part of my life.'

'Well then, you can't just let it go!'

'But - It's not quite that simple. What she said did make a kind of sense. Enough sense that I know I really ought to think about it.'

'You should do no such thing,' I said warmly. 'Absolutely not! That's your shop, Oliver, not hers. Why, you've owned that place forever.'

This time he gave me a proper smile. 'Not quite forever, Tess. Margaret and I moved in as newly-weds. And it was money from Margaret's family that allowed us to take it on.'

'But it was you who've made it a going concern. You who put in all the time and effort. You who've kept it going all this time.'

'But it was still money from Margaret's family that made it possible in the first place. And it's money that Anita inherited from Margaret that allowed her to add so many extras to all the renovations we've just had done.'

'But you didn't ask her to!'

'No, I didn't,' he agreed. 'But at the end of the day, it's Anita who's paid for quite a lot of it. And I have to take that into account.'

'But it's still your shop. Yours, not hers.'

He looked down at his clasped hands. 'Yes. I know. I do have a choice in the matter, I know I do. But when she started putting forward all her arguments, well, it did give me quite some food for thought. I can't just dismiss them out of hand.'

I bit back the words that surged into my mouth. So Anita, as well as her usual bludgeoning tactics, had now resorted to moral blackmail. How could anyone try to force their own father out of his livelihood? I wondered bitterly just when she had come to the decision to put her own money into the shop without telling him. Whenever it was, she must have realised it was a stroke of genius. Oliver was a sucker for fair play, and she couldn't have found a more effective way of manipulating him.

I glared into the dark depths of the duck-pond. I don't think I had ever before felt such red hot rage with anyone.

Oliver put his hand over mine once more. 'Don't be angry, Tess. There is some logic to it. There really is.'

'Yes?' I said coldly.

'Firstly, I *am* getting older.'

'You've just turned fifty! That's not old.'

'No, I know I'm not in my dotage. But I'm no

284

spring chicken, either. And it has crossed my mind, I'll admit, that when I finally do retire, it would be nice to see the shop continue as a going concern.' He looked at me. 'Anita's my daughter, Tess. I know it sounds egotistical, but I'd love to see Pilgrim's Antiques stay in the family.'

'But...' My voice tailed away. I could hardly argue against what was, after all, a perfectly reasonable and natural desire.

'And,' he continued, 'Whatever her faults, Anita is an excellent business woman. She'd probably run it better than I do now.'

'But the love for antiques - ' I insisted. 'She might be good at business, but she hasn't got anything like the sort of love and appreciation for them that you have.'

'True,' he said. 'But I think Todd has. It surprised me, because I wasn't expecting it. But from the first time I showed him round – and later, when I've been watching him – you know, he's got a real feel for the stuff we have in the shop. He asks me the right questions, he wants to know their history and context, and he handles them with respect. It's not something you can feign, and in any case, why on earth would he bother to? I know it doesn't take a genius to see that it's Anita who's boss in their relationship, but I think even she recognises that this is something that Todd is not only good at, but would stick at.'

'He's good with the customers as well,' I admitted reluctantly. 'Never pushy, but nicely enthusiastic.'

'Exactly.'

'But you - ' I said. 'Okay, taking over the shop may be a wonderful move for Anita and Todd, but what about you? Where would that leave *you*?'

'It would leave me,' he said, 'doing my repairs in a purpose-built workshop which would stand in place of the old shed. It would be properly heated and insulated, and with plenty of space and light inside.'

'Is this what Anita has offered you? And is she going to pay for it?'

'She is. She still has enough cash. Apparently over the last few years she's invested all the money that Margaret left her, and it's been bringing in a very good return.'

I should have known. When had Anita ever done anything that *wasn't* lucrative? Which must mean she was equally certain that, if she took over the shop, she'd be able to make money out of it.

'So,' I said slowly, 'would you still be involved with the day to day running of everything?'

'No, not to the same extent. But I would have far more time to spend on the renovations and repairs which, as you know, is the bit I most enjoy. But it would happen gradually. At first I'd still be doing the buying and going out to auctions and sales, but I'd be taking Todd with me. I'd be teaching him what to look out for, telling him what's worth getting, and what isn't. And obviously I'd be right on hand if he was serving in the shop and needed a second opinion on anything.'

'Oh.'

'So you see,' he continued gently, 'it's not quite as black and white as it first appears.'

I chewed my lip. 'So what about Anita? What's her part in this grand plan she's proposing?'

'Well,' he said, 'she'd be in charge of the admin, keeping on top of the finances, and generally expanding the empire. But also - ' He looked at me. 'This bit is what took me most by surprise. She and Todd are intending to start a family.'

I gaped at him.

'Yes,' he said. 'That was my reaction as well. I don't know why, but I've never really thought of Anita as a maternal sort of person. But I know Todd's keen, so perhaps this is all part of the arrangement. A sort of bargain between them. You know - Todd will accept coming to live in a different country and taking up a new career, and in return Anita will give him the children that he wants.'

'Oh,' I said blankly.

'I'd like a grandchild,' said Oliver. 'Now that it seems that it might actually happen, I've realised just how much I would like it.'

I summoned a smile. 'I know you'd make a wonderful granddad.'

For a while we both remained silent. Then a belated but obvious thought occurred to me. 'Incidentally, Oliver,' I said. 'If you're doing the repairs, Todd's in the shop, and Anita is doing the admin...'

For the first time, Oliver looked positively awkward. 'Yes, I know. You're wondering what will be left for you to do.'

'Yes. Yes, I am.'

'Well… I'll admit, I'm not sure that you'll be quite so needed in the shop as you always have been. But,' he hurried on, 'there is another thought. If you did marry me – or even just decide to live with me - you could be a lady of leisure. You could do what Margaret did - give up working, and have all the time you want for - well, whatever.'

'I don't think,' I said slowly, 'that I'm the sort of person who would enjoy doing nothing in particular all day long.'

'Well, there might be an answer to that,' he said. 'And do think about it before you do answer. But if Anita does start producing babies, perhaps you might like to take on some of the child-minding duties. What d'you think?'

Chapter 18

By the time I left work for the day, the weather had improved considerably. The clouds that had looked so threatening at lunchtime had dissolved during the afternoon, leaving a soft blue autumnal sky which should have raised my spirits, but didn't.

Whilst Oliver had seemed rather more cheerful after our discussion I, on the other hand, had felt more and more depressed as the afternoon dragged by. At first I'd consoled myself with the thought that after work I'd call on Jodie to chew things over with her – until I remembered that James' parents were due to arrive any time. 'They'll be staying with us till next Wednesday,' Jodie had told me. 'His mum is intending to catch up with some of the housework and prepare some freezer meals for us. She doesn't think much of James' housework skills, and to be honest, she's right. Not that he's had much time to spend on domestic stuff, poor thing, what with trying to get on top of his new job as well as everything else.'

'Well, if you need any more help after his parents have gone, do let me know,' I had urged.

'But you're busy at work too,' she had pointed out, smiling.

Remembering her words, I now felt even gloomier. It seemed all too likely that within a very short time I wouldn't be busy at all.

289

The cottage was empty when I let myself in, and I found a note from my mother waiting for me on the table.

'Gone to Hector's,' it informed. *'Don't wait dinner, I shall eat with him. Shan't be home too late. Shepherd's pie in fridge, or there's a pasty and some salad stuff if you prefer.'*

I didn't really feel like eating anything. Denied the chance to confide in Jodie, part of me had still wanted to talk about it to my mother. And part of me didn't want to talk about it at all. For I still hadn't told anyone about Oliver's proposal - and yet if I didn't, then I could hardly expect them to appreciate the full significance of today's news. But if I did tell them, then they would surely feel obliged to comment on the matter. And I didn't *want* advice, however well intentioned. It had to be my own decision.

I poured myself a large gin and tonic, adding an extravagant amount of lemon and ice-cubes. Sitting at the table, I stared into the glass, watching the tiny bubbles rise to the surface. Why was it that for the past few months, I seemed to have been hopping from ice-floe to ice-floe, each time believing I was landing on something secure, only to have it slip sideways beneath me?

And what was with this sudden spate of babies everywhere? I still wasn't sure if this is what I wanted for myself, but I did envy the sense of purpose that pregnancy must bring. After all, a baby was a real stake in the future. Whereas *my* future… I took another gloomy mouthful. At this moment it appeared that *my* future might lie in any one of a hundred different directions, and the more options that popped up, the more confused and depressed they made me. Why couldn't life just stay the same? I reached for the gin bottle again.

If, when she returned home, my mother noticed that I was more full of alcohol than food, she didn't comment on the matter. 'Cup of tea?' she offered, switching on the kettle. 'I nearly stayed to have some at Hector's, but then I realised if I hung on any longer I'd miss *Gardeners' World,* and as Hector wanted to watch some old war film instead, we decided to do our own separate things.'

'Compromise,' I said. 'That's what the world needs more of. Compromise. It'll lead to a very happy marriage, you'll see. You'll see.'

She looked at me, mildly startled. 'Yes indeed. Have you had your meal, by the way? I see the shepherd's pie is still in the fridge.'

'No,' I said sorrowfully. 'No, I haven't had anything at all.'

'Then I shall put it in the microwave for you now,' she said. 'You go and turn on the tv, and I'll bring it in for you, along with the tea.'

I did as I was told, and had already begun to doze over advice on lifting dahlia tubers, when the tray was put on the coffee table in front of me.

Mum smiled. 'I think you need some food,' she said. 'And when you've finished, I shall tell you all about my news.'

True to her word, she waited patiently until she felt she had my full attention. The steaming hot

291

shepherd's pie and gravy had revived me a lot, and I put down my knife and fork, feeling considerably more alert than I had done earlier.

My mother smiled. 'Right, now I'll tell you. Someone has put in an offer for Hector's cottage. And it's the full asking amount too. Isn't that lucky! Hector's thrilled, because it means he won't have to keep showing people round. He's hated having to live in a state of permanent tidiness. Better still, it's a cash buyer, so there'll be no problems with property chains. You hear about that sort of thing so often. And that means, fingers crossed, we can put in an offer of our own for that house we liked on the Windmill Hill estate. It's still available, Hector checked straight away.'

'Oh,' I said. 'Things are really beginning to move fast, aren't they. Does that mean you'll need a quick decision about my own plans?'

'No, no,' she reassured quickly. 'Well yes, obviously some time or other. But no hurry. After all, I imagine that you've got other, even more important, decisions on your mind. So there's no hurry about this one.'

I frowned in some confusion, wondering quite what she was getting at, and wondering if the effects of the gin were still befuddling me.

'No, you need to take your time,' she continued after a moment. 'The fact that Hector has sold so quickly, *and* for the full asking price, puts us in a strong position. Definitely strong enough for us to go and have a serious second viewing of the house. It's such a practical option, you see. Apart from the fact that it doesn't need any work doing to it, it's near enough to the village shops for us to walk there easily, which will be very useful if Hector gets to the point where he doesn't wish to drive anymore.'

I gave her a quick hug. 'It sounds absolutely perfect. I shall be keeping my fingers crossed for you. And now,' I said, standing up and retrieving the tray of empty crockery, 'I shall take this lot out to the kitchen, and leave it there. The washing up can wait until tomorrow. It's been a long day, and I really could do with an early night. See you in the morning.'

Having deposited the tray by the sink, I was already on my way upstairs when she called to me from the sitting room.

'Oh – Tessa! By the way - I forgot to tell you. There was even more good news. Hector's heard from Fraser, and it seems he'll be home in time to come to the wedding. Isn't that nice!'

Todd was already in the shop when I let myself in the following morning. He greeted me cheerfully. 'Looks like it's just you and me this morning, Tess. Oliver had a call yesterday evening from someone who has a load of books to sell. Apparently these people are emigrating in three weeks' time, and it's only just occurred to them to sort out their stuff before they go.' He raised his eyes to heaven.

'It does happen,' I laughed. 'So has Anita gone with him?'

'Yes. It was Oliver's suggestion. He thinks she

needs to know a bit more about the day to day business of running the shop.' He looked at me sideways. 'I imagine Oliver has told you about our proposition.'

I nodded.

'And what do you think?'

'I think it's up to Oliver to decide.'

'Very diplomatic,' he said. 'So just how comfortable is that fence you're sitting on?'

'Perfectly comfortable, thank you.'

He gave a mock grimace, and I relented a little. 'It's no good asking me. It isn't my decision. Nor will I be trying to influence him.'

'My, my, such restraint,' he smiled. 'Especially when I suspect that you *could* influence him, if you chose to.'

There was a silence. 'Well, either way,' I said at last, 'it has to be his choice. But there is one thing that Oliver did say - he thinks that if you chose to, you'd be very good at the job.'

Todd looked pleased. 'That's great to hear. I like Oliver a lot. He's an honest guy, and you don't meet that many of them in the world of commerce. If Anita and I take over - *if* - I'd certainly do my darnedest not to let him down.'

After the bustle of Thursday and Friday, the morning felt quiet in comparison. 'Saturday mornings often are,' I explained to Todd. 'A lot of locals take the chance to go into Taunton to pick up whatever shopping they can't get in the village. And this dull weather doesn't help bring people out. But it'll probably pick up later in the day.' I glanced round at the shop interior which still felt slightly alien in its unfamiliar amounts of light and space, and lingering smell of fresh paint. 'I daresay there will still be plenty of people who'll call in just to check out our new improved premises.'

With no immediate influx of customers on the horizon, Todd took himself upstairs to carry on with some paperwork while I manned the shop floor. From time to time people came in to look round or buy, but as the skies got gloomier, so numbers dwindled. I wished things were busier, and not just for the sake of business. Last night's news about Fraser had thrown me considerably. At least, I reflected, forewarned was forearmed -although exactly why I felt the need to arm myself, and how I was to set about it, I couldn't have explained. I only knew that the knowledge had left me feeling extremely jumpy. Thank goodness I'd have a few days' grace in which to prepare.

By lunchtime Oliver and Anita had still not reappeared. 'I guess that's a good sign,' said Todd optimistically, appearing through the inner door to see if they had got back. 'It should mean that there's plenty of interesting stuff for them to see. Anyway, you must be getting hungry. Shall I come down, if you want to go for a break?'

'I'm okay,' I assured him. 'It's still not busy, and if we do have a sudden rush, then I'll call you.'

'You're sure? I'll admit it's taking me longer to get on top of things than I'd expected. Hey, I know what - when I'm through, I was thinking of fixing myself a sandwich. I'll do you one as well. Ham and tomato okay?'

I smiled my thanks, and went back to examining yet another box of books that had been brought in earlier. I certainly need not have worried that we might not have enough to stock all the shelves. This lot was a real mixture; some good quality volumes on flora and fauna were jumbled in with several ancient greasy paperbacks fit only for the dustbin. Unfortunately, even the better volumes had a mustiness to them that spoke of years spent in storage. With head down and dividing them into appropriate piles, I gave an almighty sneeze.

'Bless you.'

The sound of the unmistakable voice above me made me shoot upright. 'Fraser?' I stared at him in total confusion. 'Why aren't you in Australia?'

He grinned. 'Well, that's a nice welcome, I'm sure.'

'But of course you're welcome,' I said, feeling myself go red. 'Yes, it's lovely to see you,' I burbled on. 'I was just a bit surprised. Mum did tell me you were intending to come, but I didn't think it would be for at least another two or three weeks. She said you'd be here for the wedding.'

'She was right,' he confirmed. 'I will be here for the wedding. But it seemed silly not to come here earlier, seeing as I got back into London yesterday.'

'I thought I wouldn't see you for ages,' I blurted.

'Well, I'm sort of playing hooky,' he said. 'I really ought to be going through all the material I collected – and it's a hell of a lot – but I decided it could wait for a few days. So I drove down this morning. It's good to see you again, Tess.'

I smiled inanely. 'You too.'

He paused. 'You know, I did try to catch you before I went off, back in July.'

'Yes, Mum told me you had. I did wonder if you'd try phoning me while you were away.'

'To be honest, I wasn't sure you'd feel like talking to me. I didn't exactly behave very well last time we met.'

I shrugged awkwardly. 'I guess neither of us did.'

'No, it was my fault. To put it plainly, I behaved like a dickhead. It took Hector to point out to me that it might have come as a shock for you to hear that he and Pat were getting married. It wasn't until it was too late that he realised perhaps he ought to have left Pat to tell you on your own. I think he assumed that you'd guessed more than you had done. But if you weren't expecting it at all, then I can see that it must have felt like a bit of a body blow at first. As if Hector was trying to muscle in, expecting to take your father's place. I suppose that, to you, it can't seem all that long since he died. Stupid of me not to see it.'

I sighed. 'But you were right, I could have behaved better. It isn't even as if I don't like Hector. He's a lovely person. But the news just caught me off balance. Once I'd got over that initial shock, I realised that Dad would have understood. He'd have wanted Mum to be happy. He'd have wanted someone to take care of her. Which I know Hector *will* do.'

'He will. Hector thinks the world of her, you know.'

We stood and smiled at each other. 'Anyway, he continued eventually, 'I really am glad to see you again. And especially glad to find that you haven't borne me any grudges.'

'Of course not.' We seemed to be standing very close, but neither of us made to move away.

Then with a jangle that made us both jump, the door opened and a cheerful stranger said, 'Don't mind me, you two. I've just come to browse for a house-warming present.'

As she turned an ostentatious back upon us, Fraser stepped back a little and gave me a wry grin. 'Oh by the way,' he said, 'when I parked up at Hector's and told him that this is where I was headed, he said to ask if you and Pat would like to eat with us at the Dragon's Head tonight?'

'Tempting fate a little, isn't it?' I asked rather mockingly, 'after the last time.'

'Ah, but this time I shall try to behave myself,' he said.

I laughed. 'Then I shall, too. It sounds a lovely idea. I'm afraid I'm stuck here in the shop for the rest of the afternoon, but if you've got nothing more urgent to do, why don't you call on Mum and issue the invitation yourself. I know she'd be really pleased to see you.'

'Then I'll do that.'

'And tonight you can tell me all about Australia,' I said. 'About how the book is going, and where you've been, and what you've seen and done…' My voice faded away as yet again we seemed to be lost in simply looking at one another.

But this time it was the opening of the inner door that broke the spell, and Todd emerged. 'Your sandwich awaits, ma'am. Ham and tomato as instructed. I even fixed some side-salad as a treat.' He stopped as he saw Fraser, and smiled a little uncertainly. 'Sorry - am I interrupting something?'

'No, no,' said Fraser. 'And in any case,' he added, perceiving that the woman was now returning to the counter carrying a toasting fork, 'I can see you've got a customer. I shall tell you all about it later, Tess.'

Todd looked at his retreating back. 'Sorry - *was* I interrupting?'

'Don't worry,' I said happily. 'I shall be seeing him tonight anyway.'

'Fraser was here for quite a long time,' said my mother when I arrived home that evening. 'It was such a nice surprise to see him back in the village already, and he was so full of interesting stories about his travels. He says he's got more than enough material for his book. And then I was telling him all about your holiday with Oliver, and the shop re-opening, and next thing I knew he was looking at his watch and saying that he ought to be getting back to Hector's.'

'He also told you that we're invited to eat with them at the Dragon's Head, I hope?'

'Oh yes. But not till half-past seven, so there's plenty of time to get changed. It is rather late, but apparently that was the earliest time that they could find us a table. That place is getting so popular these days, since they got that new chef. Still, I suppose it's better than being able to get an earlier table at a place that does horrible food.'

I laughed. 'Yes. And it'll give me time to have a bath before we go out, which is handy.'

I headed upstairs, glad that I would have plenty of time to make myself look as good as I could. I had a good soak using my special-occasion lotions, then spent almost as long ensuring my hair and make-up looked their best. What to wear took me even longer to decide, but when I finally made it back downstairs, I was rewarded by a look of approval from my mother.

'Very nice,' she commented. 'You look lovely, Tess. You should make an effort more often. Is that the dress that you bought to take on holiday?'

'Yes,' I admitted. 'Do you think it's a bit too much?'

'Not at all. It's a shame you don't get the chance to wear your best clothes more often.'

'Well, you look very nice too,' I said cheerfully. 'I just hope they both realise how lucky they are to be taking us out.'

There was a definite tinge of autumn in the air as we walked down the road in our finery, and the chill breeze made us glad to step into the busy warmth of

300

the Dragon's Head. The men had got there before us and were already waiting at the bar and, in the confusion of getting drinks and finding our table, I did not at first notice that my own glad smile was met with only a polite nod from Fraser. It was during the discussion of the menu choices, that his muted responses started to concern me. I looked at him wonderingly. At lunchtime he had seemed in the best of spirits, but now something was definitely different – and wrong. And though he appeared to behave more normally with Hector and my mother, with me he was noticeably reserved. As the meals arrived at our table, I tried to discover what had changed. What could possibly have happened in the few hours that had elapsed since our last meeting? Or had *I* done something wrong since arriving at the pub? Either way, my own spirits were plummeting by the moment.

'Well, it's good to hear that your trip went so well,' said Hector, after Fraser had finished telling him about a small mineral mine somewhere in the outback of Australia. 'Where do you think you'll be heading off to next?'

Fraser shrugged. 'Oh, I shall be heading back to Oz again. I'm becoming more and more convinced that what I've seen so far is only the tip of the iceberg. There seem to be so many sites that have been left abandoned or forgotten, and which would certainly bear being photographed and properly documented. And my publisher is keen. So I shall be heading off again just as soon as you two have tied the knot.'

He started explaining about some obscure

301

industrial railway that he thought had the potential to make a book on its own, but I couldn't concentrate.

Well, so that was that. So much for any stupid hopes I'd nurtured that we might become closer. From the way he was talking, it sounded as if he simply couldn't wait to get away again. And to stay away for as long as possible.

Glasses clinked, diners chatted, laughter floated across the restaurant. People came and went, servers delivered food and took away empty plates. Delicious aromas drifted in from the kitchen, but never before had I faced a plate of steak and chips with less appetite.

The evening dragged by. With so many diners in the restaurant, service was slow, and by the time we had finished dessert, my mother was visibly
wilting.

'Tired Pat?' said Hector. 'Let me take you home, and we'll leave the youngsters to stay and have coffee at their leisure.'

Almost before we had registered what was happening, Hector was helping her into her coat and escorting her out, leaving Fraser and I to face each other awkwardly across the table.

I stared down at my cup. To break the ever-lengthening silence I said, 'Mum was really pleased that you called in on her this afternoon.'

'Yes,' he said. 'We had a long talk.'

I risked a smile. 'I imagine her conversation was more about the wedding plans than about any

302

other topic. She's getting more excited by the day.'

'Yes. The wedding,' he said. As if coming to a decision, he looked at me meaningfully. 'And she tells me that there's the imminent prospect of more good news.'

It took me a moment to work out that he must be referring to the cash offer that Hector had just received for his house. 'Yes, that's right,' I said. 'Yes, he's a lucky man.'

Fraser looked startled. 'Well - yes. I'd agree with that sentiment all right. Who could argue?'

As I smiled rather confusedly, he stared down at the table. 'So is there a date?' he asked.

'I'm not sure,' I said. 'But I'm sure he'll be keen for it to happen as soon as possible. After all, why delay?'

I wasn't sure why he had suddenly become so fixated on Hector's house sale, but at least we were talking. Then, of course, light dawned. As he was currently staying with his uncle, it might well affect his own plans. Was that what had been preying on his mind all evening? His concern seemed a little out of character, but I was beginning to realise just how little I knew Fraser.

'In any case,' I said, 'if you're off back to Australia anyway, I don't imagine it will affect you at all.'

'Have you finished your coffee?' Fraser's tone was abrupt.

'Yes, thank you.'

'Then we might as well go. I'll walk you home.'

'No need,' I said, fighting the urge not to disgrace myself with tears.

'As you like,' he snapped. 'Well then, I'll just go and settle the bill - no, don't worry, I'd always planned to make it my treat.'

He strode towards the bar and I watched, with blurred vision, as he paid the bill. '*Treat*'? That might have been his word for it, but it certainly wouldn't have been mine. It was one of the most miserable evenings I had ever spent.

Chapter 19

'It's lovely to see that you're taking up sketching again.'

My mother smiled as she saw my pencils and pad set out on the breakfast table, ready to take with me. 'Is that what you're planning to do, while I'm off for the day?'

'I thought I might as well.'

'You don't sound very enthusiastic,' she said. 'You know, if you decided you'd like to come out with me and Hector instead, you'd be very welcome.'

I frowned. 'I'm not sure his cousin would be particularly thrilled to have an extra uninvited guest suddenly turn up for Sunday lunch. I know I wouldn't.'

Mum laughed. 'Knowing you, you'd be fine about it. Still - if you're quite sure...?'

'Yes, positive,' I said.

She finished eating her piece of toast and, with a questioning glance for my consent, donned her reading-glasses to leaf through my sketchbook. 'Ah, I remember seeing these when you got back from Scotland. They're good, you know. You should think about framing some of them.' She looked at me over the top of her glasses. 'Art was just one of the things you stopped doing when you left Bristol to come and look after me. I do hope,' she said tentatively, 'that once I'm off your hands and you've got your own life back, you'll feel free to do things that you might not have done before.'

"Off your hands?' That's just silly,' I said. 'You've never been any kind of burden on me. You shouldn't make it sound as if I made some kind of tremendous sacrifice. After all, I've made a perfectly good life for myself here in Little Bagford. Good friends, interesting work, nice boss. Not to mention all the village activities that keep me busy. What more could I want?'

'Yes, of course. You've made a very good job of it. But I'm just saying that if you do want to make your own new beginning, don't dither about it too long. Life goes by too quickly.'

'What a serious conversation this is,' I said lightly. 'But I think it's you who needs to go quickly right now. Isn't that Hector pulling up outside?'

'Oh, so it is!' Immediately distracted, she retrieved her bag and jacket and hurried to open the door. I waved her goodbye with relief, wondering what had prompted her to speak so strangely. Whatever it was, I was profoundly glad that I would not have to put on a cheerful front for the rest of the day.

It had taken me some effort of will to come up with any plan of activity for the morning, and the extra exertion of deciding exactly whereabouts I might do my sketching was too much. Instead I found myself drifting aimlessly along the footpath that followed the stream, scuffing my way through dead leaves and

306

over muddy ruts. Under a sky as listless as my mood, I could find nothing to inspire me. But I kept walking until the path widened out a little, giving a pleasant enough view over fields and distant woodlands. There was even an old wooden bench on which I could sit and spread out my drawing materials.

I opened my sketchbook and, at the renewed sight of my last artwork, was immediately transported back to that last afternoon in Scotland. At the time, I had been pleased with them, yet turning the pages now, I was vividly and uncomfortably reminded of that hillside behind the holiday house. The torrential rain. Daniel coming up the path to find me. The two of us sheltering in that little stone hut and the rain beating on the corrugated iron roof. The strange intimacy of it all. And then Daniel's obvious expectation... I bit my lip. What a good job my mother didn't know about *that* when she had admired my drawings.

To my surprise, once I started work it didn't take long before I became absorbed in my efforts. It wasn't until sometime later that I suddenly came to, and realised that I was beginning to feel cold. And yet I also felt soothed. My life might be a mess, but at least I'd kept control over my pencil. Perhaps, I thought rather wildly, I should devote my life to art and forget about any personal complications.

'May I see?' A sudden voice behind me made me jump and I looked up to find Oliver standing there.

'Sorry,' he smiled. 'I thought you must have heard me coming along the path, but you were obviously lost to the world. I knew you said you liked sketching, but this is the first time I've seen you actually at work.'

'Don't look,' I said, embarrassed. 'It's not very good.'

Disregarding me, he peered over my shoulder. 'But it *is* good. Very good. You've got talent, you know. You should be more proud of your efforts.'

'Well, it's a long way from professional standards,' I said, closing my sketchbook and putting aside my materials. 'Anyway, what are you doing here? I wasn't expecting to see you today.'

In the newly cleared space on the bench he sat down beside me. 'Okay if I join you? No, I wasn't expecting to see you here either. I just felt like a walk to clear my head. Anita's decided that she wants to do a proper Sunday roast today, so while she and Todd have taken over the kitchen, I decided to seize the opportunity for of a bit of thinking time.' He glanced at his watch. 'I have strict instructions to be back by two o'clock and not a moment later.'

'What will happen if you're late?'

He laughed. 'No dinner and sent straight to bed, I imagine. But not to worry, I've got nearly an hour. No hurry.'

It was later than I'd realised. Not that it mattered, for no-one would be at home tutting impatiently as they waited for me. 'Mum's gone out with Hector for the day,' I told him. 'She's being taken to meet his cousin, so they won't be back until after tea. The cousin lives over Leamington way, I think. Somewhere in that area anyway.' Running out of words, I stared silently at the drifts of leaves that had congregated around the feet of the bench. It was no good. If I was going to speak, I knew that I'd never get a better opportunity than this. Taking a deep breath, I said, 'Oliver, I'm glad you - '

I stopped, for Oliver had begun speaking at almost the same moment. 'Tess, I need - '

We both came to a halt, and smiled diffidently at each other.

'You first,' he said.

'No – you.'

He sighed. 'Okay. Well, as you might have guessed, I came out for a walk because I wanted to think through Anita's proposition. Her grand plan for the future of the shop. But I've realised that I *can't* think things through. Not without input from you. Tessa, my dear, I know I said that I would never press you for a quick answer to my question, but what with this massive spanner in the works from Anita - '

'Yes, I can see that. I can see you can't come to a sensible decision without having my answer.'

'It would change so many things, you see,' he said simply.

I looked at him. 'Oliver, I *have* decided. In fact I very nearly came over to see you this morning, but I didn't want to run into Anita or Todd. After all, this is just between the two of us.'

'And?'

'And my answer is no,' I said, as gently as I could.

He stared down at his hands. 'I had a feeling it would be,' he said. 'Deep inside, I think I always knew that if it was going to be a yes, then you'd have told me straight away.'

'It wasn't an easy decision,' I assured him unhappily. 'It really wasn't. Apart from anything else, I'm so fond of you, Oliver. Deeply fond of you. But I love you like a brother, like the best possible friend. But not like a husband.' I paused wretchedly. 'I'm sorry. I know it must sound as if I'm trotting out nothing but platitudes. But I'm not. I'm saying these things because they're true. You've been so good, so kind to me over the years, and I love you like the best brother in the world.'

'Then there's no need to cry about it,' he said. 'Don't get upset. Perhaps I should never have asked.'

'You had every right to…'

'Have I spoiled everything?' he asked. 'Have I ruined our friendship by suggesting we might get together?'

'No….' I found a tissue in my pocket, and rubbed at my eyes. 'No, of course you haven't. You paid me a massive compliment, and it's me who's spoiled everything.'

'No,' he said. 'No, in that case, nothing is spoiled, not unless we allow it to be.' He put a gentle arm round me. 'Anyway, there's one thing,' he said, continuing with forced cheerfulness. 'At least now that I know your answer, it simplifies my own decision about the future. I think I shall go along with Anita's plan. It'll keep the business in the family, and it'll allow me to spend a lot more time concentrating on the part of it that I like best.'

I leant against him, still stupidly tearful. 'You're

310

a good person, Oliver. You really deserve for things to work out well.'

'As long as it works out well for you too,' he said. 'I don't quite know how it's all going to pan out, but whatever Anita's plans involve, there won't be any compromises as to whether or not you keep your job. I shall make it quite clear to her that my agreement will be entirely dependent upon you being around for as long as you want to.'

Still leaning against him, I sighed. But *would* I want to? I couldn't help thinking that once under Anita's management, working in the shop would be very different from what it was now.

Chapter 20

We parted, inevitably a little awkwardly, and I sat and watched him heading back to the village, still in good time to avoid being scolded by Anita. Well, at least he would have his Sunday roast to look forward to. I bent and retrieved my drawing materials from my bag, but found that the urge to finish my picture had deserted me. I remembered gratefully that my bag also contained a thermos flask, from which I now poured myself a cup of hot coffee.

When I scalded my tongue it almost felt as if it served me right. Oh Oliver, poor Oliver. He must surely be the kindest person I knew, and the one that I would least like to hurt. But to marry him out of pity or guilt would be doing him a far greater disservice. I lifted my cup and took a more cautious, less painful sip, staring blankly at the view in front of me.

It wouldn't have worked. It was not just the age gap, nor the clouded question of where we would live together. It wasn't even the awful thought of Anita becoming a permanent and unavoidable fixture in my life. If I had loved him in the right way, all those obstacles could have been overcome. But there was one obstacle which nothing could overcome.

There was no chemistry, no spark between us. And, although I loathed admitting it even to myself, it was Daniel who had shown me that. That stone hut

in the rain, when he slid his arms around my body…
Even though I knew just how badly he could behave
- and *was* behaving…   No, I might not have liked
Daniel, but I had definitely wanted him, and with an
urgency that I'd never ever felt for Oliver.

But then, neither did I want *just* sexual
chemistry. If that had been the case, I might even
have given in.

I sighed. No, it was seeing Fraser again, that had
clinched it. If sexual desire didn't walk hand in hand
with deeper feelings then, as far as I was concerned,
any relationship would be merely second-best. And
Oliver deserved better than that. He deserved a wife
who came alive whenever he walked in the room; a
lover who wanted to spend every day and to share
every night with him. The only one on earth who
would do.

In short, someone who would feel about him just
as I felt about Fraser.

Fraser, who obviously wasn't interested in me at
all.

With sudden disgust, I threw the rest of the
coffee onto the ground, and watched the dark stain
merge with the mud and the blackened leaves.

Fraser. Why on earth had I been stupid enough
to hope that he might feel the same about me? After
all, most people would have been smart enough to
take the hint when their Beloved Object chose to
remove themselves to Australia. And yet I really *had*
tried my best not to think of him after he'd gone.

But then he had come back again.

Damn Fraser and his ability to mess up my life!

Had I really imagined that connection between us when he came into the shop yesterday? No, surely I hadn't. But then why had his behaviour been so very different only a few hours later at the pub? What could possibly have happened to cause that extraordinary change? Was it simply that he was a very moody person? But no; he had never struck me as that, not even in the days when we knew each other only as schoolmates.

I jumped up, suddenly furious with myself and the whole rest of the world.

Why on earth was I allowing myself to stay here wallowing in self-pity? Who cared if the rest of the day loomed horribly empty, and the prospect of returning to work tomorrow was even worse? So bloody what! I flung my bag over my shoulder and stomped off miserably in the direction of home.

As I came within sight of the house, I saw someone standing at the front door.

'Why are you never actually inside when I stand here ringing the doorbell?' demanded Fraser as I came close enough to hear. 'It's almost as if you know I'm coming, and decide to make yourself deliberately unavailable.'

'Don't be so ridiculous,' I said. 'How on earth do you imagine that I would know in advance if you've suddenly decided to grace me with your presence?'

I put my key in the lock, still unsure if the rudeness between us was genuine, or if he would

314

suddenly return to being the old teasing Fraser I knew best. Nothing was certain these days.

He followed me inside, and I automatically went to put the kettle on. 'Tea? Coffee?' I snapped.

He shrugged.

'Something stronger? I finished off the gin the other night, but I daresay there's some wine if you want.'

For the first time a glimmer of humour touched his mouth. 'Perhaps not wine – not after that last time.'

I allowed myself a wry smile. 'Yes, perhaps not.' I took two mugs from the cupboard. 'Tea then?'

'Yes. Thanks.'

He sat down at the kitchen table and watched in silence as I thrust teabags into mugs and plonked the milk on the table.

'So, did you come here for a reason?' I said at last. 'Oh - you haven't come with some message from Hector and Mum, have you? Although I did have my mobile with me all morning. *And* it's fully charged. I would have thought she'd have rung me direct if she needed to tell me something.'

'No. There hasn't been any message, and that isn't the reason I'm here.' He looked at me crossly. 'For goodness sake, stop flouncing about and come and sit down.'

'I am *not* flouncing. And if you actually want a cup of tea, then you'll have to put up with me standing up and moving about.'

I found an unopened packet of custard-creams and, not bothering with a plate, I shoved them in front

315

of him. Only then did I pull up a chair and sit down on the far side of the table.

'I came for a different reason,' he said.

'Yes?'

He pulled something from his jacket pocket. 'I brought you a present from Australia,' he said. 'I was going to give it to you on Saturday evening but... Oh well, I didn't.'

I took the small package uncertainly. 'What is it?'

'Like I said. A present from Australia.'

Silently I pulled back the wrappings and saw the shine of a silver chain. And then the blue-green sparkle of opal.

'Oh,' I said. 'Oh.' I turned it slowly in my fingers, feeling its cool smoothness, admiring its shape, and depth of colours. 'It's beautiful, Fraser. It's the loveliest pendant I've ever seen.'

'It's from Coober Pedy,' he said.

'And it's for me?'

'Yes, of course it's for you.' He scowled at me.

'It's just lovely.' Feeling totally wrong-footed, I fell back on the old cliché. 'But you shouldn't have...'

'You're right, perhaps I shouldn't have,' he said. 'But I did. It was a token of how I felt about you. But now I see that I should have simply got it as a present for the bride-to be.'

'You mean you've decided to give it to my mother instead?' I looked at him blankly

'No, of course not for your mother,' he snapped. 'What's wrong with you, Tessa?'

316

'What's wrong with *you?*' I demanded. 'Fraser, I really don't know what to make of you! And I liked you so much. I really, really did.'

'Then why,' he demanded, 'if you like me so very much, are you intending to marry this Oliver? I even asked you about him ages ago, and you told me that it was purely platonic. So what changed? Was it when you were in Scotland that you suddenly decided you were madly in love with him?'

'No - ' I began, but Fraser wasn't listening.

'Or is it merely that Oliver is the safe option? That he can offer you a home when Pat and Hector move out into their own place? A nice safe refuge so that you don't have to worry about anything ever changing? For God's sake, Tess, what are you playing at? I'd thought you were better and braver than that!'

I stared at him open-mouthed. 'Who told you I was going to marry Oliver? Who told you?!'

He glared at me. 'Your mother did. Yes, your own mother. Why - was she not supposed to say anything about it?'

'There's nothing *to* say about it!'

'Then why does she think there is?'

'I don't know,' I said wearily. 'Honestly, Fraser, I'm beginning to wonder if you're not some kind of weird lookalike, just beamed in from an alternative universe. I've got absolutely no idea what you're talking about.'

He spoke with studied patience. 'What I'm trying to say to you is that, whether or not your engagement to Oliver is supposed to be secret, your mother knows all about it. She told me when I was here yesterday afternoon. I don't think she actually meant to tell me, but there again, she probably didn't realise just how paranoid you are about it.'

I fought back my urge to smack him, and said with equally insulting patience, 'But it isn't true. Perhaps you need to tell me exactly what she did say that gave you that impression.'

'She said that she had asked Oliver himself,' said Fraser triumphantly.

'When?'

'She said it was at the shop reopening last week. She'd got chatting to him about her own wedding plans and got a bit carried away, and asked him if she could look forward to seeing him and you getting hitched.'

'And he said…?'

'He let the cat out the bag. He said he'd already asked you.'

'But that didn't mean I'd said yes!'

Fraser looked sulky. 'But you obviously hadn't said no, either. And then, when I saw you last night, I actually asked you directly, and you said yes, and that he was a lucky man. A little immodest of you, I thought, but nevertheless true. He *is* a lucky man. Too fucking lucky for my liking.'

I closed my eyes for a moment, wondering if, when I opened them again, normality would have been restored.

'You confirmed it,' insisted Fraser. 'Don't try and deny it. It was when we were talking about Hector and Pat's wedding. I asked if there was to be

318

more good news, and you said yes, and that he was lucky.'

I started to laugh and, once having started, found it difficult to stop. 'But I thought,' I eventually managed to squeak, 'that we were talking about the sale of Hector's house. He's got a cash buyer, and ever so quickly – oh come on, he must have told you about it.'

'Oh. Oh, yes he did mention it.'

'Then you can see why I thought that's what we were talking about.'

'But your mother seemed so sure…' He stared down into his cup, his face rather red. 'And then, when I saw him in the shop, when he'd brought you down that sandwich -   Well, he's a good looking chap. And a lot younger than I'd expected.'

Much to his discomfiture, I began laughing again. 'Oh Fraser - no wonder he wasn't what you expected. That wasn't Oliver you saw, it was Todd. Oliver's son-in-law. Anita's husband. He's a lovely guy, but I wouldn't be tempted, even if he wasn't already spoken for.'

'Oh.' He paused. 'So you're not marrying Oliver then.'

'No, definitely not. And,' I said, sobering, 'I've already told him so.'

Fraser bit his lip. 'Then I really have been making a total dickhead of myself, haven't I?'

'Yes, you have.'

He looked so downcast that I softened. I said wickedly, 'So does that mean I can keep the pendant?'

He raised his eyes. 'That pendant was always intended for you, Tess   Even when I wasn't sure you'd be speaking to me when I got back here. Even when I did think that you were the next bride-to-be.'

'And did you mean it, when you said it was a token of how you felt about me?'

This time his eyes stayed focused on mine, and there was no concealment for either of us. 'Yes,' he said. 'Yes, I did. In fact you're the reason I came back to England weeks earlier than I'd planned to. The reason I dropped off all my things in London and headed straight down to Little Bagford. The fact is, you've really got under my skin, much more than I realised when I left here. Half the time I was away I was kicking myself for not saying something when I had the chance. So as soon as I could, I got on a plane and came home.'

'I thought you'd come back for your uncle's wedding,' I said.

He grinned rather shame-facedly. 'It was a good excuse, but I'm not sure I'd have travelled halfway across the world for it. But I wanted to see you again. And then yesterday, after I'd talked to your mother, I thought I'd left it too late.'

'Oh,' I said.

'And now, thank God, I find I haven't.' Across the table, he reached to touch my fingers, and once again his eyes met mine with that breathless directness. 'Tess. Come with me.'

'Where?' I asked stupidly.

'Australia. Yes, I know it's a big decision. But come with me. Even if it isn't the permanent security that Oliver could have given you, isn't life worth a risk now and then? Even if you get there and decide that you hate me after all. And for all I know, you might hook up with some hunky Australian. Or run off with a jolly swagman, or take up a career in kangaroo racing.'

I laughed nervously. 'Is there such a thing?'

'Possibly not,' he admitted. 'And I'm not talking about taking up permanent residence anyway. But you know that I need to go back there, and I'm simply saying come with me. Get away from this village for a while, and start seeing what the rest of the world has to offer.'

'A sort of gap year, you mean?'

'A gap year – or longer.' He looked at me. 'Come with me, Tess.'

I stared at the table. 'I don't know,' I said.

'Why not?'

I gazed almost unseeingly at the pendant still on the table, half-hidden in its tissue paper wrappings. I took it out and tilted it in the light so that soft sparkles danced across its surface. It was a perfect turquoise teardrop, as green as a tropical rainforest and as blue as a sunlit ocean. I let the silver chain slide across my fingers. 'What about my commitments?' I murmured, almost to myself. 'For a start, there's Mum - '

'Taken care of,' he interrupted. 'Hector will be looking after her from now on.'

'And there's the shop.'

'Oliver will manage without you. I thought you said that Anita and Todd were intending to join him permanently?'

'And then there's Jodie's baby. I don't want to miss that.'

'Now you're just being silly,' he said. 'Jodie will have her baby with or without you being here. And when it is born, she'll be sending you more photos than you'll have time to look at.'

'And could I even afford to take a gap-year?' I wondered aloud.

He grinned. 'Australia isn't the dearest place to live in the world. And in any case, don't worry, you'll be with me. I might not be whisking you off to a champagne lifestyle, but I definitely won't be expecting you to live on crusts or doss down in a flea-ridden hostel.' He took my hand. 'Come with me.'

'But...' My voice trailed away. Was I really ready to leave my little corner of Somerset and live somewhere so upside down that even a dish as normal as summer pudding was served up in December?

Fraser kept his eyes fixed on my face and, at that most inopportune of all moments, the phone rang.

Automatically, I picked it up.

'Tessa?' demanded the voice.

'Hello Aileen.'

'Sorry to bother you,' she said. 'Especially when you've got company - yes, Maureen was walking by, and saw that nice nephew of Hector's going in with you - yes, sorry, I wouldn't have rung, but it is rather urgent, I'm afraid. You see, the reason Maureen rang me in the first place is that she's now been given a date for her hip replacement. And it's only a couple of weeks away, which means she won't be able to help with the Village Bonfire Party next month. I know it might seem we've got plenty of time, but - yes, that's right - I immediately thought of you. You're such a stalwart, Tess – so very dependable - always there whenever you're needed.'

I glanced at Fraser, whose gaze still rested steadily upon me. I took a deep breath. 'Thanks Aileen,' I said. 'But I'm afraid that I won't be available either. You see,' I added, 'I'm going away. Yes, right away. I'm having a gap year - unless,' I smiled, 'it happens to turn into something even longer.'

* * *

SUMMER PUDDING RECIPE

All the amounts given below are approximate, and can be readily adjusted to suit both your tastes and the size of your basin!

Ingredients:

800g Mixed berries (strawberries, raspberries, blackberries, blueberries, blackcurrants, redcurrants, or any other soft fruits of your choice.)
200g Caster sugar
1 loaf of white bread, **or**, for extra luxury, one or two packets of trifle sponges.

Place the fruit and sugar together in a saucepan. Cook gently over a medium heat until the juices are running, and the sugar has dissolved.

Line a medium-sized pudding bowl with slices of white bread, *or* (my personal preference) trifle sponges. Where there are any gaps in the lining, cut or break the bread or sponges to seal them.

Pour in the fruit and sugar, reserving some of the juice for later. Cover over with more bread or sponges, and pour the remaining juice over them, until the pudding is an appetising pink. Place a small plate over the top of the pudding, and weigh it down so that the contents are compressed. Place in fridge overnight. Before serving, run a knife between the pudding and the basin, in order to loosen it. Turn upside down onto its serving dish, and serve with cream. Eat and enjoy!

Acknowledgements

A bucketful of thanks to all those who nagged me to get my book into print, and particularly to those who gave practical support. Janet Jones and her fellow proof-readers, take a bow!
And thanks to the wonderful ever-encouraging, ever-supportive Minehead Writers Group.

Printed in Dunstable, United Kingdom